# "*DIO MIO!* WE ARE LOST!"

Judith turned the rock over in her hands. Musical notes, carefully replicated from what looked like a score, were painted on the rough surface—along with a much more crudely drawn skull and crossbones.

"AAAARGH!" The cry was wrenched from Mario Pacetti's golden throat. He toppled backward, falling against Schutzendorf.

Schutzendorf craned his neck for a better look at the offending rock. "Vat? A stone with drawings? A few notes? So vat?"

"But such notes," Pacetti said, struggling to right himself. "They are the first notes Alfredo sings in *Traviata*: '*Mar-che-se...*'" The stricken tenor sang the word *sotto voce*. "I am doomed!"

# MARY DAHEIM

## Bantam of the Opera

### A BED-AND-BREAKFAST MYSTERY

AVON BOOKS
*An Imprint of HarperCollinsPublishers*

AVON BOOKS
*An Imprint of* HarperCollins*Publishers*
10 East 53rd Street
New York, New York 10022-5299

Copyright © 1993 by Mary Daheim
Inside cover author photo by Tim Schlecht
Library of Congress Catalog Card Number: 93-90343
ISBN: 0-380-76934-4
**www.avonmystery.com**

First Avon Twilight printing: December 1999
First Avon Books printing: November 1993

Avon Trademark Reg. U.S. Pat. Off. and in Other Countries, Marca Registrada, Hecho en U.S.A.
HarperCollins® is a trademark of HarperCollins Publishers Inc.

Printed in the U.S.A.

20  19  18  17  16  15  14  13  12

# ONE

JUDITH GROVER MCMONIGLE Flynn peered up at the clear blue October sky through the charred ruins of her toolshed. Glancing at the cluttered shelf behind her, Judith grimaced at the boot box that contained the ashes of her first husband, Dan McMonigle. Through what was left of the window, she observed her second husband, Joe Flynn, sitting in a lawn chair, presumably thinking about raking leaves.

"Joe," she called, coming out of the toolshed, "I can't stand it any more. We've got to get rid of Dan and put Mother here instead."

Joe turned his round face toward Judith. "But she's still alive," he said, not without a trace of regret. "Shouldn't you wait until . . ."

"I mean," interrupted Judith with a shake of her silvered dark curls, "redo the toolshed, expand it, turn it into an apartment for Mother. The situation with her and Aunt Deb living together just isn't working out. I can't stand any more of Mother's bitching and Cousin Renie is driving me nuts with her complaints about their complaints." Judith plopped her statuesque form into the matching lawn chair. "When Mother said she wouldn't live under the same roof with you, she meant

*1*

it. But I don't think she ever dreamed she'd be the one to live somewhere else. In a way, it's not fair. This was her home. If we turned the toolshed into an apartment for her, at least she'd be on her own turf."

"Turf," mused Joe, sipping at the mug of coffee that had been resting on a small wooden table between the two chairs. "How fitting. Your mother with a poleax. Your mother defending the goal line. Your mother spraying me with mustard gas. How did I know it would always come to this?" The round face with the magic green eyes grew vaguely morose.

"Knock it off, Joe," said Judith. "Don't be so damned *Irish*. At least we got rid of Mike and Kristin," she pointed out, referring to her son and his girlfriend. Both were forestry majors at the state university, a convenient three hundred miles across the mountains. But through an error in job assignments, they had ended up not in Montana as planned, but working at the local city zoo. Naturally, they had settled in at Hillside Manor for the summer, disrupting Judith and Joe's hopes of newlywed privacy. Not, Judith reflected with a wince, that there was ever a great deal of privacy in a home that was also a bed-and-breakfast establishment. Still, after their late-June wedding, Joe and Judith had hoped to have the third-floor family quarters to themselves. Instead, Mike had taken over his old room and, at Joe's somewhat old-fashioned insistence, Kristin had been ensconced in Gertrude's former hideaway. The guests, as usual, used the bedrooms on the second floor, and hardly a night had passed right up through Labor Day without the B&B being full.

Joe was now staring at the toolshed, still looking gloomy. "It'd cost a bundle," he pointed out. "Plumbing, rewiring, kitchen facilities. It'd take months to get permits from the city. In fact, I suspect you'd have to start with a new foundation . . ."

"Joe . . ." Judith spoke in a soft, cajoling voice. "You work for the city. You're a big shot homicide detective.

Don't you think you could get somebody downtown to wink a bit at our plans?"

"Wink?" Joe gazed at Judith, the gold flecks in the green eyes glittering. "They'll blink. Hey, Jude-girl, I'm an *honest* cop, remember? Do you really think I'd try to pull the wool over the building permit guys' eyes?"

Judith's strong features set; her chin jutted. "Of course you would. Besides, I doubt we'd have a problem. I had this whole house redone when I converted it four years ago." She made an over-the-shoulder gesture in the direction of the blue-and-gray Edwardian saltbox that was, along with Mike, her pride and joy. Hillside Manor nestled in the shade of russet-leafed maples and two tall evergreens, high above the heart of the city, overlooking the bay, offering ease in the cul-de-sac of a stately residential neighborhood. "I didn't have that many problems. If you don't change the original exterior too much, the city doesn't make a fuss. The fireworks those kids set off didn't do any structural damage, except to the roof," Judith went on, referring to the Fourth of July accident perpetrated by their paperboy, Dooley, and some of his buddies. "And Mother wouldn't need a kitchen, just a bathroom and a bed-sitting room. It wouldn't take up much more space than the toolshed does right now."

"What about a place to park her broom?" Joe was still looking unhappy.

"Joe!" Judith was beginning to lose patience, an uncharacteristic occurrence, especially with the man she had waited twenty-five years to marry. "Look, we knew this wasn't going to be easy. We even talked about buying a condo and running the B&B from there. But that wasn't practical. Then we conned Mother into moving in with Aunt Deb, which was a great plan on paper but a terrible idea in reality. Mother and Aunt Deb get along only if there's two thousand feet of phone cord between them. The bottom line is that it isn't fair. My mother has lived in this house since she was a bride in 1936. She and my father came to stay with my grandparents to get on their feet during the Depression. They never left. Until now."

"Your father left. Quietly," said Joe, brushing at his faintly receding red hair.

"I know. He died," said Judith between gritted teeth. "And quit looking like that."

Joe's expression had changed from glum to hopeful. But he had the grace to give Judith a sheepish grin. "Hey, you and Renie sort it out. It's your mothers we're talking about. If Renie agrees they're better off on separate ground, we'll find your mother an apartment of her own. Close. You know, like Patagonia."

Judith might have been married to Joe for only four months, but she'd known him off and on for over a quarter of a century. She realized when it was time to hold and when to fold. "I'll talk to Renie. Again," she added on a resigned note. "Meanwhile, you give it some thought while you're in New Orleans at that sociopath conference with Bill."

"Hmmm," murmured Joe, warily eyeing the rake that leaned against the maple tree. In a week's time he and Bill Jones, Renie's psychologist husband, would be off to New Orleans to attend a conference called "It Starts with Hamsters," regarding the sociopathic personality, social and criminal. Bill had thought that a homicide detective would benefit as much from such a gathering as would any psychologist, psychiatrist, or sociologist, and had invited Joe to join him. To Joe's amazement, the department had agreed to pay his way as part of personal development. Bill and Joe were due to leave the following Saturday. While they were gone, Judith figured she'd ask her aging but expert Swedish carpenter to give her a bid on remodeling the toolshed. An apartment, even one somewhat closer than Patagonia, wouldn't solve the problem.

Getting up from the lawn chair, Judith started for the back porch. "That rake's not making much progress," she noted.

"It's broken," replied Joe, who had moved the little table and put his feet up. "I think I'll get one of those blower things. Or is it a vacuum?" He settled his hands over his budding paunch.

Judith's black eyes fixed on the rake, which looked perfectly usable to her. "You're in a vacuum, Flynn. No wonder your own house looked like rubble."

Joe had closed his eyes. "That was because Herself had such a big bottle collection. All of which she emptied first. Fast. First and fast-most. That was Herself . . ." His mellow voice drifted off on the crisp autumn air.

If Joe found Judith's mother a sore point, Judith thought of Herself, Joe's first wife, as an open wound. Over twenty years earlier, Judith and Joe had been engaged, with a late March wedding planned. But on a cold night in January, after seeing one too many overdosed teenagers in body bags, Joe had decided to drink to forget. Among the things he'd forgotten that frosty night was that he was engaged to Judith. In the morning he awoke in a Las Vegas hotel room with an expensive Herself at his side and a cheap wedding ring on his finger. It had proved a costly mistake for everyone concerned.

Joe hadn't given up liquor, but eventually he had given up on Herself. Unlike Joe, his first wife hadn't been merely a social drinker, unless you counted downing fifths of bourbon alone in the bathtub. Or, when she was feeling particularly cunning, filling up the garden hose in the garage and slurping out of the nozzle. After one daughter and two decades, Joe ran up the white flag, leaving Herself to a condo on the Gulf in Florida, where she could have as many cocktail parties with cockroaches as she damned well pleased. Or so Joe had put it when he filed for divorce. Judith, reflecting on the rocky road to romance that had led her back to Joe, smiled thinly. Maybe Herself wasn't a raw wound any more; maybe she was just a large scar. Poor woman.

In the kitchen, Judith searched the refrigerator for ingredients. No longer did she have to keep an eye out for green baloney, brown tapioca, or blue ham. Gertrude and

Aunt Deb had at least one perversion in common: Neither ever threw anything away, no matter how rotten, how stale, or how disgusting. At present, the only nonedible item in the fridge was a plastic bag containing lily-of-the-valley pips, which Judith was saving for Mrs. Dooley to plant at the proper time in December. Pushing them to one side, Judith remembered the six dozen tulip, daffodil, and hyacinth bulbs she'd bought the previous week at Nottingham Floral. They should be put out in the next week or so. Housework was a chore for Judith, but gardening was a joy. She looked upon it as therapy.

Deftly, Judith tossed the makings for salmon mousse into the blender. Onions. Garlic. Cream cheese. A can of sockeye. Guests at Hillside Manor were entitled not only to a full breakfast, but hors d'oeuvres and sherry circa 6:00 P.M. All four sets of couples were holdovers from Friday night, one from Portland, one from Denver, and two from in-state, spending the weekend in the city for shopping, shows, and sight-seeing. *A perfect time of year for a vacation,* Judith thought to herself as she glanced through the kitchen window at the bright red pyracantha berries and the lacy red Japanese maple. Next door, the Rankers's Tree of Heaven swayed in graceful russet splendor. A scattering of red, yellow, orange, and purple dahlias turned bright faces between the two houses, friendly guardians of the property line. Arlene Rankers was on her back steps, throwing dried bread to the birds. Her husband, Carl, was rolling their gas mower out of the garage, hopefully, Judith figured, for the last time this year. Arlene gazed at her mate, a slight smile on her lips. Carl bent over the mower.

"It's broken," he called. Judith saw Arlene frown, then watched Carl head back to the garage. A moment later he emerged, said something Judith couldn't make out through the closed window, and disappeared into the laurel hedge.

Over the whirr of the blender, Judith heard the phone ring. It was Cousin Renie, and Judith girded herself for yet another diatribe about their mothers.

But Renie was off on a different tangent. "Hey, coz, I

just realized that Bill won't be here for the opera next weekend. Want to go with me? It's *Traviata,* with that tenor who's staying with you."

Momentarily, Judith closed her eyes. She dreaded the coming of Mario Pacetti, world-renowned singing pain-in-the-ass. She had agreed to his stay at Hillside Manor only because the local opera company had offered to triple her usual fee for the two weeks that Pacetti and Company would be residing at the B&B. His reason for seeking alternative lodging was simple. The great tenor despised hotels and wished to avoid hordes of fans in the lobby. Ordinarily, he was able to move in with friends, of which he had a plethora in most other opera capitals of the world, but in Judith's hometown, Pacetti appeared to be chumless. Indeed, Renie, who had done some graphic design work for the local symphony, reported that the conductor, Maestro Dunkowitz, had hosted the tenor on his previous visit six years earlier and had taken a sacred oath on his baton never to let Pacetti waddle across his threshold again.

"Well," said Judith at last, "since he's staying here, I suppose I should go hear him sing. Sure, I'll take Bill's place. After all, Bill is taking mine. I always did want to see New Orleans."

"Me, too," said Renie, sounding a bit sulky. "I would have gone if I didn't have a deadline on this Henderson Cancer Center brochure. They're breaking ground next week on the new facility."

"Someday," said Judith, "maybe we can go for Mardi Gras. Just think, we could take our mothers and dress them up like gargoyles."

"Yeah, think of the money we could save on costumes. Say, when are Pacetti and crew arriving? I wouldn't mind sort of hanging around, you know, getting a preview."

Judith consulted the big calendar that hung by the phone, though in fact the date was inscribed on her heart, not unlike Gilda's "Caro nome" in *Rigoletto.* "Thursday. I gather somebody like Pacetti doesn't need to rehearse much. How the heck did we get him to sing here in the first place? Most of the people the local opera hires are either on their way up or going in the other direction."

"A lot of them aren't going anywhere," said Renie with some asperity. "Honestly, I get so sick of paying forty or fifty bucks a ticket every season and watching those bozos do *Lucia* in modern dress, with a set made out of Astroturf, or *Lohengrin* in L.A., where the hero shows up on the Number 46 bus to Burbank ... Well, don't get me started ..."

"Right, right," said Judith hastily, aware that once her cousin got launched on a favorite topic of derision, there was no stopping her. "Pacetti, you were saying why he came ..."

"Oh, yeah ... well, he sang here about six years ago—he'd signed up before he went global—but it was as Pinkerton in *Butterfly,* not exactly a tenor's most sympathetic role. The Cio-cio-san was wonderful, actually a Japanese soprano, and she stole the show, which is saying something considering how terrific Pacetti was even then. I heard from Maestro Dunkowitz that it ticked Pacetti off and he's always wanted to come back. I guess he felt he had something to prove to local audiences. So the opera signed him then and there, and now he's here. Or will be, come Thursday. Lucky you." Renie sniggered.

"Keep that up and I won't tell you when they get here," said Judith, propping the phone against her shoulder and using a rubber spatula to get the mousse out of the blender. "Frankly, it's a nuisance, having Pacetti and his entourage take up the whole house for two weeks. I've had to turn away at least three regulars, who always come in late October. I won't do that again at any price."

"What do you mean?" inquired Renie. "It's just Pacetti and his wife and the business manager, right?"

"Wrong. It's Pacetti and wife—who require separate rooms so he can rest his multimillion dollar vocal cords, presumably without sexual or any other kind of harassment from Signora Pacetti. Then the business manager has a so-called assistant, and with a name like Tippy de Caro,

I can only guess what she's assisting. But she, too, must have a separate room, for appearances' sake. And last but certainly not least, there is the chief executive officer of Cherubim Records who, for reasons unknown to this poor bed-and-breakfast hostess, sticks to Pacetti like Elmer's Glue. Bruno Schutzendorf, by name, and why do I feel as if the Hun Also Rises?"

"Schutzendorf!" exclaimed Renie, ignoring her cousin's pun. "Hey, I'll tell you why—he signed Pacctti to a ten-year ten-zillion-dollar contract, that's why. It was in the paper last spring. Don't you read Melissa Bargroom's culture column?"

"Only when she writes about people whose names I can pronounce without hyperventilating. Say, what time is Tom's birthday party tomorrow night?"

"Six-thirty," said Renie. "Bill and I are giving him the Apartments-Furnished section of the classifieds."

"Stop kidding yourself, coz," said Judith. "They never move out. Not permanently."

"I know," sighed Renie. "He's only twenty-two. But I sort of thought that when he graduated from college last June ... And now he's talking about law school, with Anne and Tony still to finish ..." Her voice weakened and trailed away.

"Hey, Mike's a year older and he's got at least two more semesters. Or is it three?" Judith's own voice grew faint. She rallied quickly, eyeing the clock. "Got to run, coz. See you tomorrow night."

"Great. 'Bye."

"Coz?"

"Huh?"

"Is everything okay?"

"Right, I got the cake ordered at Begelman's, we'll pick up the ice cream after church tomorrow, and Rich Beth is going to give her honey a file folder for his nonexistent investments."

"No, no," protested Judith. "I mean," she paused, catching her breath, "our *mothers*. I haven't called mine yet today."

"You haven't?" said Renie in mock surprise. "Gee, I've only talked to mine four times and it isn't even three o'clock. How could you be so lucky as to have been given life by a woman whose idol wasn't Alexander Graham Bell?"

"Then they're still alive?" inquired Judith.

"Mine is," replied Renie.

"Hmmm. Fifty percent's not bad. 'Bye." Judith's voice was breezy, but after she hung up the phone a frown creased her high forehead. The absence of controversy in Renie's manner was only temporary, no doubt induced by a number of things, including the proximity of her eldest child's birthday, the presence of Bill Jones, who didn't like to hear about other people's troubles unless he was being paid for it, and the possibility that Aunt Deb had murdered her sister-in-law Gertrude, but Renie didn't want to mention it and spoil the upcoming family celebration. Judith carefully upended the copper mold shaped like a fish and put it in the refrigerator, then headed through the rear entryway toward the back porch. Stepping outside, she opened her mouth to call to Joe. But his red head was tipped to one side, and even from fifteen feet away, she could hear him gently snoring. In the other lawn chair, a darker head, streaked with gray, was tipped in the opposite direction. Carl Rankers also slept. Judith sighed and went back inside the house.

Judith busied herself in the kitchen, emptying the dishwasher, getting out the sherry glasses, opening a box of water wafers for the mousse. Like Renie, she wasn't keen on having her husband trot off to New Orleans without her. Also like Renie, Judith had work that held her hostage. She could hardly leave Hillside Manor when such august guests as Mario Pacetti and Herr Schutzendorf were booked. And though she had initially dreaded Joe's absence during much of their stay, she realized it might be just as well. Joe had been a very good sport thus far about sharing his new home with all manner of assorted guests. But the explosive tenor, famous for his forays onstage and off, could upset even a hardened homicide cop such as Joe Flynn. After all, Joe was entitled to his peace and quiet after a rough day examining crime scenes. With Mario Pacetti on her own scene, Judith felt that there might not be a lot of peace or quiet.

She was, of course, absolutely right.

# TWO

"LISTEN, YOU LAMEBRAINED knothead, I'm not paying for Deb's damned dresser skirt! It's your cat that did the damage, and you can pony up to buy her a new one!"

Judith held the phone out from her ear a good six inches, wishing her mother's voice had grown as feeble as her legs. "You wanted to keep Sweetums with you," Judith countered, bringing the receiver back in place. "He followed you to Deb's while Joe and I were on our honeymoon. Why can't you make him behave?"

"Behave! Ha!" rasped Gertrude in her voice made of gravel. "Since when did that mange-ball ever know how to behave? I had less trouble raising you than this cat. And that's saying something, Toots. Or have you forgotten how you used to sit inside the fireplace and smoke up the chimney?"

Judith hadn't, but almost thirty years later, it seemed beside the point—particularly since she had quit smoking a few years earlier, while her mother refused even to consider giving up her favorite vice, especially now, when she knew how much it annoyed Deb.

"Another thing," railed Gertrude, "Deb says she wants to get a new parakeet. Nasty creatures, all they do is squawk and poop, which figures, because that's about all Deb does, too, but she says she can't have a bird as long as I've got Sweetums. I'd like to give her the bird all right, but to be fair—and you can't say I'm not that," she went on hurriedly, just in case Judith should try, "the least you can do is come and get this loathsome monster before Deb tries to cook him for dinner. Which, I might add, would taste better than the pot roast she fixed last night. It was like eating a ball of twine."

Judith rubbed at her temples, ruffling the new permanent she had gotten the previous week at Chez Steve's Salon. Aunt Deb was actually an excellent cook, which was no mean feat considering that she had to work her wonders at the stove from a wheelchair. Gertrude was basically fond of Sweetums. The two sisters-in-law were, deep down, fond of one other, each in her own way. But four months under the same roof was straining the fabric of affection. Obviously, matters were boiling to crisis proportions. Judith toyed with the idea of telling her mother about the toolshed, then decided to hold off. At least until Joe was out of town.

"Mike got a 97 on his forest products test," Judith said brightly. "He called me last night."

"Hunh. He didn't call *me*. I haven't heard from the little bugger since he took off for college. Not," she added hastily, "that I'm one for yakking on the phone. Like some I could name who are sitting pretty damned close listening in and eating my leftover birthday cake."

"It is *her* grandson's birthday cake," Judith noted mildly. "Didn't we have a nice time at Bill and Renie's Sunday?"

"Bill and Renie are idiots," said Gertrude. "They spoil those kids something awful. Too many presents. What does Tom need with another leather jacket? He's got three; I counted 'em in the hall closet. And that big radio thing, it looks like you could drive it home. Sweaters? What does he do, wear six of 'em at once? You got Mike a belt for his birthday last August. Now that was sensible."

"Well . . . yes," agreed Judith, rolling her eyes. Gertrude

had not known about the slacks, two shirts, four CDs, wristwatch and new car seat covers that had been sneaked past her. At least Joe hadn't pitched a fit at Judith's extravagance, but he could hardly afford to when she had lavished as many gifts on him. And on the same day, since her husband and son shared their birthdays.

"Look, Mother, I'm off to Falstaff's Market in a couple of minutes to shop for the next batch of guests." Judith shuddered at the suggested list of favorite foods submitted by the opera company. "I'll swing by and bring anything you and Aunt Deb need, okay?"

"Chloroform," said Gertrude with bite. "I'm not saying whether I'll use it on Deb or the cat."

"Look," said Judith, keeping a check on her impatience and yielding to compromise, "once this bunch of opera people, who are due in tomorrow leave, I'll bring Sweetums back here, okay?"

"When's that?" grumbled Gertrude.

"Two weeks." Judith swallowed the words.

"Two weeks!" shrieked Gertrude. "What are you doing, you stupe, adopting 'em?"

"They're staying through the duration of the production," replied Judith a bit wearily. "But I promise, I'll take Sweetums back then. And I'm going to . . . uh . . . well . . ."

"Well, what?" snapped Gertrude. "Quit mumbling, Judith Anne. What are you going to do, ship me to a pest house?"

Judith emitted as long sigh. "I'm figuring something out, Mother. Just give me time, okay?"

"You'll need it, kiddo. Any time you figure something out with that short-circuited brain of yours . . ."

"Mother, I've got to run, really. I'll get you some nice pickled pigs' feet."

"Well." Gertrude sounded temporarily assuaged. "Tongue, too?"

"Sure. And chicken gizzards."

"That's my girl," said Gertrude and slammed down the phone.

With her wide shoulders slumping, Judith didn't replace the receiver. Instead, she waited for the dial tone while she quickly leafed through her personal address book, going directly to the T's. Skjoval Tolvang's name leaped out at her. She dialed the master carpenter's number and hoped he was still alive and building.

Judith had expected a courtesy limo, a hired Rolls Royce, even a taxi. The mauve RV that cautiously backed into her driveway was at least forty feet long and so wide that it overlapped the grass. Discreetly curtained windows, one-way glass, and California vanity license plates reading "TEN-OR-ONE" allowed only the most subtle hint of the passenger's identity. Judith quaked as the huge camper eased within inches of her garage.

"What the hell is *that?*" gasped Renie as the cousins craned their necks in the living room's big bay window. "Has Pacetti got the orchestra in there, too?"

"That sucker must sleep at least six people," said Judith. "Why do they need to stay *here?*" Seeing the driver, attired in mauve livery with a snappy cap, emerge from the front of the RV, Judith hopped off the window seat and headed for the French doors that led outside. "Lord, I hope they're not going to park that behemoth *here*. We won't be able to get in or out of the garage. It's a good thing Joe's got his MG at work."

Renie followed Judith outdoors. A woman was alighting, pretty and plump, with golden hair piled high and a mink coat tossed over her shoulders.

"Signora Amina Pacetti," announced the driver, who was assisting the first arrival with the descent. He spoke her name as if she were being presented at the Court of St. James.

Judith swallowed, approached her guest, considered curtseying, and then put out her hand. *"Buona sera,"* she greeted Signora Pacetti, resurrecting a phrase from her 1964 visit to Italy. "Welcome to Hillside Manor."

Amina Pacetti's handshake was delicate, but her scrutiny of the Grover homestead was hard. "Thees ees *eet?*"

"Yeah, sorry, we couldn't tow Windsor Castle this far," murmured Renie, who, fortunately, was several feet behind her cousin.

But Signora Pacetti's hearing was acute. "Yes? You what?"

Over her shoulder, Judith shot Renie a menacing look. "This is my cousin, Mrs. Jones. She was saying that we're sorry there's a hassle about, uh ..." Judith stopped, her usually glib tongue immobilized by the sight of the enormous bearlike bearded man who came to earth with the impact of a cannonball.

"Signor Pacetti," gulped Judith, over small squeaking noises of protest from Renie, "we're honored to have you here at ...'

*"Nein!"* growled the bear, twirling a walking stick with a boar's head ornament as if it were no heavier than a pencil, "I am not the great Pacetti, I am a mere minion, a cog in the wheel, a miniscule captain of industry!" He made a courtly bow, and Judith realized her mistake. The Tyrolean hat with its jaunty black feather, the flowing green cape, the suede vest with its brass buttons bespoke a colder climate than sunny Italy.

Judith tried again. "You are ..."

"Schutzendorf!" The large man rumbled with laughter and twirled his walking stick. *"Ja, ja,* me, I am merely ... *Schutzendorf!"*

"How ... nice," said Judith, now gazing frantically at Renie for support. But Renie was engaged in what appeared to be a somewhat frosty conversation with Signora Pacetti. Her cousin's uncharacteristic loss of words was exacerbated by the emergence of a voluptuous redhead, whose short, tight skirt rode dangerously high on her thighs as she stepped down from the RV.

"Hi! I'm Tippy! Where are we?"

The pale, almost ascetic-looking man immediately behind her spoke in low, earnest tones. "This is our lodging, Tippy. It's Hillside Manor. It's a bed-and-breakfast."

"Ooooh!" Tippy bounced on the grass, no mean feat in her four-inch heels. "Bed! And breakfast! I love them both! So much! Ooooh! Cute! Ooooh!"

Renie, who had disengaged herself from Signora Pacetti, tried to get close to Judith but was almost mowed down by Herr Schutzendorf, who was now stalking the lawn, from the ruined toolshed to the front rockery. His walking stick sank into the ground repeatedly; each time, Schutzendorf yanked it out as if he were pulling a spear from an enemy's chest. Judith shuddered and greeted the pale man, who introduced himself as Mario Pacetti's business manager, Winston Plunkett.

"This is my assistant," he added, motioning vaguely at the bouncing Tippy. "Ms. de Caro."

Judith waved at Tippy, who acknowledged the gesture with a tug of her upraised right hand, as if she were ringing a bell. Judith tried to smile.

At the side of the RV, the driver was now assisting yet another personage. With bated breath, Judith waited, feeling Renie finally at her elbow. "Signor Mario Pacetti," intoned the driver, as his master disdained further help.

Pacetti was short, dapper, and rather round. His black hair was plastered to his head, parted on the side, and coaxed into gleaming waves. He wore a maroon velvet smoking jacket, a cream ascot, and sharply pressed black trousers. A diamond on his left little finger caught the October sun as he shielded his eyes. His gaze took in the house, the small patio, the garage, the garden. The toolshed.

*"Dio mio!"* he cried. *"Assassini!"* With amazing grace, he turned around and flew back inside the RV.

Judith, Renie, and Winston Plunkett had followed Pacetti's gaze. So apparently, had Signora Pacetti, who now moved hurriedly toward the others. She grabbed

Plunkett's arm, shaking it like a dust mop and speaking in rapid-fire Italian.

"I tried to explain," murmured Renie. "She noticed the toolshed, too. She thought it was anarchists."

Herr Schutzendorf had stomped back to the vicinity of the RV. Bushy brows knitted together under the brim of his Tyrolean hat. The sunlight bounced off a silver medallion that held the rakish feather in place. "Vell? Have ve a problem, Mr. Plunkett?"

Tactfully trying to free himself from the agitated Signora Pacetti, Plunkett gazed over her head to the German record magnate. "I seriously doubt it, Mr. Schutzendorf. I'm sure this minor damage can be easily explained." Plunkett's gray eyes rested hopefully on Judith.

"Absolutely," asserted Judith, finally regaining her aplomb. "It happened last summer, while my husband and I were out of town. We're going to remodel it. In fact, the carpenter is coming Monday to give me an estimate."

"Ah." Plunkett's long, thin face didn't exactly light up, but he appeared relieved. In what sounded like perfect Italian, he relayed Judith's explanation to Mrs. Pacetti. Her flushed, if flawless, cheeks began to return to normal. As she let go of Plunkett's pin-striped suit sleeve, he turned toward the RV. Mario Pacetti was anxiously peering out the door.

"No rivals? No critics? No paparazzi?" he asked in a speaking voice that was strangely unremarkable, given his reputation as a singer.

After several exchanges between the tenor, his wife, his business manager, and Bruno Schutzendorf, Pacetti alighted from the mauve conveyance. He moved lightly on his feet, chin, chest—and chubby paunch—protruding. Judith was reminded of a rooster. Indeed, she recalled hearing that because of his many quarrels in the opera world, he was known as The Fighting Cock. And to the cognoscenti, he was *Le Coq d'Or*.

At last, the group was herded inside, past the watchful eyes of Mrs. Dooley, who was putting tulip bulbs in next

to the fence that separated her property from Hillside
Manor, past Jeanne and Jim Ericson, who had come home
early from their respective jobs, and past Arlene Rankers,
who had happened to come outside to hang up her washing for the first time since she'd acquired her dryer in
1963. Out front in the cul-de-sac, the arrival at Hillside
Manor had drawn a small crowd: Gabe Porter, who lived
across the street, looked up from under the open hood of
his four-wheel drive; Dooley, the news carrier, backped-
aled on his route with the evening paper; a messenger on
a bike from Scooter's Delivery Service pulled up at the
curb next to a gray sedan Judith didn't recognize. She felt
like selling tickets.

Renie was pressed into service to help settle the menag-
erie in their new lodgings. The front bedroom, which was
the largest of the five and had its own private bathroom,
was given to Mario Pacetti in deference to his greatness.
His wife was ushered next door, overlooking the bay, the
mountains to the west, and the sharp angles of the
Ericsons' very modern house. Tippy de Caro adjoined
Mrs. Pacetti, which would hopefully work out, because the
women would have to share a connecting bathroom.
Plunkett and Schutzendorf had been assigned the two
small guest rooms down the hall. Originally one large
room, Judith had put in a movable divider as well as two
half-baths in her extended remodeling project. Judith
feared that the pared-down accommodations might not
hold Herr Schutzendorf, and said so to Renie.

"Hell wouldn't hold him either, so don't worry about
it," counseled Renie as the cousins finally collapsed at the
kitchen table. "Jeez, I don't envy you the next two weeks
with this crew. You're right; it's a good thing Joe won't be
around for most of the time. If it were Bill, he'd have to
put himself in therapy. But I'm glad I saw Pacetti up close.
Briefly."

Splitting a can of Pepsi between them, Judith shoved a
glass at Renie. "At least the RV is out of here. I guess the
driver stays at a motel."

"I'd forgotten that Pacetti won't fly," said Renie, removing the lid of Judith's sheep-shaped cookie jar and extracting a couple of date bars. "He goes everywhere by ship, train, or RV. He insists it not only cuts down on risk, but on overusing his voice. The jet plane has ruined many a voice, according to him. Too many engagements."

Judith, who was not as serious an opera buff as Renie, inclined her head. "It makes sense, I guess. I wonder why they didn't take the train from San Francisco."

Renie gave a little shrug and munched on a date bar. "Schutzendorf probably couldn't fit in a sleeping compartment. Jeez, coz, he's almost as big as Dan!"

"Nobody is as big as Dan," remarked Judith in reference to her first husband, "except a tow truck. As you recall, Dan weighed over four hundred pounds when he blew up."

"Right." Renie ate the second date bar, causing Judith to marvel, as she always did, at her cousin's appetite and how she not only could avoid weighing four hundred pounds, but remain relatively slim. "Still, you'd think Schutzendorf wouldn't have been exactly comfy in that RV. But then I didn't get to see the interior."

"It's probably plush," said Judith, on the alert for signs that her newly ensconced guests were stirring overhead. She got up and went to the refrigerator. The old schoolhouse clock's hands pointed to precisely five o'clock. "I've got chicken liver pâté and crackers, calamari, salami, olives, three kinds of Italian cheese, and something awful with anchovies. According to the opera people, these are a few of his favorite things."

"Mine, too," said Renie, "except for the calamari. You might as well eat rubber bands."

"You probably have," Judith noted dryly, hauling the pâté mold and a tray of appetizers out onto the counter. "Only Mr. Plunkett drinks sherry. The rest prefer wine except for Tippy de Caro, who is a solid gin guzzler. Surprise. Are you sticking around or just polishing off the date bars?"

"Huh?" Renie, literally caught with her hand in the cookie jar, gave Judith a faintly sheepish look. "No, I've got to go home to fix dinner. It's after five. I'm famished."

"No kidding," said Judith.

Renie wore her middle-aged ingenue expression. "No kidding. Being a voyeur is hard work. Ask Arlene."

Judith didn't have to. Arlene Rankers was in the entry-way, waving a lacy white negligee. "How did *this* get on my clothesline?" she demanded.

"Ask Carl?" Judith retorted.

But Arlene was in no mood for mirth. "It fell out your window. What kind of people have you got staying here, Judith?"

Judith started to answer, but she wasn't sure she really knew.

# THREE

"Now wait a minute," said Judith, taking the silken garment from Arlene. "How did this end up on your clothesline out back? The only windows on that side of the house are along the hallway and we almost never open them unless it gets to be over ninety. The rest of the windows facing you are down here or on the third floor of the family quarters."

Arlene lifted her chin and sniffed. "I know that. Haven't I run this place while you've been away? I daresay I know every inch of Hillside Manor as well as I know my own house."

Judith didn't doubt it for a minute. Arlene Rankers was as curious as she was kind. And she had indeed taken over the B&B while Judith and Joe were on their honeymoon in Oregon the previous summer. She and Carl had lived next door to the Grover house for almost thirty years, and were more than good neighbors. They were also cherished friends.

Arlene gave a toss of her red-gold curls. "If you must know, that saucy little item landed in the hedge, then blew into the backyard before I could get it. There's quite a breeze outside. It feels as if Indian Summer is over."

Renie, who had been about to make her exit, lingered long enough to examine the negligee, too. It was short, the European equivalent of a size eight, with a lace bodice and trim. The label was in Italian. "Mrs. Pacetti hasn't been a size eight since she was ten," remarked Renie. "Years old, that is."

"Tippy could be an eight," said Judith. "It sure doesn't belong to Schutzendorf." Wearing a puzzled expression, she took the negligee back from Renie. "Why throw your nightclothes out of a window that isn't in your room? I mean, even if Tippy dropped it accidentally from her room, it would have to have sailed over the top of the house and landed on the other side in the hedge."

"People do the strangest things," commented Renie in farewell. "See you, coz, Arlene." The screen door banged.

"She's right," agreed Judith, carefully folding the negligee and putting it on the kitchen counter. "Did I ever tell you about the guy—he was an aerospace engineer—who set one of those windup dogs outside his room for protection? Or the woman who booked the whole B&B for herself and her friends, who all turned out to be inflatable dolls?"

Arlene, who had mothered five children, didn't turn a hair. "There's no accounting for people. By the way, who belongs to that gray car that was parked in front of the Steins' house? It's gone now, but I didn't recognize it."

The question was typical of Arlene. Carl, as the block watch captain, had long ago delegated his responsibilities to his wife, who had been watching the block long before the term was invented. "I don't know," replied Judith. "A friend of the Steins, I suppose."

But Arlene shook her head. "They're in Mexico. Anyway, a man was sitting in it. Just sitting." Her blue eyes shot Judith a meaningful look.

"That RV was enough to draw anybody's attention," said Judith. "It was probably somebody who just happened to drive by and got curious." Rummaging in the liquor cabinet, she glanced over her shoulder at Arlene. "Do you want to stay and help with the cocktail hour?" Judith didn't mind asking for help; Arlene often assisted in the catering duties that were an offshoot of the B&B's hospitality services. Judith also knew that—like Renie—her friend and neighbor would love to get a close-up view of the new arrivals.

But Arlene reluctantly demurred. "I've got ducks in the oven. Mugs and her husband are coming for dinner. If you need any extra help during the next few days, call me. Where's Phyliss Rackley?" Arlene's head swiveled around the kitchen as if she thought Judith might have stashed her cleaning woman behind one of the appliances.

"Phyliss will be here Monday," replied Judith. "Her lumbago is acting up. The damp, you know."

"Damp?" Arlene sniffed. "We haven't had rain since Labor Day. Really, sometimes I think Phyliss is an old fraud."

"She *is* a bit of a hypochondriac," admitted Judith. "But when she works, she works hard."

"She should. You pay her enough." Arlene caught herself quickly. "I mean, I assume you do. You're such a generous person."

Visions of Arlene scrutinizing Hillside Manor's bank ledgers flitted through Judith's mind. No matter; she had few secrets from Arlene, though not always for lack of trying. After Arlene had hurried off to baste her ducks, Judith went into the dining room to get the cocktail glasses from the breakfront. The long oak table was already set for breakfast, except for the plates. A white linen cloth, matching napkins in Grandma Grover's silver rings, Judith's own flatware, and two golden chrysanthemum plants awaited the morning meal. Judith and Joe would, as usual, eat in the kitchen.

Unless he was working on a difficult case, Joe arrived home by six. In the latter stages of his first marriage, he had got in the habit of staying at work until 8:00 P.M., or even later. Vivian Flynn had never fancied herself as a cook. Fortunately, Joe was fairly handy around a stove.

He was also well acquainted with some moderately priced restaurants. Judith, who had constantly fought Gertrude over her mother's outmoded notion of eating "supper" at 5:00 P.M., now found herself trying to convince her new husband that six-thirty, maybe even seven, was not an outrageously early time to serve dinner. Joe was trying to conform.

Judith had just finished placing the appetizers and beverages on the round cherrywood table in the living room when the first of her current guests came down the front staircase. Winston Plunkett had exchanged his gray pinstriped suit for gray slacks, gray sweater, and a white shirt. With his pale face, he looked so colorless that Judith had an urge to sweep him up, like a dust bunny.

"Mr. Plunkett," said Judith in her most outgoing manner, "I hope everything is satisfactory for you and the others."

Plunkett's narrow chin dropped toward his chest in a gesture of assent. "Very nice. Except for the furniture."

Judith stared. "The furniture?" Certainly it was an eclectic collection of pieces, spanning four generations of Grovers. But basically it was good stuff, solid, handsome and well kept. "What's wrong with it?"

Plunkett cleared his throat. His entire being seemed quite stiff. "Mr. Pacetti says it's dangerous. Sharp corners. Heavy. Dark."

It was true that Mario Pacetti's guest room contained most of the Victorian pieces Judith had left in what had first been her grandparents', and later her parents', bedroom. They matched, they fit, and most guests exclaimed at the old-fashioned comfort. "Does he want to change rooms?" Judith inquired.

"No, no," Plunkett replied with a mournful air. "At least the front bedroom is over the porch. The other rooms all seem to have a straight drop to the ground."

Puzzled by the business manager's attitude, Judith proffered the appetizer plate. "I'm afraid," she apologized, "I don't understand the problem."

Plunkett declined food, but gazed wistfully at the sherry. Judith caught his look and poured out a glass. "Mr. Pacetti is very accident-prone," explained Plunkett. "Perhaps you've read in the opera magazines about some of the . . . incidents?"

Judith hadn't. Running her own business barely gave her time to get through the daily newspaper. It had been years since she'd subscribed to *Opera News.* One of her greatest laments was how little time she could spend on leisure reading. As a former librarian, she often felt she was betraying her calling.

Sipping at his sherry, Plunkett appeared to unbend a bit. "Two years ago, in Buenos Aires, during the triumphal procession, the wheel fell off his chariot when he was singing Radames in *Aïda.* He broke three ribs. Six months later, in Paris as Don José, he bent over to pick up the flower that Carmen had dropped and threw his back out. At La Scala last year, there was a problem with the door in the scene outside Rigoletto's house. The Gilda couldn't get it opened for the Duke, and when she finally did, it smashed right into Mr. Pacetti. He broke his nose, a terrible thing for a singer. Last winter at the Met, in the second act of *Tosca . . .*" Plunkett's eyelids drooped. "Really, I hate to go on. I'm not even mentioning the things that happen to the poor man off the stage. It's no wonder he won't risk flying."

"Well." Lost in thought, Judith caught herself almost violating her hostess code by sampling the calamari. Quickly, she clamped both hands to her sides. "I hope he's insured," she remarked, though the thought was more for herself than Pacetti. She might do well to call her agent in the morning and up her liability. She hadn't checked into her coverage since opening the B&B almost three years earlier.

"Oh, yes," Plunkett assured her. "Mr. Pacetti carries policies that cover all sorts of contingencies. Accidents. Illness. Death. Even," he added with what Judith thought was a touch of grim pleasure, "murder."

"My goodness," breathed Judith, but before she could say anything else, she heard the thundering charge of Herr Schutzendorf on the stairs.

Schutzendorf's large form literally created a breeze as he entered the living room. Pouncing on the hors d'oeuvres, he gobbled up several pieces of cheese, a scoopful of chicken liver pâté, and a dozen crackers. *"Vat? No vurst? At breakfast, maybe?"*

Judith winced. Her morning menu was aimed at Mario Pacetti's gastronomic tastes: eggs fried inside thick slabs of Italian bread topped with slices of red pepper, spicy sausages, freshly squeezed orange juice, sun-dried tomatoes, rolls, and coffee. "Saturday I'll do bratwurst," Judith promised, mentally calculating the cost at Falstaff's Market. Even at three times the usual fee, Judith was beginning to wonder if she'd show a profit from this particular group of hearty eaters. "I'll fix *grössita,* too. It's a family favorite."

Schutzendorf beamed at Judith. "You're German, *ja?"*

"My grandmother was," replied Judith. "Her parents came from Baden-Baden."

"Ah! Beautiful country! Me, I'm from Hamburg. Big city. Industrial. Port. Birthplace of Brahms and Mendelssohn. And me. But I am merely ... *Schutzendorf!"*

"Right," murmured Judith as Schutzendorf poured white wine with a lavish hand. "I've been there. Briefly." In Judith's opinion, Hamburg looked like a very old Pittsburgh. Except, it occurred to her, she'd never been to Pennsylvania—unless she'd slept through it on the train to New York. Though Judith had a logical mind, her sense of geography was sometimes skewed. "How do you like the Pacific Northwest?"

"Beautiful, like Bavaria," enthused Schutzendorf between gulps of Riesling. Judith was reminded of a Saint Bernard, slurping out of a water trough. "Only taller. Your mountains, I mean. The Alps in Bavaria are not so high."

Winston Plunkett had somehow managed deftly and discreetly to insert himself between Judith and Schutzendorf.

"This is Mr. Schutzendorf's first visit to this area. He had a meeting in San Francisco and thought it would be pleasant to journey with our little group up the coast. It's such a leisurely way to travel, though there was no chance to do any fly-fishing as I'd hoped. It's my passion," Plunkett added in a self-deprecating manner. "Still, driving permits a much better view of the scenery."

"Right," said Judith again, wondering why the usually voluble Herr Schutzendorf couldn't speak for himself. Indeed, Plunkett wasn't yet finished.

"This also gives Mr. Schutzendorf the opportunity to hear Mario Pacetti sing in person, on the stage. As a rule, he usually only hears the recording sessions. He misses the glory of a live, total performance." Plunkett's gray eyes slid in Schutzendorf's direction. Judith could have sworn that the business manager's gaze held a touch of malice.

*"Ja, ja,"* agreed Schutzendorf, draining his glass. "Always the studio, no costumes, no sets, just the music. Amazing music, but . . . how you say? . . . fragmented. Make no mistake, I love the voices. My first wish was to be a singer."

It occurred to Judith that Schutzendorf certainly had sufficient volume; perhaps he couldn't carry a tune in a bucket. "Was your family musical?"

Schutzendorf ruffled his beard, rich brown, streaked with gray. "My family had various talents. My father wished me to become like my great-uncle, the famous Emil Fischer. I learned much by studying his works, but I had no aptitude there, either. Instead, I went into business, after the war. I work very hard, twenty years ago I start up my own record company. Now we are famous, too, and Pacetti is Cherubim's greatest star, unparalleled. No other one can touch his sales. Or talent," he added hastily.

A piercing laugh of derision floated from the staircase landing. "Ha! You know who disputes that claim, Herr Schutzendorf," said Amina Pacetti, descending the last three steps into the entry hall and moving in quick little movements toward the living room. "Inez Garcia-Green would argue that point until her tongue fell off." She stopped on the threshold, as if inspired. "I wish it would. Then she could not sing. Ha-ha!"

Judith recalled that Inez Garcia-Green, who was almost as legendary a singer as Mario Pacetti, was scheduled to sing Violetta in *Traviata*. It struck Judith as extremely good fortune that the local opera company had been able to secure two such luminous stars.

"Actually," said Judith in a mild tone, "I'm thrilled that we're going to hear both your husband and Garcia-Green. Not to mention Sydney Haines, the baritone. I understand that he's one of the new American stars."

Amina Pacetti dismissed Judith's remarks with a wave of her hand before finally entering the room and snatching up half a dozen slices of cotto salami. "An American! How they maul the language! As for Inez, she is in the decline! She ages. It happens faster with women than with men."

"Inez is still fabulous," asserted Schutzendorf, glaring at Mrs. Pacetti. "She has lost nothing—oh, a little at the very top, maybe, yes. But the middle register is more lustrous than ever. You are in for a rare treat, Frau Flynn." He bowed at Judith.

"Tchaah!" Mrs. Pacetti made an expressive gesture with her tongue and teeth. "She bays like a wolf, howls like a hound! It is embarrassing for my husband to sing with her!"

Schutzendorf tensed, as if ready to spring. Amina's eyes flashed, as if in warning. Winston Plunkett made another adroit move, this time between the German record magnate and the tenor's wife. "Now, now, my friends, let's not excite ourselves. Mario Pacetti and Inez Garcia-Green are indubitably two of the greatest singers of all time. Mrs. Flynn is correct—this city's opera lovers are in for a tremendous musical thrill."

Schutzendorf rumbled; Amina snarled. But the argument was cut short by the appearance of Tippy de Caro, wearing diaphanous gold harem pants and a short red jacket that revealed her midriff at one end and a great deal of cleavage at the other.

"Hi! What's to eat?" She scampered up to the cherrywood table on her high heels. Huge clusters of metallic Roman coins swung from her earlobes almost to her shoulders. Tippy wore enough bangles on one arm to form the percussion section of a marching band. "Ooooh! Brown spread! And twisty things!" She dipped into the pâté with one hand and grabbed a couple of calamari with the other. "Yummy! Where are the chips?"

"Uh—I put out crackers." Judith checked to make sure there were some left. There weren't. "I'll get more. And chips," she added with a sigh, noting that the grandfather clock's hands were pointing to six-fifteen. She wondered what her guests had planned for dinner. Perhaps Winston Plunkett had made a reservation at some posh downtown restaurant. Judith hoped it was scheduled soon.

In the kitchen, Judith caught her breath. Ordinarily, she didn't join her guests for their cocktail hour. But the celebrity status of Mario Pacetti and Company seemed to call for her active participation, at least on their first night at Hillside Manor. Working quickly, Judith prepared two large baking potatoes for the oven, checked to make sure her rib steaks had thawed, and chopped a head of cauliflower in two. Joe should be home any minute. For one brief instant, she leaned against the counter and smiled. Four months had passed since their wedding. She still hadn't got over the wonder of waiting for Joe to come home for dinner. She had, after all, waited for twenty-five years. Now she no longer waited in vain. Judith wiped the smile from her face and went back into the living room, carrying a plate of crackers and a bowl of chips.

"Where's Mr. Pacetti?" she asked, noting that he had still not joined the others.

Amina Pacetti gave a toss of her carefully coiffed head. "He's resting. Tomorrow he must do the rehearsing. It is always the strain."

Noting that Mrs. Pacetti's English seemed to have improved since her arrival, Judith gave a nod. "I imagine it is. My cousin and I will be there Saturday night."

No one seemed particularly interested. Bruno Schutzendorf was guzzling more wine; Amina Pacetti had polished off the cheese; Winston Plunkett had finally deigned to try the pâté; and Tippy de Caro was balancing a black olive on the end of her nose. Just as Judith was wondering if she should try to renew any sort of civil conversation, Mario Pacetti made his entrance. He still wore his smoking jacket and seemed faintly unsteady on his feet.

"The motion," he explained, clinging to the balustrade. "So long on the road. I grow dizzy."

"Of course," soothed Amina, who had gone to meet her husband at the foot of the stairs. "I, too, am uncertain in the walking. We are like sailors, again on the shore." With a wide smile, she led Pacetti to the depleted hors d'oeuvres table. "Now, eat, Mario *mio,* you must keep up your strength for tomorrow."

"Eat *what?*" cried Pacetti, staring at the almost-empty platter and plates. "Where is the calamari, the olives, the many fine cheeses I was promised?" He waved an anchovy under his wife's nose. "I could starve to death! Where is the pasta?"

A faint groan escaped from Judith's lips. No one at the opera house had suggested piles of pasta as an appetizer. She was about to forage for more food when a knock sounded at the front door. *Another pest,* she thought, since only guests and solicitors used the front entrance. Friends, neighbors, and family all tended to come in the back way.

As she hurried across the entry hall, she wondered if the bell was broken. It was unusual for anyone to knock instead of ring.

Dusk was settling in on Heraldsgate Hill. The evening air held the ripe smell of damp and decay. Over the rooftops, Judith could make out a narrow stretch of the bay, and the hazy outline of the mountains beyond. But she could not see anyone on the front porch. The cluster of pumpkins and the tall cornstalks that would serve as holiday decor until Thanksgiving stood innocently between the front door and the porch railing. Puzzled, Judith started toward the four stone stairs that led to the walkway. She had taken only a single step when she stubbed her toe. Stifling a curse, she bent down to examine the obstacle in her path. It was a rock, about six inches in diameter. Judith picked it up and turned it over in her hands.

Musical notes, carefully replicated from what looked like a score, were painted on the rough surface—along with a much more crudely drawn skull and crossbones. Uttering a small gasp, Judith stared at the object, then gazed more intently out into the cul-de-sac. Except for the lights in the Porters' house across the street, she could see no sign of life. Turning, she gave the bell a quick, experimental poke; it echoed inside the house. Judith frowned. Perhaps whoever had delivered the rock hadn't knocked, but had merely thrown it against the door. Sure enough, there was a sharp dent in the screen that Joe hadn't yet replaced for the winter. Still frowning, Judith went back indoors.

If she had hoped to ditch the rock before her guests saw it, she was disappointed. Tippy de Caro and Winston Plunkett were standing in the entry hall, their eyes fixed on Judith's hands.

"The bell sounded . . ." Plunkett began, then halted abruptly as he caught sight of the skull and crossbones. "Good Lord, what's that?"

"Oh—kids, I suppose," said Judith vaguely. "A practical joke. Maybe they're rehearsing, too. For Halloween." She gave Plunkett and Tippy a weak smile.

But Tippy, surprisingly, wasn't put off. "That looks nasty to me. Let's see." Her enormous earrings jingled and swayed as she bent her head.

The Pacettis and Schutzendorf had joined the others in the entry hall. Judith surrendered the rock and closed the front door.

"Ooooh!" cried Tippy, pushing the rock at Plunkett as if it were a hot potato, "this is ugly! It's like . . . a *threat!*"

"Really, my dear," murmured Plunkett, "as Mrs. Flynn says, it's probably just a . . ."

"Aaaargh!" The cry was wrenched from Mario Pacetti's golden throat. He toppled backward, falling against Schutzendorf.

*"Dio mio!"* shrieked Amina, clutching at her husband's flailing arm. "We are lost!"

Schutzendorf, who was supporting Pacetti, craned his neck for a better look at the offending rock. *"Vat?* A stone with drawings? So *vat?"*

"No!" shouted Pacetti, still limp and allowing Amina to fan him with her handkerchief. "It is much more! See! The music!"

"A singing skull," murmured Tippy, now eyeing the rock with a keener gaze than usual, "like on an MTV video. Maybe it's an ad."

Plunkett, looking puzzled, turned the rock in his thin hands. "There are only a few notes," he said in a baffled voice.

"But such notes!" Pacetti was finally struggling to right himself. "The three in the treble—they are Alfredo's notes! The first ones he sings in *Traviata! 'Mar-che-se* . . .' " The stricken tenor sang the word, *sotto voce.* "He is meeting the guests at Violetta's party in Act I . . . I am doomed!"

Everyone, including Judith, stared at Pacetti. Plunkett made a clucking noise in his throat, Tippy squealed, Schutzendorf rumbled, and Amina had gone quite pale under her makeup.

"Brandy," mumbled Judith. "I'll get brandy." She started for the kitchen just as the water for her cauliflower boiled over onto the stove. Reaching for the burner with one hand and groping in the liquor cabinet with the other, she could hear the wails of Amina, the groans of Pacetti, the rumbles of Schutzendorf.

And Joe Flynn, coming through the back door, breezily asking if dinner was ready.

# FOUR

JOE FLYNN HAD slipped into his role as policeman. He stood in front of the fireplace, carefully eyeing the little group assembled on the matching sofas that flanked the big coffee table. Judith perched on an armless rocker, a relic of Grandma Grover's youth. She had seen Joe in action before, but the sight never failed to intrigue her.

"So at least three of you handled this rock," said Joe with a reproachful glance at his wife. He paused to let Judith, Plunkett, and Tippy nod in acknowledgment. "Then we can kiss the idea of fingerprints good-bye."

"Gloves," said Schutzendorf, who was wedged between Tippy and Plunkett. "This madman probably wore gloves."

"Maybe." Joe set the rock down on the mantel, next to a wedding picture taken of him and Judith outside of Our Lady, Star of the Sea Catholic Church. Tiny pumpkin-shaped lights draped across the stone fireplace struck a deceptively cheerful note. The carved jack-o'-lantern on the coffee table, with its faint leer, seemed more in keeping with the current atmosphere. "I'll go talk to the neighbors. Maybe the Rankers or the Porters or the Ericsons or the Steins saw something."

"The Steins are in Mexico," said Judith.

"Lucky Steins," muttered Joe, heading for the entry hall. "Jesus, I finish a day with gang shootings and crazy dopers and spouse killers and come home to find my ..." He was still grumbling when he banged out the front door.

Flinching, Judith surveyed her guests with considerable uncertainty. "Uh ... Could I get more brandy? Crackers? Chips?" A quick glance at the grandfather clock told her it was after seven. "Would you like me to call about your ... dinner reservation?"

Blank stares met her question. "Dinner reservation?" Winston Plunkett looked at Judith curiously.

"Where's the pasta?" demanded Mario Pacetti.

"I'd settle for a burger and fries," announced Tippy de Caro.

"The vurst," rumbled Schutzendorf.

"More brandy, please," begged Amina Pacetti.

"Wait a minute," said Judith, getting up from the rocker. She asked the dreaded question. "Did you plan to eat *here?*"

Schutzendorf's bushy eyebrows lifted. "The table is set, *nein?*"

"I smell food," said Pacetti.

"I could eat a horse," announced Tippy.

"Our last meal was in Oregon." Winston Plunkett's thin voice made it sound like a million miles away.

Frantically, Judith took a mental inventory of her freezer. Chicken breasts. Lots of chicken breasts. She could thaw them in the microwave. Beans. She had cans and cans of beans, from Falstaff's last special. And pasta—she always had plenty of pasta. Tortellini. Linguini. Fettuccine. She could do it ... Judith gave a brisk nod. "Thirty minutes. The brandy bottle is in the dining room. Drink up. Enjoy. You've polished off the Riesling."

Grimly, Judith marched into the kitchen, giving the swinging door an extra big shove. She would charge them for dinner, of course. Just add it to their final bill. Ten bucks a plate. That was fair. Why the hell hadn't those idiots at the opera house told this bunch of loonies that she

only served breakfast? And hors d'oeuvres? Why the hell
had they come in the first place? Why the hell had *she let
them?* Judith was as angry with herself as she was with
her guests. She stomped down to the basement to get the
chicken breasts out of the freezer.

It was eight o'clock before she and Joe sat down to their
own dinner. The guests were still in the dining room, stuff-
ing themselves with chicken, pasta, and green beans. Joe
patted butter on his baked potato and regarded Judith with
a wry expression.

"Nobody—including Arlene—saw anything or anybody.
What do you think, Jude-girl—is this some sort of operatic
ritual?"

Judith sighed. "I don't know—I'm used to ordinary
people, tourists, honeymooners, getaway couples. For all
I know, Tippy had the right idea and it's a publicity stunt.
Though why Mario Pacetti would need anything like
that, I can't imagine. And to be fair, he seemed genuinely
upset."

Joe gave Judith his engaging grin. "Hey—he's a tenor,
isn't he? He probably has a tizzy when he gets junk mail."

Judith had to admit that Joe's argument held some
merit. Still, the rock with its ugly symbol and telltale notes
disturbed her. Yet even as she tried to drop the subject, Joe
recognized his wife's concern.

"Look, if you're worried, I'll have somebody keep an
eye on the house while I'm gone, okay? Any problems,
just call Woody," said Joe, referring to his subordinate, the
capable and kindly Woodrow Wilson Price.

With a grateful smile, Judith tried to shrug off her worries. "Sure, Joe." She had one ear cocked toward the dining room. The guests should be finishing up. Maybe they
would decide to make an early night of it. She said as
much to her husband.

Joe also listened to the sounds emanating from behind
the swinging door. Schutzendorf was regaling, Pacetti was
bemoaning, Plunkett was debunking, Amina was abjuring,
and Tippy was a-tipsy. Judith held her head.

"They'll never go to bed," she complained.

Joe polished off his rib steak and gazed at Judith with the gold flecks dancing in his green eyes. "So?" He stood up, his captain's chair scraping on the kitchen floor. "We can."

"Joe . . ." Judith's black eyes scanned her husband's round, faintly florid, ever-charming face. "I have to clean up, I have to get the table ready for . . ."

Joe leaned down to put his chin on the top of Judith's head. His hands caressed her arms, her back, her shoulders. "I'll do it before I go to work," he said into her hair.

"But Joe . . ." Judith protested, albeit feebly.

"Hmmmmm?" He kissed her high forehead.

"We can't leave them . . ."

"To their own dreadful devices? Why not?" His lips sought her temple, the bridge of her nose, finally her lips.

"Screw it," murmured Judith.

"You're almost right," breathed Joe.

They went up the back stairs.

Joe didn't have time in the morning to clean up or set the table for breakfast, but Judith didn't mind. At least not a lot. By seven-thirty, she had matters well in hand, with the dishwasher going, breakfast cooking, and the dining room once again ready to serve a meal. When her guests straggled down, virtually in the same order they had arrived for the cocktail hour, she made her announcement. Dinner was not usually included in the price of a stay at Hillside Manor. Lodgers were expected to eat elsewhere. She assumed their day would be full. They might not see their hostess again until evening. Judith held her breath, waiting for outraged cries.

None were forthcoming. Mario Pacetti announced that he would be rehearsing all day; Bruno Schutzendorf said he was going on a tour of local recording studios; Winston Plunkett and Tippy de Caro were off to meet with the media on their client's behalf; and Amina Pacetti was going to glue herself to her husband's side at the opera house.

Judith drew a sigh of relief and went upstairs to make the beds.

She was working in Mrs. Pacetti's room when Amina returned from the breakfast table. "One question," she said, with surprising diffidence.

Judith looked up from replacing the bolster on the bed. "Yes?"

"If you do not serve the other meals, may we prepare little somethings? My husband, he has the outstanding appetite."

Judith hesitated. There had been a few occasions in the past when she had allowed guests with special dietary needs to use the kitchen. She supposed Mario Pacetti fell into the same category. "Okay," she said slowly. "But make sure the stove is always turned off."

"Of course," responded Amina, crossing the room to stand at the window which overlooked the bay. "We of the opera world do not eat like other mortals. Our lives are all this way and the other way. It is nothing much we require, just what you call . . . the snacks. Herr Schutzendorf is also fond of his nibbles, to eat with his Sekt." Noting Judith's puzzled expression, Amina's mouth twisted into a wry smile. "Sekt is the German version of champagne, much too sweet for serious palates. Fret not, he brings his own. It is difficult to find in this country, especially out here in the wilds. Oh, and much tea. My husband requires many cups of strong tea before a performance. We shall ask Signorina de Caro to bring us some items from the market. Where is it?"

Judith wrote directions to Falstaff's on one of the guest cards that reposed on the dressing table along with a guidebook, the B&B's official rules and regulations, and a few postcards. With a long, red fingernail, Amina tapped one of the postcards which showed the mountains in all their winter splendor.

"Lovely country. The city, too, is nice," she commented, as if bestowing largesse. "Many hills, much water, and so many beautiful flowers, especially in the spring."

"Yes," agreed Judith. "Some people think that because we live so close to the Canadian border, the English love of gardening has rubbed off on us. We take great pride in our gardens." She pointed to a Roseville vase which held a small bouquet. "Those dahlias are from my yard. I had just enough to put flowers in each of your rooms. But I got the asters at Falstaff's."

"So pretty," cooed Amina. "Bright blooms and so much greenery in the city and out in the countryside. That, too, is like England. California is very brown. Like Spain. And Italy, sometimes."

Judith picked up the laundry hamper with its pile of dirty linen. She would be very glad to have Phyliss Rackley back on duty come Monday. Running the B&B was always demanding work, but it was much harder when Phyliss was suffering from one of her many so-called spells.

"Everything's in order again now," she told Mrs. Pacetti. "Bedding, towels, and if it gets too chilly, there are extra blankets in the bottom drawer of the bureau."

Amina's dark eyes widened. "You went through the drawers, yes?" She did not look pleased.

Judith stared at her guest. "No, I put the blankets in there before you arrived. But I forgot to mention it."

"Oh." A wave of relief swept over Amina's heart-shaped face. "Very good. Thank you." She gave another nod, this time in dismissal.

With a shrug, Judith juggled the laundry hamper and headed down the hall. If Amina Pacetti was hiding contraband or cocaine or contraceptive devices in the bureau, that was her business. Or so Judith told herself. But she couldn't refrain from being curious. On the other hand, she had work to do. She had two rooms finished, and three to go. Judith hoped her guests would take off soon so she could get her work done without further interruptions.

As it happened, all five members of the Pacetti party were out of the house within the next half-hour. And, to Judith's happy surprise, they were as good as their word.

None of them showed up until well into the evening, when the first drops of rain began to fall. Winston and Tippy returned in good spirits, having dined at a waterfront restaurant where they'd watched the ferryboats come and go. Herr Schutzendorf, belching loudly, let himself in with the guesthouse key shortly before ten. And the Pacettis arrived a few minutes later, filled with good food and rare wine, dispensed by Maestro and Mrs. Dunkowitz in a spontaneous, if unexpected, gesture of artistic camaraderie.

"The rehearsal was horrible," Pacetti asserted with glee. "The worse the rehearsal, the better the performance. Only once did I have to threaten Dunkowitz with the fists, and that was during dessert."

"So splendid this *Traviata* will be," enthused Amina, brushing a speck of lint from the beaver collar of her husband's overcoat. "My Mario had only to shout to put Mr. Sydney Haines in his place. And Inez—that screeching owl is silenced when Mario does *this.*" Amina clenched her hands together, as if wringing a chicken's neck. Judith gave a thin smile. But she was pleased that the Pacettis felt all boded well.

"I shouldn't have worried so," said Judith as she watched Joe pack for the trip to New Orleans. "They'll be able to fend for themselves after all. And that silly rock must have been a prank. Some sort of musical in-joke, I'll bet."

"Maybe," said Joe, counting T-shirts. "Just in case, I've asked that a patrol car cruise by every so often while I'm gone."

Joe and Bill had tickets on a ten-thirty flight and Judith and Renie planned to accompany their husbands to the airport. Ordinarily, Judith's guests finished breakfast by nine. It was now eight forty-five. Renie and Bill were coming by about nine-fifteen. So far, only Schutzendorf, Plunkett, and Tippy de Caro had come down to the dining room. Judith gave an anxious glance at the clock on the nightstand. Either she'd have to cancel the trip to the terminal, or ask Arlene to come over and fill in.

Joe was going through the closet, his movements growing increasingly impatient. "Where's my red-and-white checked sport shirt?"

Judith had been admiring what was literally the last rose of summer, a yellow bloom she'd picked that morning and put in a bud vase on the dressing table. Suppressing a sigh, she joined Joe at the closet door. "Right there." She pointed to the shirt, hanging about eight inches from his nose. Since their marriage, the closet had been divided down the middle, with Judith's wardrobe to the left, and Joe's on the right. The bedroom's cheerful yellow and white decor, with its chintz curtains and dormer windows, had taken on a more masculine air. Especially, Judith thought with a little grimace, when Joe left his shoulder holster draped over the chair in front of the dressing table.

"I may have to renege on going to the airport," Judith said with a doleful expression. "The Pacettis haven't come down yet."

Joe was going through the bottom drawer of the maple bureau. "Can't you set breakfast out for them so they can dish up by themselves? Hey, where are my light blue socks?"

"No, it's bratwurst and *grössita*. You know the *grössita* has to be served hot, right out of the frying pan." Judith bent down to point to Joe's light blue socks, which were almost touching his left hand. *"Grössita's* like any other pancake, except you fill the pan with batter, then cut it up in little pieces when it's almost finished frying. But if it sits, it turns into a big glop of glue."

Putting his socks into a large black suitcase, Joe gave Judith a wistful look. "I'd hoped you could see me off. My first trip without you. Who then will kiss poor Joe farewell at the concourse exit?"

"Let me see if I can discreetly roust them," said Judith, starting for the door.

"Hey, Jude-girl," Joe called after his wife. "Where's my gun?"

Judith gnashed her teeth. During her four years of

widowhood she had forgotten how men, even sharp-eyed homicide detectives such as Joe Flynn, couldn't find a bowling ball in the bathroom sink. Suppressing the urge to tell her husband to look in the vicinity of his backside, Judith opened her mouth to reply. But Joe had spotted the holster and was grinning with the pleasure of discovery.

"Hey, how'd it get there?" he asked in surprise.

"Gee, I don't know, Joe. I suppose it grew little leather feet and walked, meanwhile tossing socks and shirts every which way. Are you taking that with you?" It was Judith's turn to evince surprise.

But Joe shook his head. "No need. I'll ditch it in the closet. Or what about that little safe you've got?"

Judith rarely used the safe, but considered it an excellent repository for Joe's .38 special. "It's in the basement, behind the hot water tank. I think."

"Right." Joe was filling his shaving kit; Judith headed out into the little foyer which served as a family sitting room. On her left, the door to Mike's room was closed. On her right, the door to Gertrude's former room stood ajar. As if, Judith thought with a pang, it was expecting Gertrude Grover to return at any moment. Judith consoled herself that by Monday she might have some good news for her mother. If the Swedish carpenter's estimates were relatively reasonable and his schedule wasn't too busy, Gertrude might be home for Christmas. Of course Judith must discuss it more fully with Joe, but not now, with his departure at hand.

She had just descended the short flight from the third floor when she heard a tremendous crash and a piercing scream. The sounds emanated from the front bedroom. Judith raced down the hallway and pounded on the door.

"Mr. Pacetti! What is it? What's wrong? Mr. Pacetti?" Judith's heart thumped along with her fists. Fleetingly, she wondered if her insurance agent had already increased her coverage as she'd requested the previous day. It was a callous thought, she realized, since Mario Pacetti might be in a lot more trouble than she was.

Amina Pacetti, clad in a flowing peach peignoir edged with black osprey feathers, yanked the door open. Her dark eyes were wide and her golden hair was not as neatly coiffed as usual. "My husband fell out of bed! He is killed!" She leaned against the open door, a hand flung across her eyes.

Judith tensed, then grimly entered the room. To her relief, Mario Pacetti was far from dead. He was wallowing around on the carpet, his legs tangled up in the sheets. Bending down, Judith tried to extricate him.

"Help! Help! I suffocate!" Pacetti clawed at his throat, though nothing bound him in that region. "Tonight, I sing! Where is Plunkett?"

Plunkett, in fact, was at the doorway, along with Joe Flynn. Both had heard the commotion and come running to the second floor. Seeing the holster in Joe's hand, Amina screamed again. "We're all going to die! It is the Mafia! Our blood will be on their hands! Aaaay!"

By reflex, Joe went for his badge. "I'm a policeman, remember? Now shut the hell up." Joe moved swiftly to help Judith with the struggling Pacetti.

At last they had the tenor free and sitting on the bed. He appeared shaken, but otherwise unharmed.

"What happened?" inquired Judith in as solicitous a tone as she could muster.

Pacetti eyed the bedclothes as if they had betrayed him. "I was attacked. Someone came in this room and tried to strangle me." His round brown eyes darted from Judith to Joe to Amina and finally rested on Plunkett. "Where were you when I needed you?"

Before Plunkett could respond, Amina flew across the room in a billow of peach chiffon and black feathers. *"Caro!* It was I who came in! To wake you! You must have been dreaming."

"What?" Pacetti's eyes narrowed as he focused on his wife. "No! It could not be . . ." Though he sounded certain, a shadow of doubt passed over his face. "There was no one else here?"

With a quick, anxious look over her shoulder, Amina shook her head. "No." She spoke in rapid Italian, apparently soothing her husband. At last, he rose from the bed. "Well. Then I shave and shower." With an imperious twitch of his pajama-clad shoulders, Mario Pacetti trotted off toward the bathroom.

Winston Plunkett, looking faintly frustrated, withdrew discreetly. Joe, pocketing his badge, followed, presumably heading for the basement to stash his gun. Judith waited for Amina to collect herself.

"By the way," said Judith, "do you own a white, short, lace-trimmed negligee?" In all the confusion that had ensued after the Pacetti party's arrival, Judith had forgotten about Arlene's find.

"Short negligee?" Amina wrinkled her nose in scorn. "I never wear short. Always long. Like this." Her hand fluttered over the peach chiffon.

Judith stepped aside as Amina exited the bedroom, heading for her own quarters next door. Hurrying downstairs, Judith put the bratwurst under the broiler and reheated the frying pan for the *grössita*. From the living room, she could hear Schutzendorf growling at somebody, either Tippy or Plunkett.

But it was Tippy who poked her head into the kitchen a few seconds later. She was holding her coffee cup and wearing a black bustier with bright green skintight pants and a pair of long earrings that looked like ice picks.

"The pot's empty. Is there any more coffee out here?"

Judith poured from the carafe she had reserved for herself and Joe. After offering cream and sugar, she posed the same question to Tippy that she had asked of Amina.

Tippy looked befuddled. "White? No. When I sleep, I like to go barefoot—all over." She giggled into her coffee cup.

Judith turned away so that Tippy couldn't see her hostess roll her eyes. Above her, the kitchen clock showed five minutes after nine. Her chances of going to the airport with Joe were dwindling.

"Have you worked for Mr. Plunkett very long?" Judith asked, since Tippy showed no signs of leaving the kitchen.

"Oh, yes," replied Tippy with vigor. "Much longer than for anyone else. It's been over four months now."

Judith blinked. "Really. What do you . . . uh . . . do?"

It was Tippy's turn to roll her eyes. "Everything." She set the coffee cup down and hopped up on the counter. Judith winced, remembering the endless number of times she had scolded Mike for doing the same thing. "Files. Records. Documents. Lists. Notes. I could go on and on. And they all have to be *in alphabetical order.*" She heaved a big sigh, which did strange things to the bustier.

"Wow," remarked Judith, gratified to hear footsteps on the front staircase. "That sounds rough."

"It is. And sometimes I have to answer the phone. Or even make calls. It just never ends. But," added Tippy on a brighter note, "it's kind of interesting, though."

"I should think so," said Judith, peering into the dining room. Both Pacettis were sitting down at the table, and Judith uttered a sigh of relief. She might yet make it to the airport. "It isn't everyone who gets to be around a celebrity like Mario Pacetti."

"Mmmmm." Tippy didn't sound impressed. "I don't like opera all that much. They sing so high up and you can't understand a word they're saying. Plus, they always die. It's depressing."

Judith, who was furiously turning large chunks of German pancake in the frying pan, gave a little shrug. "You either like it or you don't, I suppose. Still, there must be perks being connected to someone like Pacetti."

"Oh—yeah." Again, Tippy wasn't very enthusiastic. "I saw Robert De Niro once in New York. And Geena Davis in L.A. She was in a boutique on Rodeo Drive." Tippy pronounced "Rodeo" as if it were a horse show instead of a street.

Judith began to despair of bolstering the merits of Tippy's job. It sounded as if she was a glorified file clerk, but obviously her talents lay elsewhere. *Literally,* thought Judith not without a touch of feline venom. On the other hand, she couldn't see the bloodless Winston Plunkett bouncing around in the buff with Tippy. Or anyone else, actually. And come to think of it, she realized that on neither night of their stay had she heard telltale footsteps after lights-out on the second floor. Judith was puzzled, but there wasn't time for further conjecture. She began bringing breakfast out to the Pacettis, who were head-to-head in deep, whispered conversation. Since they spoke in Italian, Judith had no idea what they were talking about. But, she reflected, Winston Plunkett would, and so maybe would Bruno Schutzendorf. Since the two men were still in the living room, Judith had to presume that the Pacettis didn't wish to be overheard.

A horn honked outside just as Judith dished up the scrambled eggs. She hurried through the entry hall to look out the front door and make sure it was Renie and Bill. The blue Chevrolet sedan stood parked in the drive. Bill had popped the trunk open; Renie was waving through the windshield. Judith started to wave back, then noticed that she had forgotten to bring in the morning paper. She reached down to get it and saw something stuck under the welcome mat.

The sheet of paper was ordinary white stationery, torn off a writing tablet. The message, however, was not so ordinary. A crudely drawn dagger, dripping with blood, filled the center of the page. At the bottom, was another snatch of music. Judith noted there were five notes in the treble. She juggled the paper, trying not to smudge it with her own fingerprints. She was torn between showing Bill and Renie and returning to the house, when Joe came down the front stairs with his suitcase in one hand and a briefcase in the other.

"You ready?" he said to Judith, then saw her startled expression. "What's wrong?"

"This," replied Judith, holding the paper in front of him. "It was under the mat."

Joe sucked in his breath. "Oh, great!" He stared at the

paper, then set down both suitcase and briefcase before turning back into the house. "I'm calling Woody," he said over his shoulder.

Judith went out to the Jones' car. Renie had rolled down the window. "What's up, coz? You look like the pigs ate your little brother, as Grandma Grover used to say."

Judith acknowledged Bill Jones with a weak smile. She showed them the piece of paper, then recounted the story of the rock.

"Why didn't you tell me that before?" asked Renie with a scowl.

"You've been busy with your cancer research project; I've been up to my ears with this gang of goonies. No Phyliss, either. I haven't had a chance to turn around for the last two days," Judith explained. "I've only talked to Mother once."

"Lucky," sighed Renie. "The reason we're five minutes late is because I couldn't get my mother off the phone. I think she was afraid I might have a sudden violent urge to hop on the plane with Bill and Joe."

Bill leaned across his wife. "Let me see that, Judith, please. Hold it up closer." His square, solid face was more earnest than usual. "The musical part is very precise, even if the drawing isn't. But an adult did both," he said after a considerable silence. "It may be crude, but it's not child-like."

Judith wasn't comforted by Bill's words. If anyone could decipher anything out of a wretched drawing, it would be William Jones, PhD, Clinical Psychologist, University Professor, and Counselor to the Severely Disturbed.

"But is it dangerous?" asked Judith.

Bill's sandy eyebrows lifted slightly above the rims of his glasses. "That's impossible to say, on the face of it. I'd have to go more by the method than the manner. That is, the picture and those notes don't mean much in themselves. But after two of them, a pattern is being established. The problem is, nobody can really know much of anything until whoever is doing this acts out."

"You mean shows up with a butcher knife and starts hacking?" inquired Judith.

Bill nodded. "That's right. You've got some highly strung people staying here, I gather from Renie. Especially Mario Pacetti. This could merely be an attempt to upset him, throw him off his game, so to speak. It could be a rival, a spurned woman, a musician he insulted. You're dealing with artistic temperament. It's hard to say."

Renie made a little huffing noise. "The artistic temperament has nothing to do with graphics. Whoever drew that might as well have done it with his lips. Or hers."

"I mean musical temperament," said Bill, still earnest. He looked at the digital clock on the dashboard. "Where's Joe? It's almost nine-thirty. We could run into traffic . . ."

Joe was coming out of the house at a jog. He threw his cases into the Chevrolet's trunk, slammed the lid, then grabbed Judith's arm. "Let's go. Those screwballs can fend for themselves."

"But . . ." protested Judith.

Joe opened the door and practically shoved Judith into the backseat. "I told them you were going to be gone for an hour or two. I put Dippy or Drippy or Tippy or whatever her name is in charge. If that bimbo can't pour a cup of coffee, she might as well resign from the human race. Let's hit it, Mr. Jones. We're out of here."

Bill did, and they were.

# FIVE

RENIE TALKED JUDITH into stopping for an early lunch at a restaurant en route from the airport. The New Orleans flight had taken off almost half an hour late and by the time the cousins left the terminal, it was approaching eleven-thirty. Judith had protested that she should go straight home, but Renie was adamant.

"I haven't heard hide nor hair of you since Thursday," said Renie after they gave their order to an oval-faced Filipino waitress. "Now fill me in on what's been happening with the Pacetti crew."

Judith did. Renie listened, her brown eyes wide. "Wow," she breathed at last, "no wonder you've been busy! Where are they all going today?"

Judith dashed a little salt and pepper over her shrimp Caesar salad. "Pacetti is resting for tonight's performance. Mrs. Pacetti is watching him rest. Plunkett—and I suppose Tippy—are doing something at the opera house, probably regarding Pacetti's contract or whatever. Schutzendorf said he was going to the zoo."

"A good place for him," remarked Renie, bolting down a large mouthful of French bread. "Maybe they'll keep him. Did you say he was Emil Fischer's nephew?"

Judith grimaced at Renie. "Great-nephew, I think. You know who he is?"

"Sure," Renie replied. "Very famous, turn-of-the-century German opera singer."

"Hmmmm." Judith fingered her chin. "Is that right?"

"Of course it's right. Look it up in your biographical dictionary." Renie sounded vaguely irked that Judith would question her knowledge about anything operatic. But soothed as always by food, she shelved her sudden pique. "So you never found out who the white negligee belonged to?"

Judith shook her head. "Both Tippy and Amina deny it was theirs. It wouldn't fit Schutzendorf, and somehow I can't see the other two . . ." She gave Renie a wry look as her voice trailed off.

"You never know," said Renie, munching on a fat french fry. "I suppose it could have blown over from one of the neighbors'."

"Not Arlene's style," said Judith. "Jeanne Ericson wears T-shirts to bed. And Mrs. Dooley is into flannel. It beats me. I think Tippy or Amina must be lying. But why?"

"They're nuts, that's why. They're all nuts." Renie dipped a piece of deep-fried halibut in tartar sauce. "Is Woody Price really going to keep an eye on the house?"

"Somebody is," said Judith. "Look, coz, let's cut to the serious stuff."

Renie looked up from the mess she had made in her lap. For Renie, eating wasn't exactly a spectator sport. "Like what?"

Judith edged closer on the booth's vinyl seat. She gazed across the table at her cousin. "You know—like what are you wearing to the opera tonight?"

Renie laughed. Crumbs flew. Tartar sauce spilled. Coleslaw dripped. The cousins were back in synch.

Judith had spent a busy afternoon, with trips to the grocery store, the liquor store, the bakery, and a quick call on Gertrude and Aunt Deb, who were arguing over which of their husbands had died with the most hair. Aunt Deb was right, but Gertrude had won by virtue of a phone call to Alice Wilinski, a mutual friend and longtime dipsomaniac who, Judith figured, probably couldn't remember if her own husband, Gus, had ever had any hair at all.

Upon her return to the B&B, Judith had worked like a whirlwind, cleaning the second floor, making a quick pass with the vacuum cleaner in the living and dining rooms, and doing two loads of laundry. Her attempt to organize the kitchen had to be postponed. By the time she came up from the basement, it was almost four o'clock and her guests had congregated for preperformance snacks. Judith grimaced as she witnessed the plundering of the refrigerator. Amina was boiling pasta, tossing salad, mixing dressing. Mario was sitting at the table, napkin tucked under his chin, knife and fork at the ready. Tippy was removing a pile of barbecued jo-jo potatoes from the microwave and smothering them with catsup. Bruno Schutzendorf was frying at least six sausages, ritualistically turning them every ten seconds, then adding a splash of water from the teakettle to increase their sizzle. Even Winston Plunkett was foraging in the bread box. Amina and Bruno vied for control of the stove, she waving a pasta ladle, he brandishing a meat fork. Judith decided it was too dangerous to stay in the kitchen. She could clean up later.

By contrast that evening, Hillside Manor was singularly quiet. Judith was left alone in the house—no husband, no mother, no son, no guests, no cat. The Pacettis had gone to the opera house around five, with Mario muffled to his nose in scarves under his cashmere overcoat, and Amina carrying a sable muff that matched her hat. Tippy and Plunkett accompanied the Pacettis. A skimpy scarlet dress showed off every curve of Tippy's figure, and the feather boa she had slung over her bare shoulders gave the impression that she was headed not for the opera house, but a cathouse. Plunkett, as usual, wore gray. Bruno Schutzendorf was the last to leave, resplendent in white tie, tails, and top hat, though the effect was somewhat diminished by the green Tyrolean cape.

Judith had hoped to get some of her bulbs in, but ran out of time. The rain, which had begun on Friday, pattered softly against the windows. It was not sufficient to daunt a native Pacific Northwesterner such as Judith from working outside, but by the time she finished her other tasks, it was beginning to get dark. Wistfully, Judith looked through the kitchen window. In the garden, the remaining flowers drooped on their stalks. The grass, which had turned brown during the long, unusually dry months of summer, was restored to its lush green state. The old apple tree, a remnant of the original Grover orchard, still sported fruit. The rain kept falling, filling the stone birdbath, washing over the small statue of St. Francis and the birds, giving a silver sheen to the white picket fence that separated Hillside Manor from the Dooleys' property.

Fortunately, Joe had put the lawn furniture indoors before leaving for New Orleans. Unfortunately, he had never got around to raking up the leaves. Judith watched more of them drift down from the maples and the hawthorns and the mountain ash. Maybe Dooley would do it for her—if she paid him enough.

After many mental gymnastics, Judith had decided on wearing a taupe high-necked silk jacquard blouse with a straight black flannel skirt under a black and taupe tiger-print jacket. Renie, she knew, was going with draped red wool crepe. Judith preened in front of the long mirror in her bedroom, wondering what Joe was doing about now. It was ten o'clock in New Orleans. Maybe he and Bill had retired to their hotel room. Bill Jones liked to keep strict hours; Joe Flynn wasn't acquainted with the concept. Judith wondered who would win the war of wills.

Heading downstairs, Judith paused on the landing between the first and second floors. She thought she heard a noise from somewhere in the vicinity of the guest bedrooms, but decided it was only the wind, making the old house creak. Since none of her guests had been at Hillside

Manor when she returned from the airport, she had not shown them the piece of paper that had been slipped under the welcome mat. It was probably just as well, she reasoned, for if Bill Jones was right, perhaps only mischief was intended. There was certainly no reason to upset Mario Pacetti further just before a performance.

As promised, Woody Price had sent a squad car by at regular intervals. About 3:00 P.M., Officers Perez and Doyle had stopped to collect the rock and the sheet of paper. Corazon Perez and Ted Doyle had both looked curiously at Judith when she'd asked them to get a musical expert to identify the five notes at the bottom of the page. But this was Lieutenant Flynn's wife, they were following Woody Price's instructions, and they might as well humor her. Still, Judith knew they thought it was a joke. She hoped they were right.

Nonetheless, Judith checked the front porch again. It was pristinely devoid of threatening missives. The corn tassels stirred in the wind. Going back into the house, she settled onto one of the matching sofas and waited for Renie.

In the corner, the grandfather clock ticked on toward 7:00 P.M. The curtain was at seven-thirty, but Renie said Maestro Dunkowitz never started until at least seven thirty-seven. The rain continued to spatter the windowpanes. Judith glanced around the big, comfortable living room—the baby grand piano, the tall, crammed bookcases that flanked the window seat, the fireplace mantel with its array of family photos: Gertrude and Donald Grover holding hands in the early years of their marriage; Grandpa and Grandma Grover, cutting the tiered cake for their fiftieth anniversary; Bill and Renie posing in front of a Reno pawnshop; Mike as a baby; Mike on his first day of kindergarten; Mike in his high school graduation picture; Mike with Kristin by the Christmas tree; and the latest addition to the collection, Judith and Joe cheek to cheek next to the carved wooden doors of Our Lady, Star of the Sea. There was a picture of Dan McMonigle, tucked behind

Uncle Vince and Auntie Vance sitting on the deck of their beach house. Judith had considered taking it down when she married Joe Flynn. But that wouldn't have been fair to Mike. Dan had been Mike's father—at least as far as Mike was concerned. Judith got up to scrutinize the most recent picture of Mike. The red hair was darker—and much thicker—than Joe's. Otherwise, the resemblance was unremarkable. Mike's features were the spitting image of his grandfather, Donald Grover. And, by coincidence, Dan's mother was a redhead. Joe and Judith had agreed there was no need to tell Mike the truth about his parentage. At least not yet.

Judith ambled over to the bay window, the three large panes displaying black silhouettes of a cat, a bat, and a witch. It was almost dark, with the lights of downtown glowing amber in the rain. Two big freighters were tied up in the bay, superferries crisscrossed the water, and a tug was hauling a big barge into port. In the cul-de-sac, Judith saw the headlights of Renie's car. She shrugged into her coat, picked up her handbag, and started out toward the entry hall. A smile touched her lips as she took one last look around the living room. Warm. Cozy. Peaceful. Mike was content to be away at school, a solution for Gertrude's dilemma was in the offing, and best of all, she and Joe were married. A sense of serenity came over Judith as she went out through the entry hall.

It would, of course, not last long.


"What," demanded Judith with a gasp as she and Renie settled into their front row center seats in the first balcony, "did you and Bill pay for these?"

"We sold one of the kids," replied Renie, laying her black raincoat over the plush red chair. "Actually, I hammered out a deal when I designed that symphony brochure last summer. Bill and I weren't that keen on going to the symphony more than once or twice a year, but we definitely wanted to upgrade our opera seats. I told Maestro Dunkowitz I insisted on having a better view than our orthodontist had. This is it. Dr. Feldman is around the corner, to your left, second row. Ha-ha."

Judith cast a discreet glance in Dr. Feldman's direction. He, like several of the other men in the boxes, was wearing a tuxedo. Judith couldn't imagine Bill Jones, who taught his university classes in a sport shirt and washpants, going to such bother. She said so to Renie.

"You're right," agreed Renie. "On the other hand, Dr. Feldman wears his tuxedo when he works on his patients." Seeing Judith's startled look, she laughed. "I'm kidding, but believe me, he could afford to. Not only is he raking it in as an orthodontist, but his wife is a throat specialist. In fact, she's the family star, or so Feldman tells me. Pretty, too." Renie nodded in the Feldmans' direction.

"At least you're past the braces stage now," said Judith, taking in Mrs. Feldman's black shoulder-length hair, classic profile, and chic white evening gown. "So am I, thank God. I guess you finish off with teeth just in time to start with college."

"How true," agreed Renie, glancing through her program. The opera house, which was located at the bottom of Heraldsgate Hill only five minutes away from Hillside Manor, was rapidly filling up. The rich paneling gleamed under the houselights; the heavy red curtain shrouded the stage; the murmur of three thousand voices echoed around them. The air of anticipation was tangible. Not only was this the opening night of the season, but serious opera lovers knew how rare it was to hear two singers of the first magnitude perform on the local stage. Judith had not been in the opera house for years. Wryly, she noted that it had changed considerably less than she had.

A wave of applause broke out as Maestro Dunkowitz stepped up to the podium. A moment later, the poignant strains of the prelude filled the opera house. Judith sat back to enjoy an exceptional musical treat.

As the curtain parted to reveal a handsomely decorated Paris salon of the 1840s, the orchestra shifted gears into Verdi's mood of revelry. A glittering chandelier hung above a long table set with crystal and china. Silver epergnes perched at each end, while in the middle a floral arrangement of exotic blooms held sway. Second Empire furnishings in rich green and blue velvet reposed against a backdrop of tall, arched windows. Half of the chorus was greeting the other half, while Inez Garcia-Green, in layers of white tulle, glided across the stage to welcome the mezzo-soprano. The mood on stage was festive, and Judith caught herself tapping her foot. Inez's lyrical voice floated effortlessly into the farthest reaches of the house. As far as Judith could tell, Amina Pacetti's claim that the soprano was in decline did not appear to be true.

In the background, the servants prepared the table with food and drink. Renie had her opera glasses trained on the action. "Hey," she said in a low voice, "is that Tippy de Whoozits as one of the supers? Gray and white maid's costume, big frilly thing on her head." She passed the glasses to Judith.

Judith focused. Even with the opera glasses, it was difficult to be sure, but the young woman arranging champagne bottles on the supper table certainly resembled Tippy. "Could be," said Judith, handing the glasses back to Renie. "Maybe that's one of the perks."

Tippy, or her look-alike, melted in with the other supers. A moment later, Mario Pacetti and another man entered the salon. Pacetti was impeccably dressed in a black frock coat and a ruffled white shirt.

"He's lost weight," Renie whispered. "Or else he's wearing the world's tightest girdle."

Judith gave a slight nod, then caught Pacetti's first notes: *"Mar-che-se . . ."* She frowned, thinking of the rock.

The revelers began to seat themselves at the table. Pacetti was next to Garcia-Green. A tiara sparkled on the soprano's head; white camellias descended from décolletage to hem. Wine was being poured; plates were passed. Inez and the tenor who was playing Pacetti's friend were doing most of the singing. It seemed to Judith that Inez's exaggerated gestures with a huge ostrich-feather fan did much to obliterate Pacetti from the audience's view. At last, he sang again, five short notes. Judith looked up at the supratitles. "Yes, it is true." She wondered . . .

Everyone but Pacetti now seemed to be taking turns singing as the guests exchanged flippant remarks. Inez was giving Pacetti a coquettish look as she poured him a glass of wine. The tenor made a gallant toast to the soprano. Everyone seemed to be urging Pacetti to sing a drinking song. He demurred, then surrendered. The rousing notes of "Libiamo" bounced off the opera house walls. Judith smiled; the set piece was one of her favorites. At the conclusion, enthusiastic applause erupted. The singers turned to the audience as if toasting their listeners, then drank.

Renie nudged Judith. "Lucky us, both Pacetti and Garcia-Green are in good voice. I'm anxious to hear Sydney Haines when he comes on in Act II."

"That's right, the father doesn't appear until then," Judith whispered back. "I was waiting for him to show up at the party in a Yellow Cab."

The choristers milled about the stage in various attitudes of convivial party attendance. Pacetti and Inez were left alone to argue over love and pleasure. From offstage came the sounds of another, smaller orchestra. Everyone began heading for the center door, presumably to dance. Or so Judith deduced from the supratitles.

Inez Garcia-Green staggered and uttered an exclamation. Her guests evinced concern, but she sang her reassurances.

"Don't worry about me," murmured Renie, loosely translating the opera singer's phrase. "She sounds like my mother." Judith grinned.

Inez sat down, a hand to her impressive bosom. More concern, more reassurances. At last, everyone exited from the stage except the tenor and the soprano. Pacetti was ardent; Garcia-Green, cynical. They were close together, Inez in her chair, Mario at her side. Renie passed the opera glasses back to Judith.

"Look—they're kicking each other."

Judith adjusted the glasses again. Sure enough, it appeared that Mario Pacetti was trying to stomp on Inez Garcia-Green's feet. She, in turn, was attempting to strike his shins from under the voluminous tulle hem of her ball gown. "Yikes!" breathed Judith. "Pacetti looks like he's foaming at the mouth!"

Verdi's score, however, conveyed a much more idyllic relationship. Inez, as Violetta, was beginning to succumb. Mario, as Alfredo, was turning up the heat meter in his ardor. Stepping directly in front of his leading lady, he began to sing the familiar duet, "Un Dì Felice Eterea." His body seemed to twitch and his voice sounded uneven. Judith tried to see if Garcia-Green was on the attack. But the soprano was getting to her feet, preparing to join in. Just as she faced Pacetti, his arms and legs seemed to go every which way. Before he could utter the next phrase, he collapsed at Inez's hem.

Judith, Renie, and the rest of the audience let out a collective gasp. Not to be outdone, Garcia-Green emitted an ear-shattering shriek. Maestro Dunkowitz put down his baton. The notes from the orchestra died away as the curtain was quickly drawn.

"Is he sick?" asked Renie, half rising from her seat. "Did Inez stab him or something? What on earth . . . ?"

There was a great rustling and much murmuring in the audience. On the main floor, Judith could see several ushers moving uncertainly down the aisles. Maestro Dunkowitz had left the orchestra pit. The errant notes of a violin floated eerily across the house.

Renie had sat down again, chewing on her lower lip. "Why don't they tell us something? Where's that effete yet ineffectual drip who manages the place, Creighton Layton?" She paused to flip through her program. "Why don't they turn the houselights on? I want to see who Pacetti's understudy is."

"Here," said Judith, taking her keychain out of her purse. "Use this little flashlight."

Renie flicked the flashlight on. "An American, Justin Kerr. I think he sang the tenor lead in *Don Pasquale* here last season. Bill and I missed it because they did a modern production set at an AMA convention in Anaheim. There were Disneyland characters all over the place. I resent Goofy and Pluto singing Donizetti." With a snort of annoyance, she handed the little flashlight back to Judith.

The audience was growing increasingly restless. Several patrons were now standing, stretching their legs, but keeping their eyes on the closed curtain. The orchestra members were also moving about, talking to each other, trying to look out into the wings.

At last, a tuxedoed figure appeared on stage, entering from the left. "Layton," whispered Renie.

"Ladies and gentlemen," said Creighton Layton in a cultured, if nervous, voice, "we regret to inform you that there has been a serious accident. Mario Pacetti is very ill. Given the gravity of his condition, and the disconcerting effect it has had on the rest of the cast, we regret to inform you that this performance is canceled. Please retain your ticket stubs. You may call the opera house Monday after 9:00 A.M. for information concerning remuneration. Thank you." Layton raced from the stage.

"Drat," said Renie, with a scowl. "What did the little twerp do, eat too much calzone?"

Judith, her face etched with concern, turned to Renie. "We should go backstage. I need to know if any of them will be coming back to the B&B or if they'll be keeping watch at the hospital or . . ."

Renie waved away Judith's suggestion. "Not a chance. It'll be a zoo back there. Security, emergency types, the press. Somebody will call, I'm sure."

A single word had caught Judith's attention. "The press? Don't you know the music critic, Melissa Bargroom?"

"Sure," replied Renie as their seatmates in the center box swirled about them. "So what?"

"She'd know what's happening. Why don't we try to find her?"

Renie rolled her eyes toward the farthest reaches of the opera house. "She's doing her job. She's got a deadline to meet. We'd never catch her in this . . ."

But Judith was already pressing her way up the steps that led to the nearest exit. With a resigned sigh, Renie trotted along behind her cousin. " 'Easygoing,' " Renie muttered. "That's what they always called her when we were kids. Ha!"

Renie was right, however, about getting close to the action. After fighting their way through the main lobby, the cousins discovered that ushers were guarding not only the stage, but the side entrances that led to the Green Room and the backstage area. Judith's request to speak with Melissa Bargroom was met with a clamped-jaw refusal by a female usher.

But Judith wasn't giving up. To Renie's chagrin, Judith found a policeman in the atrium foyer. Identifying herself as Mrs. Joe Flynn, she tried to coax the patrolman into letting her go backstage. He, too, refused, but his rejection was phrased politely.

"Rats," groaned Judith as the cousins began to wend their way through the dwindling crowd toward the parking garage across the street. "You're right—we'll have to wait." She stopped at the curb where the stoplight had turned amber. "Hold it, coz—there's an ambulance at the rear of the opera house. And a fire truck, and more policemen. Let's go."

But even as she spoke, the red lights on the ambulance began to flash through the rain, the siren shrilled over the sound of traffic, and the screech of tires resounded as the vehicle pulled out into the thoroughfare. Two squad cars followed, also with lights ablaze and sirens screaming. Only the fire truck remained.

Reluctantly, Judith followed Renie and the rest of the herd as the corner light changed to Walk. During the long wait for the cars to move down the ramps in the big parking garage, Judith was uncharacteristically subdued. As they started up the steep Counterbalance that led from the crest of Heraldsgate Hill almost to sea level on the outskirts of downtown, Renie made an effort to cheer her cousin.

"Build me a drink and I'll stick around until you hear something, okay?"

"Sure," said Judith with a flicker of enthusiasm. "It's only eight-thirty. We, too, can sing a drinking song."

Entering as usual through the back door, Judith made straight for the front. But again, there was no sign of anything untoward on the porch. Judith slipped out of her tiger-print jacket and checked her answering machine. There were three calls, two for reservations in mid-November, and one from Phyliss Rackley, announcing that her lumbago was better, but her neuralgia was acting up something fierce. Still, she'd try to come in on Monday, God willing.

"Poor God," murmured Judith, going to the liquor cabinet. "He gets blamed for more things than I do."

Renie accepted a bourbon and water. Judith carried her scotch into the living room where the cousins sat down opposite each other on the matching sofas.

"It's cool enough to build a fire," Judith noted, but made no move to do so. "I've got to get my bulbs in before we have a frost."

"We may not get one this year," said Renie, removing her shoes and tucking her feet under her bottom. "What's the point? The squirrels and the raccoons eat the damned things anyway. Next year, I'm going to stick to perennials. Say, did you have any extra lily-of-the-valley pips? I could use some of those."

"I was saving them for Mrs. Dooley, but I could dig up a few more for you. You can't put them in until almost Christmas."

Renie gave a nod of assent. "I'll probably forget. It's such a hectic time of year around then. Hey, when's your carpenter coming?"

Judith started to reply but the phone rang. She got up to answer the extension on the little table next to the window seat. Winston Plunkett's thin voice sounded very wobbly.

"Mrs. Flynn? I have some terrible news. Mr. Pacetti has ... passed away." Plunkett's voice broke on the last syllable.

With a gasp that made Renie jump, Judith clutched at the phone. "You mean ... *he died?*" she said, aware that her remark was idiotic.

"Yes." Plunkett apparently had regained control of himself. "In the ambulance, on the way to the hospital."

"Oh, dear." Judith had her back to Renie and couldn't see her cousin's frantic gestures. "What was it—heart?"

"It would seem so," said Plunkett. "I wanted to let you know in case some of the rest of us don't return tonight. Mrs. Pacetti has been sedated. Mr. Schutzendorf is being examined for a possible stroke. And Ms. de Caro is hysterical. Naturally, we have our keys. Please don't wait up for us." He rang off.

Judith replaced the receiver and turned to Renie in a daze. Renie was on her feet, holding her drink with both hands. Her brown eyes were very wide. "Toes up?"

Judith nodded.

"Heart, I gather?"

Judith nodded again.

"Damn!" Renie sat back down, spilling bourbon on her red wool cape. "He wasn't that old," she remarked, her face puckered with dismay under the fringe of chestnut hair. "Mid-forties, I think. But look at Caruso, he died at about the same age."

Slowly, Judith made her way back to the sofa. "Right." She sat down and took a sip of her scotch, aware that her hands were shaking. After a long pause, she met Renie's gaze head-on. "Coz, I'm a terrible woman."

Renie's expression changed from dismay to puzzlement. "Why?"

"That poor man with his wonderful voice and talent for giving so much joy to people is dead, and all I can do is thank God that he didn't die *here*. I don't think I'll ever get over having all those emergency vehicles show up on the doorstep after the fortune-teller was killed in my very own dining room." She saw Renie start to interrupt and made a shushing gesture. "I know, I know, the notoriety may actually have helped, not hindered, my business. But even so, if it had happened more than once, I would have felt that this place was hexed."

"Don't be silly," said Renie. "With all the people you have coming through the doors, something awful is bound to happen. Illness, accidents, even something fatal like a heart attack or an aneurism." She got to her feet again, reaching for Judith's half-empty glass. "Here, let's freshen our drinks. I don't want to drive home stewed, but it won't hurt to have another shot."

Judith didn't argue. "Maybe you're right," she said as Renie headed for the kitchen. "Still, I don't want to get the reputation of being a high-risk bed-and-breakfast. The next thing I know, guests will be bungee-jumping out the windows."

"What?" called Renie from the kitchen. She'd missed most of what Judith was saying. "Hold on."

"I said," Judith yelled, "that I don't want to . . ."

"Yipes!" exclaimed Renie, passing through the dining room and glancing out through the entry hall to the street. She stopped, getting a firm grip on the glasses.

"What's wrong?" Judith swiveled on the sofa.

Renie skittered into the living room, hastily depositing their drinks on the coffee table. "It's not an ambulance," she said in a rapid delivery. "It's not the fire department or an aid car. But," she went on with an air of apology, "it *is* the police."

Judith groaned.

# SIX

IN THE BRIEF time it took Judith to open the door, she hoped to see Woody Price, Joe's second in command. Or even Officers Perez and Doyle, whom she had at least met that afternoon. Instead, she was confronted with a very small woman and a very tall man she had never seen before in her life.

Officer Nancy Prentice was possibly in her late twenties—or maybe her early forties. Her expressionless face made it hard to tell. No makeup, mousy hair pulled back in a ponytail, pale blue eyes cool as the autumn air, Prentice had a no-nonsense manner and a voice to match.

"Mrs. Joseph Flynn?" At Judith's affirmative response, Officer Prentice asked to enter. Judith stepped aside.

The policewoman surveyed the entry hall with its big bouquet of dahlias, Victorian hat rack, ebony umbrella stand, guest registration table, and the door that led to the downstairs bathroom under the main staircase. On the newel-post at the end of the carved balustrade reposed Judith's tiger-print jacket. Officer Prentice looked as if she did not approve, either of the jacket itself or the careless manner in which it had been tossed.

"Would you come into the living room?" asked Judith, gathering her aplomb along with her hostess skills. "My cousin and I were just having a drink."

"Uuum." The comment, if it could be defined as such, came from Officer Prentice's partner. Stanley Cernak was upwards of six-four and probably weighed no more than a hundred and seventy pounds. His straw-blond hair grew in a cowlick and his gray eyes seemed to be constantly narrowed, as if he expected to find something suspicious in even the most ordinary items of daily life. Judith guessed him to be about thirty, but again, it was difficult to be sure.

Judith introduced Renie to the police officers, whose dark blue uniforms were spattered with rain. Renie raised her glass; Prentice gave an abrupt nod; Cernak grunted.

Disdaining Judith's offer to sit down, Nancy Prentice stood at ramrod attention and delivered the goods. "Mario Pacetti, internationally known opera singer, who has been residing at Hillside Manor for the past three days, has died of an apparent heart attack. To determine whether or not an autopsy will be performed, we must ask you a few routine questions. We will be brief and we expect your full cooperation." She gave a little jerk of her small body. Judith expected her to salute.

"We heard," Judith said quietly. "Mr. Pacetti's business manager, Mr. Plunkett, called us a few minutes ago. We were at the performance. Naturally, we were shaken." She tapped her glass, as if she needed an excuse for being caught drinking an alcoholic beverage in the privacy of her own home on a Saturday night.

"Uuum," said Officer Cernak.

"According to Sergeant Woodrow Price, we understand that certain threatening messages were sent to this address in the past two days," Officer Prentice said as if Judith hadn't spoken. "Officer Cernak and I have not seen them. What was the nature of these threats?"

Judith explained, first about the rock, then about the sheet of paper. "I asked the two patrolpersons who came by this afternoon to have a music expert decipher the notes. Since Mr. Pacetti said that the ones on the rock were . . ."

"What made you think these alleged threats were intended for Mr. Pacetti? Were they addressed to him?" Prentice's interruption crushed Judith's words like a steamroller.

"No, they weren't." Judith fingered her upper lip. It had never occurred to her that the threats, if such they were, had been intended for anyone other than Mario Pacetti. But of course it was possible.

"You are certain that you have no idea where these items came from or who might have sent them?" Prentice was still standing at full attention. Judith noted that Stanley Cernak had a tendency to loll, his tall, thin frame looking a bit like a bendable straw.

"None." Judith was getting a bit impatient with Nancy Prentice's rat-a-tat delivery. "Look, Mr. Pacetti never saw the second delivery. My husband—Lieutenant Joseph Flynn of your homicide division—had me turn the items over to Officers Perez and Doyle this afternoon. That's really all I can tell . . ."

Again, Prentice broke in on Judith. "Did Mr. Pacetti at any time or in any way behave as if he thought his life was being threatened?"

Judith glanced at Renie who was looking annoyed. "Mario Pacetti was a very high-strung performing artist. Mrs. Pacetti is also quite excitable. Both acted as if they thought the rock's message was aimed at Mr. Pacetti. Maybe it was. But what I'm trying to say is that just because the Pacettis got worked up, doesn't necessarily mean . . ."

"Why didn't they call the police?" To Judith and Renie's amazement, it was Cernak who asked the question.

Judith frowned at both officers. "I told you, my husband *is* the police. He handled the matter."

"Did Lieutenant Flynn file a report?" Prentice looked as if she didn't approve of Joe, either.

"I don't know," Judith replied honestly. Joe hadn't mentioned it, but she really had no idea. So much of her husband's time was spent on paperwork that he very well might have gone through the official motions.

"Thank you." This time Prentice actually did raise her hand to her head, as if in salute. The police officers started for the front door.

"Wait a minute," called Judith, getting up. "You mentioned an autopsy. Is there some reason to suspect that Pacetti didn't die of natural causes?"

Prentice, despite an eight-inch disadvantage in height, somehow managed to make Judith feel insignificant. "We can't discuss that. Good night." The officers left, Prentice marching down the front steps, Cernak loping at her side.

Judith went straight to the phone. "I'm calling Woody," she said. "He won't act like such a jackass."

But Woodrow Price was not in. In fact, he was not assigned to the case. There was no assignment, a crisp male voice told Judith, because there was no case. Yet. Judith hung up with fine lines etched on her brow.

"Relax," said Renie. "Pacetti had a heart attack. Maybe he's been dieting too strenuously. Certainly he led a demanding life. It happens. Sad, but true."

Judith gave a little shrug. "Maybe they're talking about an autopsy just so that the family will know for sure what happened. Do the Pacettis have kids?"

"I don't know," answered Renie. "Wait. Yes, they do, all more or less grown. The reason I remember is because they were boy, girl, boy, like our Tom, Anne, and Tony, and just about the same ages. I read it in a magazine a couple of years ago. The Pacettis must have married very young."

Judith's commiserating remarks were cut short by the doorbell. She gave Renie a puzzled look. "Stiff and Stick are back? What did they forget, to arrest us for using incomplete sentences?"

"Maybe it's some of your guests," Renie said as Judith headed once again for the front entrance.

"They all have keys." Judith peered through the curtained oval glass in the old oak door. A man and woman stood on the porch, but they didn't look much like the recently departed police officers. A bit hesitantly, Judith opened the door. "Yes?"

The young man of about thirty was not as tall as Stanley Cernak, but he was an inch or two over six feet. Under the tan suede jacket and casual slacks, Judith could tell that his physique was broad through the shoulders and chest, fairly narrow at the waist and hip. He was handsome, with chiseled features and wavy, dark brown hair. Over one arm, he carried an enormous bouquet. Judging from the tropical blooms, it had come from a florist. His companion was almost Judith's height, a carefully preserved forty-plus, with raven black hair pulled back from sharp features. Fleetingly, Judith guessed her to be quite attractive when she was in full makeup, but at the moment, she looked pale, pinched, and rather plain. She also struck Judith as somewhat familiar.

Despite the fact that the woman clung to his right arm, the handsome young man held out his hand. "I'm Justin Kerr," he said in mellifluous voice. "This is Madame Inez Garcia-Green."

Still clutching at her escort, Inez inclined her head, as if she were a queen acknowledging a lowly subject. Judith ushered them inside. Recognizing the famous soprano at once, Renie bolted from the sofa.

"Señora Garcia! This is a pleasure!" She stared more closely at Justin Kerr. "And Mr. Kerr, I think?"

Justin appeared to be in pain. "These aren't pleasurable circumstances, I'm afraid, Mrs. . . . ah . . ."

"Jones," said Renie, looking faintly shamefaced, but still managing to pump the tenor's hand. "Sorry, I was so surprised to see you here. We were at the opera house tonight." She made an agitated motion with her hands. "Naturally, we're still stunned about Mario Pacetti."

"We, too." Inez Garcia-Green hung her head, though the brief smoldering glance she darted at Justin Kerr conveyed something other than sorrow. Diamond studs sparkled at her ears. She had changed from her white ball gown into a black woolen dress with a matching coat trimmed in fox. The dark aspect of her costume accentuated her pallor. When Judith offered the sofas, Inez seemed reluctant to relinquish her grasp on Justin, but grateful to collapse.

Justin Kerr, however, remained standing. "We brought these," he said, indicating the armful of ginger, lobster claw heliconia, bird of paradise, and protea. "Is Mrs. Pacetti here?"

"No," said Judith, thinking that the flowers were not only wildly exotic, but somehow familiar. "We heard from Mr. Plunkett and it appears Mrs. Pacetti may be staying at the hospital for the night. Possibly Mr. Schutzendorf, too. And Ms. de Caro, maybe." Judith winced. It sounded as if, with the exception of Winston Plunkett, her entire guest list had fallen apart. But then, she realized, they had every right to do so. Pacetti's sudden death must have come as a tremendous shock. Certainly the two newcomers before her also seemed distraught.

Justin Kerr gave Judith a sympathetic look. "It's a terrible tragedy. A real loss to the world of opera. Pacetti had at least ten more years of giving his talent to his fans."

"Five, anyway," put in Inez Garcia-Green, though her expression remained mournful. "He—and I—revived Verdi. True Verdi voices have been much lacking in recent years, you know."

"Interesting," remarked Renie, who felt she should have known as much, but didn't.

Justin Kerr rustled the flowers against his broad chest. "If you don't mind—may I put these in Mrs. Pacetti's room?"

"Oh," said Judith easily, "I'll take care of them. Let me get a vase from the kitchen." She hurried out through the dining room.

Renie, smarting a bit from her ignorance over the state of Verdian affairs in the music world, made an attempt to save face. "Actually," she began, trying to phrase her remarks as tactfully as possible, "despite the paucity of outstanding Verdi singers, you and Pacetti haven't sung much together in recent years, isn't that so?" The question was put to Garcia-Green.

The soprano gave a toss of her raven black hair. "It is a question of individual commitments. Our paths have not crossed for several years, that is true. Now, of course, we shall never sing together again. What sadness this brings me!" Her limpid black eyes seemed to fill with emotion.

"It makes me sad, too," agreed Renie, feeling somewhat vindicated. "I was so looking forward to tonight's performance. Everybody was. I couldn't believe our good fortune when they announced the season last year. How did we get so lucky?"

The question was rhetorical, but Inez took it literally. "Mario asked me to sing this *Traviata* with him. Six years ago, I believe. I agreed." A touch of bitterness was in her lilting Spanish voice.

Renie tried not to stare. At that moment, Judith came back into the room with a tall, widemouthed cut-glass vase. "Here, I'll put the flowers in this and then fill it with water."

But Justin Kerr clutched the bouquet against his broad chest as if it were a shield. "No!" The mellifluous voice was sharp. "That is, you mustn't bother. They're already in water." He shifted his grip on the bouquet to reveal a plastic container. His tone grew more mellow and a charming smile spread over his handsome face. "Just tell me where Mrs. Pacetti's room is located. Please." He made it sound as if Judith were granting him a great favor.

Judith shrugged. "Okay. It's the middle door at the near end of the hall."

As Justin Kerr headed for the front stairs, Renie returned her gaze to Inez Garcia-Green. "I have a Cherubim recording of you and Pacetti doing *Tosca*. That must have been some years ago."

"That is so. In 1982, I believe. We cut two more complete works after that—*L'Elisir d'Amore* and *Faust*. That must have been 1983 and 1984."

"No Verdi?" Renie was like a terrier, worrying a bone.

"Only *Rigoletto* in 1981," replied Inez, a hand touching her right eye. "A pity, I think." With a graceful motion, she got to her feet. "Pardon me, I must adjust my contact lens. The bathroom is upstairs?"

"Yes," said Judith, who had remained standing by the rocker. "But you needn't go all the way up to the second floor. There's one down here, right off the entry hall . . ."

But Inez had glided out of the room and headed straight for the staircase. She was almost on the first landing before Judith finished speaking.

The cousins eyed each other curiously. "What's the thrill about going upstairs?" demanded Judith in a low voice.

Renie frowned. "I don't know. Could they be checking something out?"

Judith shook her head. "It's odd. In fact, it's distinctly odd that these two have come at all. Why not just send the flowers from the florist? Obviously, that's where they bought them."

"Should we check on them?" asked Renie as the rain began to fall harder.

Judith's mouth twisted in an expression of uncertainty. "I don't want to be rude. They may be innocent—of whatever we suspect them of. What *do* we suspect them of, coz?"

Renie fingered her short chin. "Damned if I know. Looking for a short white nightie, maybe?"

"And so what if they are?" Judith shifted from one foot to the other.

"Are all the bedroom doors unlocked up there?" Renie gestured in the vicinity of the ceiling.

"I imagine. I ask guests to leave them unlocked while they're out so that I can clean or deliver or do whatever. It saves me having to carry around a bunch of keys."

"But if any of these people had anything to hide, they'd lock up, right?" Renie was looking very serious, wearing what Judith always referred to as her boardroom face.

"True." Judith pricked her ears for the sound of foot-

steps. She heard a creak above her head, possibly in the
area of Mrs. Pacetti's room. "Unless they start carrying out
Grandma and Grandpa's headboard, it's none of our business, right?"

"I suppose not." Renie replanted herself on the sofa.
"You got anything to eat? All of a sudden, I'm hungry. It's
after nine-thirty, and time for my elaborate snack."

"Sure," said Judith. "Let's forage in the fridge."

Renie eyed the prosciutto, the kielbasa, and the truffles.
"I could make a sandwich out of that. Where's the
cheese?"

"That stuff's not mine," replied Judith. "Tippy got it for
the others up at Falstaff's, along with the green peppers,
the red cabbage, and the goat cheese. They've been doing
a spot of between-meal cooking on their own. I've got
Havarti, though. How about slapping it on some pastrami
and a French roll?"

"Sounds good," said Renie.

It did to Judith, too. With Joe gone, she had not bothered to make herself a full dinner. She rummaged in the
refrigerator, trying to find the mayonnaise, and let out a
small curse when she discovered it had been shoved far to
the rear of the bottom shelf.

"These food-crazed fiends I'm hosting have got this
thing so crammed full of their own stuff that I can't find
mine," she complained. "I shouldn't have let them do their
own cooking. I knew it was a bad idea." Wrestling with
jars of mustard, barbecue sauce, salad dressing, and horse-
radish, she finally managed to extricate the mayonnaise.
As she stood up, a sheepish look crossed her face. "Oh,
dear—there I go again, being mean-minded. Most of this
was for Pacetti, and now he's dead. I wonder if they'll all
move out tomorrow."

Renie, who had found the French rolls in the bread box,
considered the idea. "They might. Certainly they won't
stay for the whole two weeks. There'll be a funeral, in Italy, I imagine, and that'll be handled by Mrs. Pacetti and
Plunkett. So there goes Tippy, too. As for Schutzendorf,

there's no reason for him to stick around. He'll probably attend the funeral."

Judith was trying very hard not to think greedy thoughts. "If they leave," she said carefully, "maybe I could call some of those regulars I had to turn down. Otherwise, I'm out a bundle. I can't expect them to pay if they take off early."

"Did you get a deposit?" asked Renie, buttering the rolls.

"For the first night only," replied Judith, slicing pastrami. "They were supposed to pay up at the end of their stay." Hearing footsteps on the stairs, she went out into the dining room. Justin Kerr was in the entry hall, his broad shoulders hunched.

"Is everything all right?" asked Judith.

"What?" He turned with a jerky movement, then straightened his carriage. "Oh, yes, fine, thank you. I'm not much good at arranging flowers, though. I'm afraid they don't look very artistic."

"I'm sure Mrs. Pacetti will appreciate the thought," said Judith in a soothing voice.

Inez Garcia-Green was descending the stairs, also looking troubled. Seeing Judith in the entry hall, she composed her features and smiled faintly. "Thank you. My vision is much improved. Your bathroom is charming. I like the Spanish galleons in the wallpaper. You do not show the English sinking them, *gracias a Dios*."

"Oh, right, I don't. I mean, the wallpaper doesn't." The comment caught Judith off-guard. Judith actually hated the galleon motif, but had had a hard time matching the border of clipper ships in the bedroom itself. The galleons had been on sale as a remnant.

"We go now," announced Inez, latching onto Justin Kerr and making for the door. "We thank you for your graciousness."

"Certainly," said Judith, her brain still not quite on track. "It's been a pleasure meeting you."

Justin Kerr opened the front door. The rain was falling

hard and fast, in straight heavy drops. "Would you like me to walk you to your car with an umbrella?" asked Judith.

"No, no," replied Justin Kerr, looking faintly uncomfortable as Inez nestled closer. "Our car is right there, in front." The two singers made a dash for it. Judith stood in the doorway, waiting to wave them off. The headlights came on and the car started down the cul-de-sac.

Although it was hard to see through the heavy rain, Judith was almost sure that the car was gray.

"Great pastrami," commented Renie, chomping on her sandwich. "So what's this about a gray car?"

Judith reminded Renie that Arlene Rankers had seen a man sitting in a gray car on Thursday afternoon, presumably watching the house when the Pacetti party arrived at Hillside Manor. Renie was not impressed.

"There are probably about ten thousand gray cars in a city this size," Renie pointed out between attacks on her sandwich. "Tony's car is gray, the Dooleys' van is gray, Father Hoyle drives a gray Mercedes, our previous Chevrolet was gray, and Mike used to have a gray Honda. Need I go on?"

"Please don't," said Judith, surrendering. "You're right, I'm hallucinating. And I don't even know why. A famous singer comes to stay at my B&B, he gets a couple of goofy messages—or somebody does—then he dies of a heart attack, and suddenly I'm trying to make a big deal out of it. I'm probably being overly suspicious about Justin Kerr and Inez Garcia-Green showing up. Where else would they take flowers?"

"Right. They wouldn't deliver them to the hospital because they didn't know Mrs. Pacetti might be staying overnight." Renie popped the last bite of pastrami into her mouth. "Say, didn't I see a lot of German beer in the fridge? Do you think Herr Schutzendorf would mind if I borrowed one? It would wash this down pretty good."

"So it would," agreed Judith. "Actually, I bought that

for him, though he seems to prefer his Sekt. Want to split one?"

Renie allowed that would be just fine. Judith went back to the kitchen, got a bottle out of the refrigerator, opened it, and poured the contents into two small glass steins. As she came back into the living room, she posed a question to Renie.

"Was I imagining things, or did Inez display a proprietary air toward Justin?"

Renie smirked. "You bet. It looked to me like Inez was making the passes, but Justin didn't think he was the intended receiver. She must be at least ten years older than he is."

"Older women, younger men—it's in," Judith remarked. "It's smart, too, if Justin wants somebody to help him with his career. Do you know if he's any good?"

Renie shrugged, a dollop of mustard just missing the front of her red wool crepe. "I told you, we skipped his performance last season. But they wouldn't hire a no-talent to back up Pacetti. Potentially, the understudy may have to sing with Inez and with Sydney Haines."

Judith reflected on Renie's words. "Big stuff, huh?" Judith mused, then gestured with the last bite of her sandwich. "Say—it just dawned on me. Where does the Green come from in Inez's name? That doesn't sound very Spanish."

"She married an Englishman a long time ago," answered Renie, hoisting her stein. "Or maybe it was an American. I think they split up. He was some kind of businessman, whose money helped get her launched. I suppose that's why she kept the name."

"Green," mused Judith. "I remember enough of my Spanish to know that translates as *verde*. And in Italian, as *verdi*. That's kind of odd, isn't . . . oh!"

"What?" Renie stared at Judith over the rim of her stein.

"That's what was bothering me—not Green, but Spanish, I mean," said Judith rapidly. "Inez was remarking about the Spanish galleons in the bathroom upstairs. That's the *front* bedroom, where Mario Pacetti was staying. Now why would she go in there instead of Mrs. Pacetti's room, where Justin Kerr was doing his floral bit?"

"Coz . . ." Renie spoke as if to a small, dumb animal. *"Stop.* Maybe she wanted to piddle and preferred more privacy. Don't tie yourself into knots over nothing."

"Right," said Judith. "Absolutely right. I'm being a goose. More beer?"

Renie declined, saying she should head home. Feeling guilty about the spring bulbs still sitting on the back porch, Judith offered to split them with her cousin.

"I told you, I signed an unconditional surrender with the squirrels," said Renie. "But I'll take some of those pips."

"They're for Mrs. Dooley," said Judith, then gave a wave of her hand. "What the heck, I'll give you the ones in the fridge and pull up some for her tomorrow. If nobody's around, and it's not coming down like cats and dogs, I might even get the damned bulbs in. Hold on."

But Judith's initial perusal of the refrigerator produced no lily-of-the-valley pips. She started to search among the shelves, but Renie told her to forget it.

"You'll have to haul most of that stuff out to find them," said Renie, indicating the B&B guests' horde of gourmet treasures. "Frankly, I might never plant those pips if I have to do it around the holidays. You know what a madhouse it's like. I'll get some starters from Nottingham's in the spring."

Judith didn't argue. After briefly musing on what their husbands might—or more likely might not—be doing in New Orleans, the cousins said good night. It was still pouring, but the wind had picked up. Leaves swirled around the yard, tree branches groaned, shrubs rustled against the side of the house. Judith waved Renie off, then locked the front door. It was going on eleven o'clock. Perhaps she'd treat herself to a good book.

Shortly before midnight, Judith put down the spy thriller she'd never found time to read five years earlier when it had run amok on the best seller list. Her eyes were tired and so was her body. Judith turned out the light. The house seemed very empty. Not only was Joe gone, but it was rare that Judith had any rooms vacant, let alone all of them. The rain pelted her window; the wind blew through the eaves. Judith struggled to find a comfortable position in the queen-sized bed that suddenly felt enormous without Joe beside her.

The old house creaked and groaned as it always did, especially on a stormy night. At first, Judith thought the noise she heard was merely the wind. Then she realized there was someone downstairs. She sat up, listening. Had one of her guests returned after all? If so, should she get up?

Reaching for the light switch, she noted that it was almost twelve-thirty. If someone from the Pacetti party had come back, he or she would not expect her to greet them. Indeed, whoever it was would no doubt be exhausted and head straight for bed. There was no reason for Judith to go downstairs.

Grabbing the blue bathrobe she'd bought for her trousseau, Judith got up and headed for the first floor. Winston Plunkett was in the kitchen, drinking a glass of mineral water. His gray pin-striped suit was rumpled, his solid navy tie was askew, and his face looked haggard. Judith offered her condolences.

"How is Mrs. Pacetti?" she asked, genuine sympathy in her black eyes.

"She's sedated, as I mentioned. Or did I?" Plunkett stared at Judith as if he'd never seen her before. "I've made so many calls . . . all over the world . . . Good God, I still can't believe it! Pacetti's career was my life's work! It should have gone on for years!" Plunkett swayed, then caught himself on the sink counter.

Judith grabbed at his arm. "Mr. Plunkett, please, come sit down. Wouldn't you like something stronger than water?"

Discreetly, he shook her off. "I'm all right. I'm just . . . tired. Alcohol goes straight to my head. A little sherry, that's all I can take, but not this late . . ." He collapsed onto the floor.

Judith knelt, feeling for his pulse. It was strong, if a bit rapid. She gave Plunkett a slight shake. He opened his eyes and gazed vacantly into Judith's face.

"Just sit still for a few minutes," she urged. "Then I'll help you get upstairs. Or, if you prefer, I can make up a bed on one of the sofas down here."

Plunkett exhaled a quavery sigh. "I'll make it on my own. I just need . . . to collect myself."

"Of course." Judith stood up, wondering what else she could offer besides brandy. "What about a strong cup of tea?"

But Plunkett shook his head. "No. No, thank you." He was gazing up at Judith, his eyes coming into focus. "I just can't believe it. It's so . . . horrible."

"Yes, it is. But you and Mrs. Pacetti and his family have to go on. Think of the heritage he's left. Someone will have to carry the torch." Judith, looked away, feeling inadequate.

"Horrible," muttered Plunkett. "Horrible." He was clinging to the edge of the stainless steel double sink, trying to stand up.

"My father died of heart trouble," said Judith. "My cousin's father did, too. Very unexpected in his case. He was always so fit."

Plunkett was now on his feet, one hand trailing in the sink. "Oh, no," he breathed. "Heart attacks aren't so horrible—alas, they're all too common." His thin, ashen face seemed to crumple. "I'm talking about murder."

# SEVEN

Tippy de Caro scoffed at Winston Plunkett's announcement. She had let herself into Hillside Manor just as the business manager made his startling statement to Judith.

"Honestly," said Tippy, straightening Plunkett's tie and looking as if she wished she could do the same to his backbone, "that's just too crazy! Why would anyone murder poor Mr. Pacetti?"

Plunkett, valiantly trying to regain his aplomb, cleared his throat. "I agree, Ms. de Caro. But when I went back to the opera house after I left the hospital, the police were carrying away some things in evidence bags. I have to assume they suspect foul play."

"Well, of course!" Tippy removed her short, chartreuse vinyl raincoat to reveal the feather boa and skin-tight scarlet dress. "That's what the police do, don't they? Police-type things, like . . . *evidence*," she added brightly. "It probably doesn't mean a thing. They were looking here and poking around there, but what's to find? Poison in the champagne?" She giggled, on a jarringly high-pitched note. "The police have to earn their money, like the rest of us."

Judith was about to point out that it didn't work quite that way, but Winston Plunkett was in no shape to argue with Tippy. "I'm utterly exhausted. Perhaps," he said dolefully as he went out of the kitchen, "we can learn more in the morning."

"Oh, bother!" exclaimed Tippy, flipping her feather boa over one shoulder. "He can be soooo stubborn! Have you got any gum? I ran out at the hospital."

Judith rarely chewed gum, but she kept it on hand in case she got one of her urges to resume smoking. Opening her junk drawer, she offered Tippy a small pack. "How are you doing? I understand you were very upset earlier this evening."

Tippy's green eyes grew round. "Oh, I was! One of the nurses had to give me a good shake. But life goes on, you know. I'm okay now. Still, it seems like only yesterday that Mr. Pacetti was alive and singing."

"It *was* only yesterday," Judith said dryly. Tippy didn't react to the remark, so Judith continued speaking. "How is Mr. Schutzendorf? Is he coming back tonight?"

"No," responded Tippy, chewing hard on the gum. "He's spending the night under . . . what do you call it? Observation, I guess. He was pretty cut up by Mr. Pacetti dying and all that."

Judith didn't comment, hoping that her silence would give the hint to head upstairs. But Tippy seemed inclined to linger, ostensibly admiring the old schoolhouse clock, the religious art calendar from Our Lady, Star of the Sea, the pasta cookbook that lay open on the kitchen counter.

"I could use a drink," Tippy said, giving Judith an ingenuous look. "You know, like some gin."

Judith, who had been thinking in terms of hot milk or cocoa, suppressed a little sigh and went to the liquor cabinet. "Okay, I'll fix it and you can take it upstairs with you. Ordinarily, I discourage guests from drinking in their rooms, but this is certainly an unusual situation, so I'll make an exception." Judith was being truthful about cautioning visitors against consuming food or beverage abovestairs, but for all she knew, half of her guests had a flask taped to their thighs and were freebasing cocaine in

the bathrooms. Schutzendorf had, after all, been guzzling
his German wine, and as far as Judith could tell, he must
have brought a case with him. Empty tumblers appeared
on the sink counter at regular intervals. It had occurred to
her that his jocular air might be induced by an overdose of
Sekt. But she had to admit he never seemed drunk, which
was more than she could say for some of her guests in the
past. Except for keeping ever-vigilant, there was no way to
stop them. But for insurance purposes and Judith's peace
of mind, they had been warned. "Ice? Tonic? Vermouth?"
asked Judith.

"Just ice," said Tippy. She took the glass from Judith
but made no move to leave the kitchen. "You have a nice
place. This is a nice city. I like the water and the mountains and all the greenery."

"Thanks," said Judith. "Is this your first visit?"

"Yes." Tippy's eyes again roamed about the kitchen,
studying the high ceiling, the collection of pots and pans
that hung from hooks above the stove, the new green
mixer Judith had recently purchased on sale at a downtown cookware shop.

Judith considered returning to bed, but made one last attempt at being gracious. "Are you from the East Coast?"
It was a guess, based on the hint of a New England accent
in Tippy's voice.

"Boston." Tippy snapped her gum and sipped her drink.
"I went to Harvard."

Judith's jaw dropped. "Really?"

"For a picnic. It was during semester break." Tippy
gazed again at the ceiling.

Judith had to exert considerable effort to keep from
grinding her teeth. "I wonder what Mr. Plunkett was talking about, regarding the police. Did you go back to the
opera house tonight?"

"What?" Tippy looked more vague than usual. "No. I
came from the hospital. I took a cab. Mr. Plunkett had to
go back to collect Mr. and Mrs. Pacetti's personal things."
At last, Tippy seemed ready to go upstairs. "Mr. Plunkett

is nice enough to work for, but he's a real fussbudget. I'll bet the police were just getting valuables together. Or making sure nobody stole anything in all the excitement. It was pretty wild backstage after Mr. Pacetti collapsed."

Judith could imagine the scene, with the turmoil among the singers, supers, stagehands, and other opera house personnel. Then the arrival of the emergency crew, the announcement by Creighton Layton, the dispersing of the audience. She was still mulling over the aftermath when she finally headed back to her bedroom.

Tippy was right, of course. It was unlikely that anyone would want to murder Mario Pacetti. Winston Plunkett must be mistaken about the police carrying off evidence from the backstage area. Judith switched off the light and tried to put her mind at rest.

But it wasn't easy. Judith knew too much about people not to realize that murder was always a possibility.

With only the two Americans on hand for breakfast, Judith kept to her usual Sunday morning menu of waffles, eggs, ham, juice, and coffee. Tippy gobbled up her food as if she hadn't eaten in weeks, but Plunkett picked at his, apparently forcing himself to take nourishment in order to keep up his strength.

By the time Judith returned from ten o'clock mass, there was no sign of her guests. She assumed they had taken a cab or hired a car to fetch Mrs. Pacetti and Herr Schutzendorf. Judith used the spare time to peruse the Sunday paper. Since Pacetti's death had occurred so close to deadline, Melissa Bargroom's front-page story was brief. Death was attributed to heart failure, according to the article. Pacetti had died in the ambulance en route to Bayview Hospital. A brief résumé of his career was given in the next to last paragraph, including his previous appearance at the local opera house six years earlier. Bargroom concluded the piece by saying that funeral services were pending.

Judith had just finished the front section when Renie

called. The cousins had seen each other in church, but had been sitting on opposite sides of the altar. They had waved, but not spoken.

"Guess what," began Renie. "I stopped to see our mothers and mine won this morning's bout in the third round. It was a TKO, stopped by Mrs. Parker, who came by with a desiccated coffee cake she'd picked up off the day-old rack at Begelman's Bakery."

"What are they fighting about now?" Judith asked with a weary sigh.

"Whether Great-Aunt Opal had a boil on her butt in 1946. My mother said she did because when she came to my dad's birthday party, she couldn't sit down. Your mother said she didn't because not only did she sit down, she won the cakewalk. Your mother said that wasn't in '46, it was '47, and she remembered because that was the year your dad came down with the three-day measles over Thanksgiving. But my mother said . . ."

"Stop!" Judith shrieked into the phone. "I can't stand it! Their bickering drives me crazy in person. Why do I have to listen to a secondhand account?"

"Do you want me to tell you what happened to the coffee cake?"

"No."

"Mrs. Parker's poodle, Ignatz, ate it. Serves the ugly little mutt right." Renie chuckled evilly, then turned a bit more serious. "How are your guests, if any?"

Judith explained what had been going on since she and Renie had parted the previous evening. Renie, naturally, was mildly interested in Winston Plunkett's report of alleged police activity. But, like Tippy, she dismissed it as procedural.

"I've got to pick up my new slacks from Nordquist's alterations department this afternoon. If everybody takes off, why don't you come over tonight and have dinner with me and the kids?" asked Renie.

"Maybe," said Judith, pleased at the prospect. Even if

she lost money on the deal, she wouldn't be sorry to see the Pacetti party check out early.

But Judith had scarcely made it to the regional section of the newspaper before she heard a clamor at the front door. Winston Plunkett, Tippy de Caro, and Bruno Schutzendorf were on the porch, arguing over whether they had over- or undertipped the cabdriver who was just pulling out of the cul-de-sac. Judith let them in, then gaped through the rain as an ambulance came to a cautious stop in front of the B&B. Two uniformed attendants got out and went to the rear double doors.

Plunkett gave Judith an apologetic look. "Mrs. Pacetti," he murmured. "She's still very weak."

"Uh . . ." Judith bit her lip. "Where are you going to put her?"

Tippy gazed blandly at Judith. "Why, in her room, of course! She has to recuperate. Here comes the nurse now."

A beige compact had pulled into the spot vacated by the taxi. A tall, thin woman wearing a white uniform under her black car coat strode purposefully through the rain. She carried a valise in one hand, a suitcase in the other, and had a large handbag slung over her left shoulder. Judith felt herself go pale.

"This," said Winston Plunkett in his eternally contrite manner, "is Edna Fiske. She's a registered nurse, and comes highly recommended."

"By who, Hitler?" murmured Judith as she took in Edna Fiske's homely features and stern expression. But as the nurse tramped up the front steps, Judith moved to greet her. "I'm Mrs. Flynn. How do you do?"

Edna Fiske ground Judith's hand like a nutcracker. "In the pink. You look peaked. Do you want me to take your blood pressure?"

"No, thanks, I'm just swell," croaked Judith, giving her fingers an experimental shake to make sure they were still attached to the rest of her arm. "You're moving in?"

But Edna already had. At least she had penetrated the entry hall and was surveying the stairwell. "I've been advised to take the deceased's room. Don't fret; I'm not superstitious. My work has trained me to think of the dead only as former patients." Edna stepped aside as the ambulance attendants wheeled Amina Pacetti into the house.

Judith tried to catch a glimpse of the stricken widow, but a plastic hood had been put over her face to ward off the rain. Her hands were encased in the sable muff, which looked incongruous against the background of the coarse brown ambulance blanket. Expertly, the two men carried the stretcher upstairs with Winston Plunkett at their heels. Edna Fiske waited a respectful moment, then also ascended to the second floor.

"Vell!" boomed Herr Schutzendorf, who had remained uncharacteristically quiet until now. "Vat next? My heart, it is still racing! I must sit." He charged past Judith into the living room where he dropped onto the nearer of the two sofas.

Tippy, meanwhile, apparently had just discovered the front parlor, which faced the street. Judith usually reserved it for small private parties.

"Oooh!" exclaimed Tippy. "This is cute! More bay windows! Another fireplace! *Darling* furniture! Why can't we sit in here?"

"It hasn't been cleaned in a week," Judith responded tersely. Given Phyliss Rackley's ongoing ill health, it was closer to two. Judith stood in the doorway, beckoning to Tippy. "I'll make some hot cider. Why don't you join Mr. Schutzendorf in the living room?"

Reluctantly, Tippy left the parlor. Kicking herself for resorting to bribery, Judith went into the kitchen to make the cider, adding a few spices and a lot of wine. By the time she was finished, the ambulance attendants were leaving and Winston Plunkett had joined the others. Edna Fiske, apparently, was tending to her patient.

For once, Judith had decided to join her guests. Waiting for the cider in her mug to cool, she tried to probe tactfully. "How long will it take for Mrs. Pacetti to recover?" she asked, realizing she didn't sound so tactful after all.

Plunkett gave a slow shake of his head. "It's hard to say. The difficult part is that no funeral arrangements can be made until she's able to cope with them. We hope to ship the . . . body to Italy in the next day or two. Of course it will have to go by train and ship. Mr. Pacetti didn't fly, you know."

"But . . ." Judith began, then gave herself a little shake. It would do no good to argue that a dead Pacetti wouldn't know the difference between a 747 and Noah's Ark.

"So," Plunkett continued, carefully stirring his cider with a cinnamon stick, "Mrs. Pacetti will have the luxury of regaining her strength over the next week or two. Ms. de Caro and I will stay on to conduct her affairs and that of the late . . . great . . . Mario . . . Pacetti." Plunkett's voice cracked; he seemed close to tears. It occurred to Judith that Winston Plunkett was the sort of person who either showed no emotion at all—or too much. There was no in-between.

Judith turned away. "And you, Mr. Schutzendorf?" she asked a bit breathlessly.

Schutzendorf was guzzling his cider as if it were a cold beer. "Me? I, too, recuperate. But of course there are business matters I must attend to. Tuesday, Wednesday, I must fly to your East Coast. Arrangements will be made tomorrow." He glanced at Plunkett who gave a faint nod. "My recording company had recently signed Signor Pacetti to a new contract. We must do the sorting out, rescheduling, all the rest. That I must take care of in Hamburg. But first . . ." He had set the cider mug down and was spreading his beefy hands. ". . .There are the more delicate affairs, in this country. Such a tragedy! Will this sadness ever leave my soul?"

"Oh, probably," chirped Tippy. "I remember when my Aunt Willa died and I thought I'd never stop bawling. But a couple of hours later, I was at the mall, scoping guys. You just have to be strong."

Schutzendorf glowered at Tippy. Plunkett wiped his eyes with a white handkerchief. Judith was relieved to hear the doorbell ring. Excusing herself, she hoped it was Renie, making a rare appearance at the front, rather than the back door.

To Judith's surprise, Woodrow Price stood on the porch, wearing a navy blue all-weather jacket over maroon sweats. His tan Nissan was parked in front of the nurse's beige compact.

"Woody!" Judith gave her husband's partner a warm hug. "Come in! I haven't seen you since the Labor Day picnic. Speaking of labor, how's your wife? Two weeks to go, right?"

Woody smiled, revealing very white teeth. His skin was the color of cocoa, his walrus mustache was jet black, and his manner, as ever, was stolid, taciturn, and somehow disarming. "November 6 is the due date. Sondra's pretty uncomfortable."

"I'll bet." Judith ushered Woody inside, noting that he seemed a bit reluctant to follow her. She paused in the entry hall and cocked a quizzical eye in his direction.

Woody inclined his head toward the living room. "Your guests?" Judith nodded. Woody pointed to the front parlor. "Could we go in there?"

"Sure," said Judith, leading the way. The door that led into the living room was already shut; Judith closed the entry hall door behind them. Indicating one of the petit-point covered chairs, Judith sat down in its mate. As always, the cozy room seemed to wrap its arms around her. The small stone fireplace was flanked by converted gaslights. An English hunting print hung over the mantel, which was adorned by a pair of seventeenth century pewter candlesticks unearthed at a garage sale, a sterling silver crucifix Judith had bought at the Vatican in '64, and an arrangement of dried autumn flowers from Nottingham's. A brass warming pan of the same vintage as the candlesticks hung at one side of the hearth, where a trio of carved pumpkins showed off happy grins.

"Who's here?" Woody asked, keeping his voice low.

Judith told him, lamenting that her guests were probably

going to drive her insane before they all finally departed. "At least Schutzendorf intends to leave in the next couple of days," she concluded. The German record magnate could be heard bellowing in the adjoining room. "That will bring the noise level down to almost bearable."

But Woody was frowning. "Maybe he'll leave—and maybe not." Noting Judith's look of apprehension, Woody gave her a weak smile. "That's why I drove my own car here. I don't want your guests to know I'm a policeman. An autopsy is being done on Mr. Pacetti tomorrow." He paused, his gaze roaming to the big armoire where Judith stored extra linens, books, records, and tapes. "If you weren't married to Joe, I couldn't tell you this, of course." His dark eyes were now fixed on Judith's tense face. "In fact, if he were here, I wouldn't do it. Probably he wouldn't either, unless he felt it was absolutely necessary."

"Right." Judith compressed her lips. She wished Woody would get to the point.

"A routine check of the opera house was made last night. An empty vial of Strophanthin was found backstage."

"What's that?" Judith had never heard of it.

"It's like digitalis or digitoxin, usually used in the treatment of heart patients," Woody explained in his careful manner. "It's much more common in Europe than it is in this country. Like most drugs, if too much is taken, it can be fatal. Given the fact that Mr. Pacetti had no history of heart trouble—and in fact had just had a physical last winter—his death from cardiac arrest was unexpected."

"But it happens," Judith put in, feeling a need to buffet herself against what was coming. "Renie's dad, Uncle Cliff, seemed in perfect health and just keeled over from a massive coronary."

Woody cocked his head at Judith. "He wasn't in his forties, was he?"

"No," Judith admitted, "he was over seventy. But he'd had a physical a month before he died."

Woody nodded, his dark eyes sympathetic. "Yes, but

even an EKG can't predict if you're going to have a heart attack. The point is, Pacetti's business manager—Plunkett, is it?—described his employer as a man who was concerned, even overly concerned, with every facet of his well-being. He was a great singer who pampered himself. So when he drops dead virtually in the middle of a performance, people are going to ask questions. That's why our men took a look around the opera house. Sort of guarding our own backsides, as it were. If your Uncle Cliff had five million dollars' worth of engagements in the next three months, had just signed a fifteen-million dollar recording contract, was going to get paid another two million for an Easter TV special on PBS, *and* was only forty-seven years old when he keeled over, wouldn't your family have asked a few questions, too?"

"Uncle Cliff couldn't sing a lick," murmured Judith.

"There you go. Anyway," continued Woody, still keeping his voice down, "finding that Strophanthin vial raised even more questions. Nobody laid claim to it, which made *us* ask questions. An analysis of Pacetti's stomach contents will give us some answers."

For a moment, Judith reflected on Woody's words. The rain pattered against the small bay window; leaves from the maple tree in the front yard fluttered to the ground; a pair of squirrels leaped from branch to branch; and in the living room, Herr Schutzendorf rumbled on.

"Where," Judith asked at last, "did they find this stuff?"

"The Strophanthin?" Woody paused again, apparently considering how far he could go without violating law enforcement ethics. "Actually, it wasn't backstage. I misled you a bit there. It was onstage. The long table, with the food and drink? The bottle was lying there, empty."

Judith's mind flew back to Act I of *Traviata*. There was something she should remember, but it proved elusive. Later, it would come. So much had happened in the past few hours; it seemed like more than a week instead of less than a day since she and Renie had settled themselves into their front row center seats in the first balcony.

"Could Pacetti have drunk the stuff onstage?" she asked, still feeling faintly stunned by Woody's news.

"Maybe. It works very fast. But," Woody inquired more of himself than of Judith, "how could anyone be sure he would choose a certain glass? There were dozens of them on that table. That's assuming, of course, that Pacetti was the intended victim. And that's also assuming he *was* a victim. I'm telling you this just in case." Woody's face grew very grave. "If Mario Pacetti was poisoned, it's possible—not probable, of course—but possible that the killer may be staying under your roof. I couldn't *not* tell you and ever look Lieutenant Flynn in the eye again."

Judith gave Woody her most ironic gaze. "Gee, thanks, Woody. And all this time, I thought we were *pals.*"

If it were possible, Woody appeared to be blushing. "I don't mean it that way—I'm in a peculiar position. You see, none of this is my business in the first place. I'm not even assigned to the investigation."

*"What?"* Judith gaped at Woody. "Well, why not? I don't want some run-of-the-mill bozo from homicide running this show! If Joe's not around, why not you?"

Still looking embarrassed, Woody was getting to his feet. "Honest, Mrs. Flynn, there are plenty of really fine police personnel on the force. Right here on your beat, Prentice and Cernak have an excellent reputation . . ."

"Hold it!" Judith had grabbed Woody by his all-weather jacket. "Don't fob those two off on me! I've got enough problems already without having Ms. Stiff-as-a-Board and The Man Who Can Only Grunt for Himself being a back-up for Homicide. If it *is* a homicide," she added hastily. "Can't you put yourself in charge, and some of your own people Woody? *Please?*"

Woody seemed unable to look Judith in the eye. "Well . . . I . . . ah . . . as you say, maybe it isn't anything, maybe somebody just dropped that bottle and forgot . . . With Lieutenant Flynn out of town, I'm pretty tied up for the next couple of weeks . . ."

Abruptly, Judith released Woody. "Oh, well, I understand." She gave him her most charming smile. "I'm being silly. By the way, did you ever get a music expert to identify those notes on the sheet of paper?"

Woody's face showed both surprise and relief. "Yes, in fact, I did." He reached inside his jacket, apparently digging into an inner pocket. "Whoever did this said it wasn't too hard to figure out once he knew what the notes on the rock were from. Here, my Italian isn't so good."

Judith stared at the small slip of paper. *"Si, egli è ver"* was written in small, but precise, letters. "My Italian isn't so good, either. What does it mean?"

"Something about 'Yes, it's true.' If memory serves, it's Alfredo's second line in Act I of *Traviata.*" Woody Price, who knew almost as much about opera as he did about police procedures, hummed the phrase in his melodious baritone. "It's pitched too high for me, of course," he added apologetically.

"Uh-huh," responded Judith a bit absently. She tucked the little piece of paper inside the pocket of her dark green flannel slacks. "Sorry I was crabby. It's been a rough few days. Especially with Joe gone." Again, she bestowed her sweetest smile on Woody.

"That's okay," he smiled back. "I just wanted to make sure you understood what might be going on. We'll keep the patrol cars cruising, of course."

Judith gave Woody a kiss on the cheek. "Thanks." She took hold of his jacket again, this time more gently. "And stop calling me Mrs. Flynn! You stood up for us at our wedding, remember? You and Sondra are practically family!"

Woody beamed. "We *will* be a family in about two weeks. All three of us."

"That's right," said Judith, walking him to the front door. "Give Sondra my best. And let us know as soon as the baby gets here, okay?"

"Sure," agreed Woody, heading back out into the rain. "Only two weeks to go!"

Judith waved and smiled some more. She waited until

Woody had pulled away from the curb before going back inside. "Two weeks, my foot," she muttered as she hurried upstairs. "First babies never come on time." She kept climbing, all the way to the family quarters on the third floor. Tucked into the top drawer of her dressing table was the address and phone number of the hotel where Joe and Bill were staying in New Orleans. If Woody Price wanted to back off and wait for his baby to come, that was fine. But if Mario Pacetti really had been murdered, Judith was sure that the killer would be apprehended long before Sondra Price went into labor. Even as she dialed the hotel number in New Orleans, she knew that she just might end up having to help solve the crime herself.

And if she did, she wanted Woody Price at her side. In an off-key voice, Judith hummed a little Verdi as she waited for the hotel operator to come on the line. Judith knew Woody couldn't say no to Joe.

# EIGHT

THE EXPLOSION OVER the phone line had practically deafened Judith. Joe Flynn could not, would not, absolutely refused to believe that his wife had got mixed up in another murder. No, he had not seen the local newspapers or turned on the TV. He was off duty, out of town, recreating himself. There was nothing he needed to know except how to get from the Hyatt-Regency to Jackson Square, Goddammit.

When Joe finally stopped yelling into the receiver and his voice had dropped to an almost-normal level, he asserted that crime had got out of control back home, that nobody was safe any more, that the homicide rate had skyrocketed to unbelievable proportions, and that somebody ought to kick the police in the butt.

"Joe," Judith had finally interjected, "you *are* the police, remember?"

Joe knew that, but he meant his superiors up the line. Or something. The weary sigh indicated he was finally coming to grips with reality. And after fulminating against tinkering with police department procedures, he agreed to call headquarters and request that Woody Price be put in charge of the investigation.

"I suppose it's logical," he had grumbled. "Woody

knows something about music. Most of the other homicide detectives think *The Ring* is something around their bathtubs."

Joe gave the usual cautions, though it was obvious from his tone that once Judith had the bit between her teeth, he knew she'd gallop straight for the finish line, heedless of danger. She, in turn, found out that he and Bill were enjoying themselves, having gone to mass at St. Louis Cathedral, taken a sight-seeing tour of the city, met the other conferees at a cocktail party in the hotel, and were now about to stuff themselves at Mr. B's Bistro. The convention would begin in earnest the following day. On a note of longing that was tinged with envy, Judith clicked Joe off, then dialed Renie.

"I suppose I'll have to offer to feed this crew tonight, if only because they're suffering from trauma," said Judith after filling her cousin in and regretfully declining the invitation to dinner.

"Make something easy," suggested Renie. "Like stew."

It wasn't a bad idea. She had boneless sirloin in the freezer, enough vegetables in the fridge, and she could whip up some of Grandma Grover's dumplings. Arriving on the second floor, Judith decided to inquire after Mrs. Pacetti. Edna Fiske opened the door a crack, her long nose thrust at Judith like a buzzard's beak.

"How's the patient?" asked Judith, keeping her voice to a sickroom murmur.

"Resting," replied Edna. She turned just enough to cast an eye in the direction of the bed.

The patient sat up. *"Dio mio,* my back, it is killing me! Rub, rub, please, Nurse! I agonize!"

Edna Fiske moved away from the door just enough so that Judith could squeeze into the room. "Really, Mrs. Pacetti, we've had one back rub already this afternoon," Edna asserted in her no-nonsense voice. "I'm a registered nurse, not a masseuse. It would be much better for you if you tried to get out of bed and walk a bit. In fact, I must insist on it before the day is out."

Sitting among the linens that Grandma Grover had embroidered with butterflies and roses, Amina Pacetti looked more distressed than ill. Without makeup, her skin was sallow. The usually well-coiffed golden hair hung limply around her shoulders. Given the fact that she had been recently—and shockingly—widowed, Judith felt Edna Fiske was being a trifle harsh with her patient.

"I was wondering if you feel like eating anything, Mrs. Pacetti," Judith said, sympathy swimming in her black eyes. "I'm going to fix dinner for the others, and I thought you might like soup or some other light nourishment."

Amina collapsed against the pillows, trailing a manicured fingernail down her cheek. "Oh—I have not the appetite. Hot tea, maybe. Or orange juice."

Edna Fiske was hovering directly behind Judith. "I know the patient's preferences. I'll fetch it," she said, and promptly left the room.

Judith sat down on a ladder-back chair that the nurse apparently had pulled up next to the bed. The bouquet Justin Kerr had brought sat on the dressing table, the exotic blooms jammed haphazardly into the cut-glass vase. Judith thought it looked as if it had been arranged by an uncoordinated chimpanzee. She couldn't help but wonder what had taken Kerr so long upstairs. But this was not the moment to speculate. "I can't tell you how sorry I am about your loss. I'm a widow, too." Seeing Amina's curious expression, Judith hastily explained. "I mean, I was before I married Mr. Flynn. My first husband was only forty-nine when he died."

"My Mario was forty-seven." Amina's eyelids drooped. "He was a man of great genius. Did your husband have a gift?"

Thinking that Dan's greatest gift had been to avoid work, Judith gave a faint shake of her head. "Gift, no. Girth, yes. He weighed over four hundred pounds when he died."

Unlike most people, Amina Pacetti didn't seem surprised at Judith's announcement. "That is large, yes. But

Mario was no small man. Two hundred and eighty in pounds, I believe. Perhaps that is what killed him."

It could, of course. The excess weight had killed Dan, who had been at least half a foot taller than Pacetti. But Woody Price thought otherwise. Judith, however, would not say so to Amina Pacetti. At least not now. It was interesting, reflected Judith, that despite the purported threats, murder hadn't seemed to have entered the widow's mind.

"You're very fortunate to have someone as capable as Mr. Plunkett to look after your affairs," Judith said, switching topics, lest she inadvertently give something away.

For the merest instant, Mrs. Pacetti's glance hardened. Or was it wary? Judith wasn't sure; the change had passed too swiftly. "Plunkett, yes, he is capable. He will see to everything. The requiem. The burial. The insurance."

Judith's eyebrows raised slightly. Funeral and burial, yes, as Mrs. Pacetti would say. But insurance? It struck Judith as an odd, even tasteless, inclusion. But then she mustn't judge. Such matters had never occurred to her because Dan had no insurance. He couldn't qualify for a policy, and Judith had been left with nothing except social security for Mike until he turned eighteen. Obviously, Mrs. Pacetti was in a different league.

"It will be a moving occasion," Amina was saying, as Judith mulled. "Flowers, so many flowers—my husband loved them, though they gave him the sneezes. I adore them, too—I worked in a flower shop when I was but a young girl. It is where I met Mario. So romantic!" She folded her hands and rested them against her cheek in an attitude of loving reminiscence. "Thus, we must have the very best, only the most beautiful. Lilies, hibiscus, jasmine, orchids—and what are those clusters of purple blooms you have around here? Red, too, and pink and yellow and even blue I once saw, with dark waxy leaves."

Judith frowned. "On a stalk?"

"No, no. A bush. Huge, some of them, to the housetops." Amina gestured with her hands. Her enthusiasm for the funeral decor seemed to improve her color.

"Oh! Rhododendrons," said Judith. "They're the state flower. They grow wild in the woods, mainly pink, but only in the spring when the hybrids bloom."

Amina sighed. "A pity. I would love those, whole shrubs of them, all over the altar in the cathedral at Bari. And the music—his favorite arias, or maybe the Verdi *Requiem.*" She cocked her head in concentration. "Who to sing, I wonder? Pavarotti? Carreras? Pons? Te Kanawa? Norman? We shall need four, then a conductor . . . let me think . . ."

Amina's thoughts were interrupted by Edna Fiske, who entered the room carrying a tall glass of orange juice. "That German is eating a ham," said Edna, depositing the juice on the night table next to the bed. "He's a very large man and it's a very large ham, but I shouldn't think it would be good for his digestion."

"Or for my budget," murmured Judith, taking her leave. The ham was intended to last at least through midweek. Judith headed for the kitchen.

Herr Schutzendorf was indeed seated at the kitchen table, knife in one hand, fork in the other, assaulting Judith's bone-in ham. She approached him with a smile. "Here, let me carve that for you. It's tricky with that bone." Judith reached out, but Schutzendorf pulled the ham closer, as if it were a cherished trophy.

"No trouble! Your cutlery is superb!" He beamed at Judith. "German, no?"

"Yes, Henckels," sighed Judith. "I got the set on sale at La Belle Epoch two years ago." She pulled up a chair and sat down opposite Schutzendorf, wondering how she could separate him from her ham. "What," she inquired, by way of diversion, "will happen with the opera performances now that Mr. Pacetti is dead?"

Schutzendorf gave a shrug of his broad shoulders. "There is an understudy, the young American, Justin Kerr. He will sing amid greatness. Garcia-Green and Sydney

Haines. Let us hope he disports himself with brilliance. It could make or break his career." Schutzendorf chuckled darkly.

"You've heard him sing?" asked Judith.

Schutzendorf wrinkled his nose and twitched his mustache. "No, I hear only . . . reports." He spoke musingly, and a gleam of what might have been malice flashed in his eyes. Schutzendorf gobbled another hunk of ham. "Such big shoes he will have to fill! But Inez will help him with the gaps." He chewed lustily.

Giving up hope of salvaging the ham from Schutzendorf's burly clutches, Judith decided to prod him for information. "Do you think that rock was meant to scare Mr. Pacetti?" She was careful not to mention the second missive; presumably, no one in the Pacetti party knew it existed.

Schutzendorf tipped his head from side to side, chomping away all the while. "Alfredo's notes . . . that is the clue. I should think yes, but not to be taken seriously. A joke, maybe. Who would want to frighten Mario Pacetti, eh? He is—excuse me, Frau Flynn—he *was* a great man. So someone teases him a little. It is not enough to scare him to death."

Judith felt Schutzendorf was probably right. It was not enough. Killing Mario Pacetti had also required poison . . .

Phyliss Rackley arrived promptly at nine o'clock, her gray sausage curls sprouting all over her head and her squat figure draped in a pastel striped housedress. As usual, her slip showed and her sluggish blue eyes didn't miss a trick.

"Your last guest went to meet the Lord, huh?" said Phyliss, getting the vacuum cleaner out from the broom closet by the pantry. "I tell you, Mrs. McMonigle, you've got to stop serving real butter. Too much cholesterol. The last time I had mine tested, it was just under one hundred and eighty, which is pretty good for a woman of my age and poor constitution. My blood pressure was a hundred and twenty-six over seventy-five. Just like a teenager." She shook a stubby finger in Judith's face. "You know why? No drinking, no smoking, no carousing after hours. When the sun goes down, I spend my time with the Lord."

Judith felt like saying that she didn't know how the Lord could stand it, but held her tongue. Phyliss's obsession with her health and her Pentecostal fervor would have driven Judith nuts a long time ago if she hadn't also been a top-notch cleaning woman.

"Now that doesn't mean I'm in perfect health," Phyliss went on, speaking above the roar of the vacuum as she headed for the dining room. "Far from it. My varicose veins have been giving me fits, my sinuses are a mess, and I'm pretty sure I've got hammertoes. I'll find out next week when I see the doctor."

Judith nodded, then slipped back into the kitchen. She'd made a big pot of beef stew the previous night, with potatoes, carrots, onions, and celery topped with fluffy dumplings. Tippy and Schutzendorf had eaten without restraint, Plunkett's appetite seemed to have revived, and even Amina Pacetti had condescended to having a tray brought up to her room. Edna Fiske had come down later to polish off the leftovers. Judith had fixed herself a grilled cheese sandwich and an apple. It was time to restock at Falstaff's.

Judith was heading through the rain for her car when a battered pickup truck pulled into the driveway. As it came to a halt, several items fell out of the back end, including a big pail, a saw, and a small metal box. They clattered onto the wet concrete just as Skjoval Tolvang descended from the cab.

"Howdy-do-do-ya?" mumbled Tolvang, adjusting his grimy painter's cap on his full head of white hair. "You got a busted toolshed, ya?"

"Exploded, actually," said Judith, who had forgotten that her Swedish carpenter was due so early. "Fireworks," she explained. "But I don't want it merely reroofed. As I explained to you on the phone the other day, I'd like to convert it into . . ."

"A doghouse," Tolvang finished for her. He was tall and lean, with a spot of high color on each wrinkled cheek. "For your mother, ya, sure, youbetcha?"

Judith never knew whether Skjoval Tolvang was kidding or not. "Sort of," she replied, a bit uneasily. "A small apartment is more what I had in mind. Can you give me an estimate?"

Tolvang took off his painter's cap and moved closer to the dilapidated toolshed. The rain was coming down quite heavily, the temperature had dropped into the low forties, and the wind had picked up again during the night. Despite the inclement weather, Tolvang wore only a light cotton long-sleeved coverall, its creases dark with the stains of hard work. He wore the same outfit in the summer. Tolvang seemed impervious to the elements.

"Okay," he was saying as he walked into the toolshed and took out a metal tape measure. "You got a floor, you got no I beam. You sure as hell got no roof, py golly. You vant extension?"

"To within a yard or so of the birdbath," answered Judith who'd already done some calculating. "Five, six feet, maybe?"

Tolvang was wielding his tape measure, but didn't bother to write anything down. He led the way outside, still measuring. "Five feet, seven and three-quarter inches. Let's call it five and a half." He jabbed at the two-foot width of garden area between the toolshed and the grass. "What you got, wild dogs? Or raccoons?"

Judith followed his gesture. The garden area in front of the toolshed did indeed show evidence of recent digging. "Damn," breathed Judith. "That's where I was going to put most of my spring bulbs, along with my lilies of the valley and some ranunculus. The squirrels must have found the daffodils and tulips from last year."

Tolvang shook his head. "Them ain't no squirrels.

Squirrels are cunning, tidy little sonsuvitches. Raccoons, I'm a-telling you, come all the way from the gully."

Judith frowned. She didn't think so. The gully was over a mile away, on the northeast side of the Hill, three blocks from Renie and Bill's house. Renie was both amused and annoyed by the raccoon families that traipsed through their yard, looking for snacks, wreaking havoc—and posing for would-be benefactor-victims in the most appealing wide-eyed manner.

"A dog, I'd guess," said Judith. "Probably Dooleys'."

Tolvang was digging about in the dirt. "Pipes," he muttered. "Ve got to see vere to dig for the plumbing. A dog, you say? Vere's that goddamn cat?"

"My cat's gone," Judith replied. "Sweetums is living with Mother." But, Judith realized, the Return of Gertrude would also mean Sweetums Revisited. Would the dreadful cat be satisfied living in the revamped toolshed or insist upon having the run of the house? For that matter, would Gretrude? Judith couldn't cope with that problem just yet. She looked up through the falling rain at what was left of the toolshed roof. "I don't suppose we could raise the ceiling to allow for storage?"

"Storage?" Tolvang's blue eyes raked over Judith. "You got four stories in that house of yours and you vant storage? Why don't you *clean?* You got enough yunk for an army."

Tolvang was right. Judith still clung to family belongings that dated back more than a century. But his timing was unfortunate. Phyliss Rackley stood on the back porch, shaking out a dust mop.

"Clean?" she screeched. "Listen, Mr. Tolvang, there's nobody on Heraldsgate Hill who cleans better than I do, if I do say so myself! It's a gift from the Lord! If you and your demented Lutheran ways think I don't know how to keep a house clean, you'd better think again!" She gave the dust mop a menacing shake.

It was not the first time Phyliss Rackley and Skjoval Tolvang had butted heads. Judith remembered their wrangling all too well from the months that the carpenter had worked on the B&B's original renovations and subsequent improvements. Judith moved to nip their latest quarrel in the bud.

"He was talking about *me,* Phyliss," Judith said with a lame little laugh. "You know I'm a bit of a pack rat."

Phyliss paid no heed. "Wax," she declared. "He said I should *wax.*" The cleaning woman spoke from the porch, like a whistle-stop candidate for public office. Her manner ignored Tolvang's presence. "Now I ask you, in a house with a poor old crippled woman on a walker, *who would wax the floors?* It'd be criminal, that's what. And not very Christian, either." Phyliss gave the dust mop another shake, shivered dramatically, and stomped back inside. Judith resumed conferring with the carpenter.

Five minutes later, Skjoval Tolvang had given his estimate, $7500, materials included. Judith hemmed and hawed. She knew it was a fair price, but she didn't want to move ahead until she'd talked to Joe.

"Well?" demanded Tolvang. "You vant your mother back home or a-scrapping and a-snapping with her sister-in-law? Make up your mind, I have three other projects to do between now and Thanksgiving."

Judith swallowed hard. "Don't I need a permit?"

Tolvang's eyes narrowed. "For a toolshed? If anyone asks, remember, it's a doghouse. You don't need no permit for Fido."

Judith gave a faint nod. "When could you start?"

"This afternoon. At least I could get some of the lumber." He had replaced his hat and looked down at Judith with his sharp blue eyes. "Vell?"

"What about next week? You see, my husband is in New Orleans at a . . ."

But Tolvang was shaking his head. "I tell you, I've got other jobs. Next veek, I do Donahues. This veek, I can do you. But you gotta tell me now, py golly."

With a sinking feeling, Judith surrendered. If she didn't commit herself now, there was no hope of getting

Gertrude home before the holidays. It was an arbitrary deadline, but she had fixed it in her mind. Some time in the New Year sounded too vague. Judith wanted to be able to promise her mother an early return. At Gertrude's age, three or four months could sound like a lifetime—or at least the rest of it.

"Okay," said Judith in a uncharacteristically feeble voice. "Go ahead."

Tolvang gave a single nod. "Ya, sure, youbetcha." He climbed into the cab of his truck, started the engine, reversed, and ran over his implements. Judith yelled after him, but he kept right on going, out into the cul-de-sac and down toward the corner. With a sigh, Judith trudged through the rain to move the dented pail, the bent saw, and the crushed metal box. Typical, she thought, of Skjoval Tolvang's single-mindedness. She had started again for the garage when Tippy de Caro called out from the back door.

"Mrs. Flynn! You're wanted on the phone!"

Judith waved an arm. "I'll call back. I've got to get to the store."

But Tippy shook her head, red curls bobbing from side to side. "It's urgent. This guy says it's a matter of life and death."

*Woody,* thought Judith, hurrying back to the house. *Or Joe, in an accident on the levee. Gertrude, even, finally decked once and for all by Aunt Deb.* She snatched the phone from Phyliss Rackley who had somehow managed to comandeer the instrument.

"Yes?" gasped Judith in a breathless voice.

"Hi, Mom," said Mike. "Can you send me a new VCR? Mine broke."

Judith gritted her teeth. There were times when she almost understood the urge to kill.

# NINE

ONE HOUR AND ninety-five dollars later, Judith was home from Falstaff's, unloading groceries. She had made a quick stop at Aunt Deb's apartment, but had not been able to tell her mother about the plans for the toolshed. Mr. and Mrs. Ringo, eucharistic ministers and fellow SOTS, as members of Our Lady, Star of the Sea were known, had brought holy communion to the shut-ins. Judith couldn't interrupt the informal little service. Nor did she want to upset the brief truce that always occurred between Gertrude and Deb when the Ringos made their weekly visit with the sacrament.

Phyliss, who was working on her third load of laundry, informed Judith that in her absence there had been two calls for reservations, both from in-state. With a flip of her striped housedress and sagging slip, the cleaning woman headed upstairs to start in on the guest rooms.

Schutzendorf, Plunkett, and Tippy had all gone out, presumably to attend to business matters. Judith was relieved. It was almost noon, and she'd been afraid she'd have to prepare lunch if they stayed around the house. As it was, she'd have to check on Mrs. Pacetti's needs.

The widow had not been awake yet when Judith had left for Falstaff's.

After putting the groceries away, Judith returned the two reservation calls, then dialed the number of her appliance man. She had been very firm in telling Mike he could not get a new VCR. It was a luxury, especially for a student who was supposedly studying far into the night. Mike had argued that that was the very reason he so desperately needed the equipment—how could he watch informative PBS programs in prime time when he was hitting the books? But if he could tape them and replay them at a more convenient time, say between 4:00 and 5:00 A.M. while he ate his sparse breakfast of burned toast and thin gruel, he could even rewind and repeat the most vital pieces of information. On the slight chance that he might not really be watching reruns of "The Beverly Hillbillies," Judith called Rex at Bluff TV to find out if they were having a sale. They weren't.

"Honest to God, I'm going broke," Judith said to Renie over the phone. "Seventy-five hundred bucks for the remodeling job, three hundred for Mike's VCR, and this gang of gluttons is eating me out of house and home. I'm going to have to start selling my body parts to break even."

"Try selling your body first," responded Renie. "Even at our age, we ought to get fifty bucks a trick. More, if we could still move fast."

Judith smiled weakly, but didn't have a chance to make a retort. Renie was off on another subject. "I called the opera house ticket office a few minutes ago. They've rescheduled the Saturday performance for Wednesday. Can you go with me?"

Judith debated with herself. "Gee, coz, I'd better not. I really couldn't leave the B&B with Mrs. Pacetti recuperating and Skjoval Tolvang whanging away at the toolshed. As you may recall, once he gets started, he works all hours of the day and night." She did not mention her greatest concern, which was the possibility of leaving a murderer on the loose at Hillside Manor.

Renie, however, understood. In that unique form of unspoken communication that made the cousins more like sisters, she was well aware of Judith's worries. "That's okay. I'll call Madge Navarre and see if I can pry her loose from the insurance company for an evening. Honestly, that woman puts in twelve-hour days, six days a week. I don't get it."

"She likes it," said Judith, referring to their longtime mutual friend and sometime traveling companion. "She can afford to work like that. She doesn't have kids. She can probably even afford luxuries, like shoes." Judith's voice had turned into a little bleat.

"Say," said Renie, ignoring her cousin's whimper, "could you get free for lunch tomorrow with Melissa Bargroom? I forgot until I looked at my calendar this morning that we have a date at Randall's Cove."

"I'll see," temporized Judith. "Maybe by then Schutzendorf will have left."

There was a brief pause at Renie's end of the line. "You mean you haven't heard from Woody?"

"Not yet."

"Hmmm. How long does it take to do an autopsy?"

"Yuck, I don't know. If they have to analyze ... *stuff,* it probably takes several hours. Maybe I won't hear anything until this evening, or not till tomorrow."

"Well, think about your own stomach contents, as in lunch. Noon, straight up. I'm anxious to hear what Melissa makes of all this. She's pretty savvy. Maybe she'll have some dirt for us," said Renie, sweetening the pot.

Judith was tempted, but she made no promises. After all, there was no official pronouncement on whether Mario Pacetti had been murdered. Maybe, if the Fates were kind, the poor man had died of natural causes. Judith consoled herself with the fact that a lot of people did.

The schoolhouse clock indicated it was after twelve-thirty. Judith hurried upstairs to inquire after Mrs. Pacetti's breakfast and/or lunch requests. Phyliss was still on the second floor, no doubt cleaning like crazy. She had, after all, been up there for over half an hour.

But Phyliss hadn't so much as lifted a dustcloth. She was standing at the door of Mrs. Pacetti's room, engaging Edna Fiske in earnest conversation.

". . . For my cuticles. Now you might think that was a small thing, but as a nurse, you know how one little part of the body can show that something's wrong with the whole system. In this case—that was late '83 as I recall—it turned out to be my thyroid. Then, in early '84, the second week of January . . ."

Judith glanced at Edna Fiske, whose eyes had glazed over. "Phyliss!" called Judith. Her voice had the effect of snapping Edna out of her trance and temporarily halting Phyliss's spate of symptoms. "Aren't you overdue for your lunch?"

Phyliss looked at her watch which had a face the size of a Spanish doubloon. "You're right!" She practically curtsied to Edna Fiske. "Excuse me, Nurse, I have to get going. If I don't eat on time, it plays havoc with my digestion. I always bring my own food, not that I'm criticizing Mrs. Flynn here, but I have to be careful. This is my week for beets." Sausage curls flying, Phyliss scurried downstairs. Judith got no farther than opening her mouth before the doorbell rang.

"Tall woman with a fur," shouted Phyliss, apparently unwilling to detour from her kitchen-bound route.

Judith sighed. "Let me know what Mrs. Pacetti—and you—would like for lunch," she said to Edna Fiske, heading back for the staircase.

Inez Garcia-Green appeared to be admiring the corn-stalks and pumpkins as Judith opened the front door. The famed soprano was wearing a coffee brown cashmere coat with a black fox neckpiece. Her head was covered with an ugly plastic rain hat, which she removed as soon as she saw Judith.

"I have come to call on Señora Pacetti," she announced,

giving Judith a smile that somehow mingled graciousness with sorrow. "My respects, as it were, to the bereaved. Is she receiving visitors?"

Given Amina Pacetti's earlier caustic remarks about Inez, Judith thought not. But it wasn't her place to say so. "Let me check," she temporized, ushering Inez inside. "Have a seat. Please." Judith indicated the small settee next to the staircase. Inez sat down with a graceful motion.

Edna Fiske was coming downstairs. "The patient feels like a steak," she announced.

Judith suppressed an urge to say that the patient looked more like a pork chop. "There are some in the freezer," Judith said in passing. "You can thaw one in the microwave."

"Two," Edna threw back over her shoulder. "She wants to regain her strength."

Amina Pacetti was sitting up, wearing yet another beautiful peignoir, in deep pink with black lace trim. She was flipping through an Italian fashion magazine and had applied cosmetics moderately. Her golden hair was also combed, pulled back into a French roll. Judith gauged that she was fit to welcome callers.

"Inez Garcia-Green is here," said Judith, with a hand on the doorknob.

Amina looked up from the pages of her magazine, eyes slightly narrowed. "Inez? Tchaah!" Her gaze returned to the periodical.

"Is that a no?" inquired Judith.

"It is a comment only." Amina gave a nod. "Send her up."

Judith did, leading the way for the soprano. Discreetly, she closed the door, then slipped next door into Tippy's room. It wouldn't hurt to start cleaning, since Phyliss hadn't yet begun. And it certainly wouldn't seem strange if she started with the adjoining bathroom. Judith leaned against the door that led into Amina's bedroom.

At first, she could hear nothing except the murmur of female voices. Then, they both began to shout, Amina in

Italian, Inez in Spanish. Judith was lost. She knew virtually no Italian, and even if her Spanish hadn't been so rusty, Inez's rapid-fire delivery was too much for Judith. But she knew fury in any language—and the two women were definitely irate. Judith decided to scrub the sink and worry about translations later.

She was flushing cleanser down the drain when she heard the door slam. A final burst from Amina floated into the bathroom. Judith grabbed a towel, wiping her hands as she hurried into the hallway.

"Madame Garcia?" Judith said, uncertain as to how to address the soprano's retreating form. "May I . . . uh . . ."

Inez paused, her hand on the balustrade. She turned to look up at Judith on the landing. "Ah! *Muchas gracias,* I appreciate your kindly hospitality. I leave Señora Pacetti feeling comforted. *Pobre mujer,* she suffers so! Treat her well, for the days ahead will be dark. *Adios.*"

*Poor woman indeed,* thought Judith as Inez Garcia-Green escaped through the front door. Inez and Amina had sounded as if they were coming to blows. There was no love lost between them, that was for sure. But why, Judith wondered as she watched Inez pull away in a sleek beige limo. Had a rivalry between Mario Pacetti and Inez Garcia-Green carried beyond the grave? If so, why had Inez bothered to call on Pacetti's widow? Inez had already accompanied Justin Kerr and his bouquet to Hillside Manor.

Edna Fiske was broiling steak while Phyliss Rackley resumed her litany of health problems. "It was right around Easter of '86 that I first noticed the fungus between my toes," Phyliss was saying over a half-eaten plate of beet greens.

Judith interrupted. "Ms. Fiske, your patient sounds distressed. You might want to check on her."

Edna gave Judith a dubious look. "Well . . . if you'd be so kind as to watch the meat. Mrs. Pacetti would like it medium rare, but that's nonsense, of course. Undercooked beef isn't suitable for a person in her condition. I've also prepared a small salad." She pointed to a plate of lettuce, tomatoes, and cucumber on the counter.

As soon as Edna left the kitchen, Judith picked up the phone. "Hey, coz," she said as Renie answered at the other end of the line, "count me in tomorrow with Melissa. I've got a few questions for her."

"Great," said Renie. "What changed your mind?"

"Inez Garcia-Green," replied Judith, as she heard a crash and a clatter in the driveway. "I'll explain later. Skjoval Tolvang has arrived."

Bruno Schutzendorf returned around 5:00 P.M. with an airline ticket to New Haven. He was scheduled to leave the following morning and Judith uttered a sigh of relief. Winston Plunkett and Tippy de Caro arrived at Hillside Manor a few minutes later. Plunkett hastened to Amina Pacetti's bedside while Tippy lingered in the kitchen. Judith, who had just waved Phyliss Rackley off for the day, was making hors d'oeuvres but had held firm in her resolve not to fix another dinner, except for the patient and her nurse.

"What's that?" asked Tippy, pointing to an open tin of smoked mussels.

Judith told her. Tippy wiggled her red eyebrows. "Like clams, aren't they? We have lots of good seafood back home in Boston. Especially lobster."

"How did you and Mr. Plunkett make out today?" Judith asked, then realized the question was no doubt too aptly phrased.

But Tippy didn't seem to notice. "Fine. We went to a sporting goods store. He bought more fishing flies. I got a hot pink Spandex leotard. Here, let me help," she began putting crackers around the edge of Judith's bone china serving plate.

Seeing Tippy perform a domestic chore jogged Judith's memory. "Say, Tippy, did you get to be a super in the performance the other night? I thought I recognized you dressed as a maid." Under cover of emptying the mussels onto the plate, Judith tried to catch Tippy's reaction.

But Tippy, as usual, seemed unconcerned. "Yes, that was me. It's fun. I got to be a courtier once in *Rigoletto* and I wore the most fabulous green brocade dress. I was supposed to be part of a mob in *Andrea Cheniér* at the Met next month, but I guess I won't be doing that now. The French Revolution will have to go on without me." Her eyes widened and her mouth curved into a huge grin. "Hey! That's funny! Do you get it? The French Rev . . ."

"Right," said Judith quickly. "That's good, that's great, that's . . . hilarious. How do you manage to get a job like that?"

Tippy gave a little shrug. She was wearing a huge bronze sweater that apparently was intended to fall off one shoulder. The gesture made it fall off of both. Hooking a thumb into the garment, Tippy hitched it back up. "Mr. Plunkett arranged it for me. Most of the supers are volunteers, but they do have to rehearse. I'd gone through my stage directions at the dress rehearsal Friday."

Judith's expression exuded interest. "What did you get to do on stage the other night? You don't actually sing, do you?"

"Not in *Traviata*," said Tippy, resealing the box of crackers. "I just fiddled around with the stuff on the table. You know, like I was preparing for the guests. But I did get to sing in the *Rigoletto* chorus. That was neat."

Judith was impressed. "You must be talented," she said. "They wouldn't let you do that—even if you worked for Mr. Pacetti—if you didn't have a good voice."

Tippy shrugged again, as the sweater slipped another notch. For the first time, Judith noticed a wary spark in the other woman's eyes before she looked away. "Oh—I guess. My family's kind of musical. I mean, we all took piano lessons and stuff like that. I paid for half of mine by working at the corner drugstore. You got to know a lot about guys that way. You know, which ones bought what contraceptives. Shall I put this plate out in the living room?"

Judith had the feeling that Tippy wasn't so anxious to help as she was to avoid further questions. Perhaps Tippy de Caro was embarrassed about her background. Judith suspected that she came from a working-class Boston family whose roots probably didn't quite measure up to the elite company in which she now found herself. But at least, thought Judith as she checked on the steaks, the de Caros had been able to afford piano lessons . . .

Her reverie was cut short by the phone. Woody Price's pleasant voice came over the wire. "I've got a surprise for you," he said, sounding not quite as restrained as usual. "I've been assigned to the Pacetti investigation."

Judith was glad Woody couldn't see the smug expression on her face. "Really? I am surprised!"

"Are you?" There was an ironic note in Woody's voice.

"Well, sure," said Judith smoothly. "I just hope it doesn't interfere too much with your . . . other duties. I mean, the baby probably won't be here for at least a couple of weeks and maybe it'll help keep your mind off of worrying about Sondra."

"Maybe." His tone was now noncommittal. Indeed, he paused, apparently waiting for Judith to make a remark. When she didn't, he finally spoke again. "Mrs. Flynn— that is, Judith—aren't you going to ask me something? Anything?"

"Huh?" Judith frowned into the receiver.

*"I've been assigned to the case."*

"Oh!" Judith clutched at the phone, the significance of his words sinking in. "You mean—it *is* murder?" she breathed.

"That's right," said Woody. "We got the stomach contents analysis back about half an hour ago. Mr. Pacetti died from an overdose of a digitalis-like poison. No doubt the Strophanthin that was in the empty vial we found onstage at the opera house."

Judith sucked in her breath. Now she was surprised, not

by Woody's assignment to the investigation, but by the fact that she had never doubted that Pacetti had been murdered.

Yes, a lot of people died from natural causes. But somehow she had known all along that Mario Pacetti wasn't one of them.

# TEN

FOR THE NEXT four hours, while waiting for Woody Price to show up, Judith felt edgy. Skjoval Tolvang had delivered the lumber and other materials he would need for the remodeling, torn out what remained of the old roof, and insisted that Judith remove whatever stored items she wanted to save. Otherwise, Tolvang would haul everything off to the dump in his pickup truck. Judith had spent almost two hours in the rain and wind sorting through her belongings, the most important of which was Dan McMonigle's ashes. With a grimace, she moved the boot box in which they rested to the basement. She would deal with Dan later. For now, she had to worry about the possibility that a killer might be living under her roof.

Schutzendorf and Tippy went off to dinner together, but Winston Plunkett remained at Hillside Manor. He spent most of the time with Amina Pacetti, much to the consternation of Edna Fiske, R.N.

"Too much stimulation isn't good for the patient," complained Edna when she brought Mrs. Pacetti's dinner tray back to the kitchen. "Moderation is the key to recovery."

"Winston Plunkett isn't exactly a whirling dervish of

excitement," Judith pointed out, rinsing off plates before putting them in the dishwasher. "I'm sure they need to discuss the details of Mr. Pacetti's funeral. Not to mention unfinished business. There must be a lot of that, given the kind of career the man had. Inez Garcia-Green is another matter, but at least she didn't stay long."

Edna gave Judith a patronizing look. "That's true, but I must tell you that Mrs. Pacetti wasn't in the least distressed as you reported to me. Quite the contrary, she was both moved and comforted by the visit."

Judith managed to keep her jaw from dropping. Unless Mediterranean culture was far different than Judith realized, angry high-pitched screaming bouts didn't usually signify camaraderie. But it wouldn't do any good to argue with Edna. It occurred to Judith that for some reason, Amina Pacetti wanted everyone to think she and Inez Garcia-Green were on good terms.

By eight-thirty, Skjoval Tolvang called it quits for the day, clattering out of the driveway with a load of junk that Judith was certain she'd need desperately within the next forty-eight hours.

"I should have had a yard sale," she told Renie over the phone. "At least I might have made some money off of that stuff."

"Like what?" countered Renie. "I've been in your toolshed, coz. It's like our so-called storage room. What did you have in there besides Dan? A broken bicycle pump, ten dozen cracked geranium pots, and your father's air raid warden's hat?"

"I might have got three dollars for the hat alone," said Judith. "You never gave the toolshed a close look. I had treasures in there that would make an antique collector drool."

"That old crap made me want to puke," retorted Renie. "Stop whining, you never throw anything away. You're turning into your mother."

Judith was aghast. "Coz! What a horrid thing to say!"

Renie was unrepentant. "It's true. We all turn into our

mothers. It's one of the things I love telling Anne. Then *she* wants to puke. Just wait thirty or forty years, I tell her. She'll see. So will you. Ha-ha."

Judith felt it was more likely that she would turn into Aunt Deb while Renie became Gertrude's clone. Each niece's personality was more like that of her aunt than her mother, and both cousins were aware of it. But Renie was right about Judith's reluctance to throw away any item that held the least hint of sentiment or nostalgia. Judith decided to shut up.

"Why don't you come over?" she asked Renie, switching subjects. "Woody's due around nine."

But Renie was already in her bathrobe, eating a tub of microwave popcorn. "Give him a hug from me and call after he leaves, okay?"

Judith agreed she would. Still on edge, she puttered around the kitchen, emptying the dishwasher, wiping up the floor, wondering how Woody's announcement would affect the other inhabitants of Hillside Manor. Schutzendorf and Tippy were still out. Mrs. Pacetti was resting, as usual. Plunkett had finally retreated to his room, presumably to work. He had requested the prolonged use of the B&B's telephone line, assuring Judith that he would use his credit card to charge long-distance calls. To Judith's knowledge, he had not eaten, unless he'd shared some of Amina Pacetti's dinner tray.

By 9:00 P.M., Judith was downright jumpy. She had stayed on the main floor to wait for Woody, instead of going up to the family quarters as she usually did in the evening. Sitting in the front parlor with a snappy little fire in the grate, she found she couldn't concentrate on the spy thriller she was reading. Maybe she needed new reading glasses. On the other hand, she'd scarcely heard a note of the Brahms violin concerto that played on her CD. All she could think of was that Mario Pacetti had been poisoned. Why? Who stood to gain? Amina Pacetti had mentioned insurance, but surely her gifted husband was worth more to her alive than dead. Plunkett had lost an employer.

Schutzendorf had been left without a star tenor. And Tippy seemed out of it in more ways than one. But she had been on the stage of the opera house Saturday night. Had someone placed her there for a devious purpose? Winston Plunkett had arranged her role as a supernumerary. Had he somehow manipulated her to plant the poison in Mario Pacetti's champagne glass? How? Why? Judith's brain whirled 'round and 'round. Inez Garcia-Green. Justin Kerr. Who else among the cast and crew? Except for Maestro Dunkowitz and Sydney Haines, Judith didn't even know who the rest of them were. The list of suspects could reach as many as a hundred.

The doorbell buzzed. Judith jumped. It must be Woody Price. She hurried into the entry hall.

So caught up in mulling over the mystery was Judith that she had not noticed that the wind had died down and the rain had all but stopped. The sidewalk gleamed under the streetlights; the night air smelled of damp earth. Woody Price stood on the front porch with Officers Corazon Perez and Ted Doyle flanking him. Judith felt a sense of relief wash over her. She greeted the trio warmly, leading them into the parlor.

Woody's top priority was to speak with Mrs. Pacetti. He went upstairs while Judith made hot cocoa. Perez and Doyle had downed half of theirs before Woody returned, his usual composure ruffled.

"She's not taking it well," he said. "Neither is the business manager. He came racing in after she let out the first shriek."

Judith nodded in sympathy. "I could hear her in the kitchen. I assume the nurse has things under control?"

"More or less. She and Plunkett are trying to cope." Woody picked up his mug and sipped thoughtfully. "Their reactions seem genuine. But you never know."

Corazon Perez, a petite young woman of Filipino ancestry, shook her head. "Murderers can be so cunning. I've only worked as liaison with homicide for a year, but I've already run into a couple who practically passed out when they learned—or pretended to learn—that their victim was dead. I think their instincts for self-preservation give them the ability to make themselves believe they're innocent."

Ted Doyle's short chin bobbed up and down. "That's right. In this business, you have to assume that everybody is lying. Not just the perps, either, but the victims and the witnesses." His steady hazel eyes met Judith's gaze. "Your husband taught me that, Mrs. Flynn."

"Great," breathed Judith, thinking that maybe she didn't realize how cynical Joe's view of humankind really was.

"We've got one thing figured out," said Woody, who was looking a bit tired around the eyes. No doubt he'd put in a very long day. Judith felt vaguely guilty. "Mr. Pacetti had his own champagne glass. So did Inez Garcia-Green. It seems that singers in their league don't want to risk picking up somebody else's germs—catch a cold or a sore throat or whatever. Pacetti's was monogrammed. Garcia-Green's had a gold rim."

Judith leaned forward in the chair. "Were the contents analyzed?"

Woody's expression conveyed chagrin. "Someone had taken the glass away and rinsed it out. Plunkett's assistant, I think, but we'll have to ask her. When do you expect Ms. de Caro and Mr. Schutzendorf to get back from dinner?"

Judith had no idea. They hadn't left until almost seven-thirty. "How," Judith inquired, trying to re-create the scene in her mind, "could someone have slipped the poison into the champagne glass without being seen?"

"There's a lot going on in Act I," replied Woody. "All eyes are on the principal singers, as a rule. And, as far as we know, the Strophanthin could have been put into Pacetti's glass before the curtain went up. There's even more confusion then."

Judith considered Woody's statement briefly. "But surely someone would have noticed if say, Mrs. Pacetti or Plunkett or somebody who didn't belong onstage had been out there before the performance?"

"Not necessarily." Woody set down his mug and

stretched his legs. "They had a right to be backstage. Pacetti is such a big star that the members of his entourage wouldn't be questioned. They could probably do cartwheels in the orchestra pit and nobody would criticize."

"I'm not saying they'd get in trouble for mooching around," responded Judith, "but that they'd be *noticed*. Surely if Inez Garcia-Green went out before the curtain went up, her own entourage would see her."

"They did." Woody gave Judith an ironic look. "She was checking on her own glass, making sure it was where she could reach it at the right moment. We've just come from her suite at the Cascadia. She readily admits she was there. But of course she denies she poisoned Pacetti and to prove the point, she passed out."

"Oh." Judith fingered her chin. "What about Sydney Haines? He doesn't come on until Act II."

Corazon Perez responded in her perky manner. "Ted and I talked to Haines—he's at the Cascadia, too—but he didn't arrive at the opera house until after Pacetti went off in the ambulance. It makes him nervous to wait around until after the first intermission for his cue in the second act." She glanced at Woody for confirmation. "That's where he sings his big piece, right?"

"That's right," said Woody. "The baritone's moment in the sun, 'Di Provenza il mar.' It's the kind of thing that would make any singer nervous. Tenors have a habit of trying to steal the scene from the baritone because the aria's so beautiful. I heard about a performance years ago where the tenor actually came up to the baritone in the middle of the aria and made bunny ears behind his head."

Judith, Corazon, and Ted all laughed, temporarily lightening the mood. "What about Mrs. Pacetti?" inquired Judith when their mirth had subsided. "Did she go onstage?"

"I don't know," said Woody. "She wasn't in much shape to give out information just now. If she did, nobody's mentioned it yet. But we've got a lot of interrogating to do."

Getting up to throw another log on the fire, Judith remembered to tell Woody and the others about Tippy de Caro's role as a super. Woody was making a note when Judith heard the front door open.

Bruno Schutzendorf did not look pleased to see the three police officers. Tippy, however, expressed excitement. "You mean, like *foul play?*" she asked in a breathless voice. "Wow! Are we suspects?"

Woody, looking far more pained than amused, assured her that they were. "Everyone is, I'm afraid. I'll have to ask you not to leave town for a few days."

*"Vat?"* exploded Schutzendorf, getting very red in the face and yanking off his snap-brimmed houndstooth cap. "Impossible! I have much business to conduct, and not in this place of rain and fish!"

Woody, who was an even six feet, had to look up at Schutzendorf, but he didn't yield an inch. "I'm sorry, sir. We'll try not to inconvenience you any longer than we have to. But there are questions we must ask. Routine, of course, but necessary."

Schutzendorf started to glare at Woody, thought better of it, and began to simmer down. "Of course, of course. I shall cooperate with your police procedures. But I know nothing," he added, now almost benign. "I am merely . . . . *Schutzendorf!*"

"Yes, certainly," said Woody, wincing as the German accidentally spit in his eye. "Perhaps we could go out into the living room where there are more chairs?" Woody cast an appealing look at Judith. She started to lead the others out of the parlor, but Woody asked Officer Perez and Tippy to remain. When Judith, Schutzendorf, and Ted Doyle had made their exit, Woody closed the door to the living room. Obviously, he was going to conduct his investigation in private. Judith was a little disappointed.

"Terrible, terrible, terrible!" muttered Schutzendorf, pacing the length of the living room from the French doors to the grandfather clock. "What of Frau Pacetti? Is she in shock?"

"She's pretty upset, I gather," Judith replied from her place on the sofa. "So is Mr. Plunkett."

Mr. Plunkett, however, appeared reasonably composed as he entered the living room. Although his long face was drawn and his tie was askew, he otherwise appeared to have his emotions under control. He took one look at Officer Doyle and frowned.

"This ordeal isn't over yet?" Plunkett asked, more of the room in general than of anyone in particular.

"No, sir," said Doyle.

*"Nein,"* growled Schutzendorf.

"I'm afraid not," replied Judith.

Plunkett waited for Schutzendorf to make the next turn in his pacing, then sat down in the rocking chair. "The nurse has given Mrs. Pacetti a sedative. Poor thing, it's been one tragic blow after another."

Before anyone could respond, the phone rang. Judith considered picking up the receiver in the living room, but decided to take it in the kitchen instead. Just before it switched to the answering machine on the fourth ring, she said hello. An unfamiliar, but lilting voice came on the line.

"Judith Flynn? This is Melissa Bargroom of the *Times*. I understand we're having lunch tomorrow. Is it true that Mario Pacetti was poisoned? I just got the word from one of our police reporters."

"You got it right," said Judith, perching on the stool next to the swinging door between the kitchen and the dining room. "The police are here now. Did you talk to my cousin, Serena?"

"Not since this afternoon," said Melissa. "I figured I'd go straight to the horse's ... uh, mouth." She gave a throaty little laugh.

"As well you might," chuckled Judith, understanding why Renie and Melissa were friends. "Don't tell me you're doing the story on Pacetti? Isn't that an odd assignment for a music critic?"

"I'm doing it with one of our regular police beat people," answered Melissa. "How is Mrs. Pacetti taking all this? Are the police there now? Shall I come over?"

Judith bit her lip. If she let Melissa come, it would open up a field day for the rest of the media. Judith had already been through that once, when the fortune-teller was murdered in her dining room. It was almost 10:00 P.M. Of course there was no way to keep Melissa away from Hillside Manor, nor did Judith want to put her off completely.

"You don't have a deadline until tomorrow, right?"

"Right," said Melissa. "Eleven o'clock. But that's before we do lunch."

Inspiration struck Judith. "Then how about breakfast? Say around eight-thirty?" By then, she would have her guests taken care of, or so she hoped.

Melissa turned dubious. "Well . . . what about Serena? She's never conscious before ten."

"I'll get Mrs. Pacetti's nurse to run a caffeine IV into her," said Judith breezily. "Cheers To You Cafe, eight-thirty?"

"Got it," said Melissa, and rang off. Hurriedly, Judith dialed Renie's number. Renie groaned at the change in plans. Judith reminded her that they were involved in a murder case. Renie groaned some more. But she gave in, sort of.

"I'll never forgive either of you two jerks for this," she fumed. "I'll have to get up at seven-fifteen! I don't even know what it's like at that time of day! Are there people around or what?"

Judith chortled and hung up. Out in the living room, Schutzendorf had finally sat down on the piano bench, but he was still in a state of upheaval. Plunkett, meanwhile, was drumming his thin fingers on his trousers. Only Ted Doyle looked at ease, though Judith guessed it was part of his professional stance. Certainly the tension in the room was palpable.

"So you are saying someone poisoned the great Pacetti?" Schutzendorf appeared to be grilling Officer Doyle instead of the other way around.

"That's right," said Doyle, his expression revealing nothing.

"When? How? Explain, *bitte.*" Half a room away, Schutzendorf glared from under his heavy eyebrows.

"You'll hear the details soon enough from Lieutenant Price," said Doyle. He folded his arms across his chest, as if to ward off further questions.

Judith had resumed her place on the sofa, across from Doyle. "You were backstage before the performance, weren't you, Mr. Plunkett?" she asked, trying to sound casual. "How did Mr. Pacetti seem before he made his entrance?"

The business manager's fingers paused just above the fine wool that covered his knees. Carefully, Plunkett considered the question. "He performed his rituals, warming up his vocal cords, holding the relic of St. Cecelia, the patroness of musicians, against his throat, invoking Beniamino Gigli's ghost, reciting Giuseppe Verdi's name backwards and forwards seven times, all of his regular habits. He was as usual, drinking hot tea and being on edge. That is, he was having his customary case of nerves, what outsiders might, I suppose, mistakenly call having a fit. There was a row with Dunkowitz, some sort of heated exchange with Inez Garcia-Green, a snubbing of Creighton Layton, a stern warning for the prompter, some words with the stage director, the chorus master, the choreographer—as I said, the usual." Plunkett concluded his recital with a slight shrug.

The catalog of Pacetti's extreme rituals and excessive behavior caused Judith to grimace, but only one phrase stuck in her mind. "Mr. Pacetti always drank hot tea before a performance, isn't that so?"

Plunkett nodded. "It somehow soothed him while also invigorating him. Mrs. Pacetti brought it in a big thermos."

An idea was igniting in Judith's brain. "She made the tea here, in the kitchen?"

Plunkett was looking a bit puzzled by Judith's question. "I believe so. That's what she usually does."

Ted Doyle was obviously following Judith's train of thought. "Where was the thermos kept? That is, was it left in the dressing room?"

"Oh, no," said Plunkett. "Mrs. Pacetti carried it with her at all times. Mr. Pacetti drank out of the plastic cover. You know, a cuplike thing that's made for drinking but fits on top of the thermos."

Schutzendorf also had apparently caught on to what Judith was thinking. "There might be poison in the tea? Vat an idea! It's too terrible!"

Ted Doyle made no comment. Judith figured he wasn't going to give anything away until Woody had spoken privately with the others. But it wouldn't hurt for her to do a little more probing of her own.

"Did you see Mario Pacetti before the performance, Mr. Schutzendorf?"

With a sad shake of his head, Schutzendorf leaned against the piano, the keys jangling unharmoniously. *"Nein,* I saw him last under this very roof when he and Frau Pacetti were going out to their limousine. I went later to the opera house, where I sat in the front row center. Too close, some would say, but fine for me. I like to see as well as hear. I am next to music critic, Frau Barfly."

"Bargroom," corrected Judith, but Schutzendorf didn't seem to hear her.

The door to the front parlor opened and a much subdued Tippy de Caro appeared. "Golly," she said in a travesty of her usual exuberant voice, "this is *serious!* It's like . . . *death!"*

Woody appeared, beckoning to Schutzendorf. The German pulled himself up from the piano bench and tromped across the living room. "The interrogation," he muttered, "like Nazis. It is a good thing that I am merely . . . *innocent!"* He banged the door behind him, rattling the china on Judith's plate rail.

Tippy, meanwhile, made as if to join the others, then abruptly swung around and headed toward the stairway off the entry hall. "I'm beat. G'night, all."

Judith noticed that Winston Plunkett didn't even bother to look up. "Ms. de Caro seems a bit shaken," Judith remarked, her eyes on Plunkett. "Is she the type who has a delayed reaction?"

Plunkett moved slowly back and forth in the rocker as he considered the question. "Possibly. I don't know her very well. She's only worked for me since July. Some would think her a trifle flighty, but that's merely a mannerism. She's actually quite efficient."

Judith tried to conceal her surprise. "Then she must have come with excellent references."

Plunkett nodded. "Very much so. She worked for the Boston Pops previously. Ms. de Caro has quite a solid background in classical music. I suspect that she sometimes pretends otherwise because as a child she was afraid of having her peers make fun of her."

The explanation made some sense to Judith, but she didn't understand why Tippy would deliberately adopt such a lamebrained image as a professional. Judith also wondered if her surmise about a romantic link between Tippy and Plunkett had been wrong from the start.

Schutzendorf reappeared, mopping his brow. *"Mein Gott!* Such questions! My heart is pounding like the whumpa-whumpa machine! Now I must postpone my departure for at least three days. My business affairs will turn into a shambles!" He, too, headed upstairs.

Winston Plunkett went off to the front parlor with the air of a man headed for a root canal. Judith was left alone with Ted Doyle.

"How much is Woody telling them?" she asked the young policeman.

"Not much at this point," said Doyle who apparently had been skimming through a travel magazine, but in fact had never diverted his attention from the others in the living room. "Lieutenant Price has to reveal that Pacetti was poisoned, but other than that, he'll let them do all the talking."

Her brain already off on another tangent, Judith gave a

faint nod. "Look, Ted—may I call you that?—it seems crucial to me to figure out how Pacetti ingested the poison. Or maybe I should say *where,* because I'd feel a lot better if I knew that my guests weren't serious suspects. Call me selfish, but I've already had one murderer staying under my roof."

Ted Doyle gave Judith a rather shy, boyish smile. "I remember that case. I had only been on the force a year when it happened. Lieutenant Flynn and Lieutenant Price sure wrapped that one up fast. They're both really sharp cops."

Judith tried not to make a face. As far as she was concerned, Joe and Woody might still be combing the Rankers's hedge for clues if she and Renie hadn't done some deep digging into the suspects' backgrounds. But her husband and his partner were pros, she was merely the owner of a B&B, and she supposed that in the long run, it was a good thing that credit hadn't been given where credit was due. But it was still annoying. She would remember to mention it to Joe one of these days.

"Yes, right, sure," she agreed, picturing Joe and Woody with their chests puffed up, accepting congratulations from the police chief on down to the lowliest panhandler informant. "Let's get back to the poison. If it was in the tea, probably only Mrs. Pacetti could have put it there. Did you get a chance to analyze the contents of the thermos?"

Ted gave Judith an embarrassed look. "We couldn't find it. And Mrs. Pacetti hasn't been in very good shape to ask what happened to it after the curtain went up."

It occurred to Judith that Amina Pacetti had been coping remarkably well, at least up until Woody had informed her that Mario Pacetti had been poisoned. "Okay, then there's the champagne glass which was cleaned. That would be tricky to poison, but not impossible."

"It makes sense," said Doyle, tossing the magazine back onto the coffee table. "That's where the empty vial was found, next to the centerpiece. The glasses were lined up in front of the flowers. I call that suggestive."

"So would I," remarked Judith, though she realized that something was bothering her. "Almost too suggestive, maybe. How big was that vial?"

Ted Doyle held his thumb and index finger about an inch and a half apart. "It was small. Are you thinking it could have been easily concealed?"

"Yes—unless you had no place to put it." She pictured Inez Garcia-Green's white tulle ball gown. Tippy's costume as a maid. The men in their frock coats and ruffled shirts. Did anyone have real pockets? Certainly not Inez, who had also plied a huge fan. "It'd be risky to carry the vial around in your hand after the fact, I suppose."

"But you could," Ted Doyle pointed out. "You wouldn't have to go very far backstage to ditch it."

"Except that it was ditched onstage." Judith grimaced. "I hate things that don't make sense. There's no logic to this case. And how does anybody get hold of Strophanthin in the first place?"

"It's used widely in Europe," said Doyle. "At least that's what the medical examiner told us. I'm afraid I don't know much about how tight the laws are over there concerning medical drugs. I imagine it varies from country to country. The label was scratched off, so we couldn't tell where the stuff came from."

Judith heaved a big sigh. "It sounds impossible to track down. All of these people have been in Europe recently, I'd guess. At least within the last few months."

"We've checked on that," said Doyle. "They've all spent quite a bit of time abroad. Even Ms. de Caro was in Austria this summer. Pacetti sang at some festival, I guess."

"Probably Salzburg," said Judith, staring at the fireplace where the pumpkin lights gleamed and two pots of China chrysanthemums anchored each end of the mantel. "Say," Judith said suddenly as the mums evoked a new idea. "I just realized something. When Inez and Justin came to pay their respects, they brought a huge bouquet. The blooms were really unusual. Now that I think about it, I could

swear they were pulled right out of the centerpiece from
Act I."

Doyle's mouth worked in the effort of deduction.
"Meaning ... what?"

But Judith wasn't sure. "Meaning there were no florists
open that late on a Saturday night, so Inez and Justin were
forced to swipe the props. I guess I'm reaching a bit," she
added in apology as Winston Plunkett emerged from the
front parlor.

"Why," he asked as if Judith and Doyle should know
the answer, "do the police want to know if Mr. Pacetti
had heart trouble? He'd just had a physical last December. All his vital signs were excellent, except for a bit of
hypertension. I should have such a strong constitution!"
Plunkett spoke with unusual force, then grew more pale
than ever. "That is, he *had* a strong ... Dear me, how
callous. Here I am, complaining about my weaknesses
when poor Mr. Pacetti is dead. I do believe I'll turn in.
Good night." He made a stiff little bow to both Judith
and Officer Doyle.

A moment later, Woody Price and Corazon Perez came
back into the living room. Woody was stifling a yawn,
while Corazon had lost the spring in her step.

"That session wasn't a lot of help, I'm afraid," said
Woody, declining Judith's offer to sit.

"They must have said *something*," remarked Judith with
a touch of impatience. It was almost eleven, and she, too,
was tired. "People always do." She fixed inquiring black
eyes on Woody's face.

"Well ..." Woody shifted his stance, clearly torn between official procedure and the demands of his partner's wife. "Ms. de Caro did rinse out Pacetti's glass.
She said Mr. Plunkett asked her to do that. Schutzendorf
didn't go backstage until after Pacetti collapsed. He's a
pretty conspicuous type, so if he had been there, somebody would have seen him. Plunkett was the one who
actually set the glass on the table before the opera
started. It contained mineral water. Garcia-Green, by the

way, always drinks cognac, but insists she only sips a bit. However, she admitted to downing the whole thing after Pacetti passed out. For medicinal purposes, of course. She had to have Schutzendorf assist her to her dressing room. And nobody noticed any tampering with glasses or placing of objects on the table." Woody lifted his palms. "That's what I mean, not much help. I wish we could find that thermos. We've got men crawling all over the opera house, but nobody's called to say it turned up."

Judith, along with Doyle, had also risen. "Woody, what else had Pacetti eaten or drunk in those last few hours?"

Woody fingered his thick black mustache. "Let me think—I don't have the report with me—some sort of salad, cheese, sausage, bread, orange juice, chocolate, throat lozenges, mineral water. There may be more on the list, but those were the main things he ingested in the last twelve hours."

The items were consistent with Judith's refrigerator contents. She recalled the ironic thought that had passed through her mind as she'd watched her guests thrashing about the kitchen Saturday afternoon: It was *dangerous* in there. A sudden sense of sadness overcame her as she walked the police trio to the door. On Saturday morning, Mario Pacetti had awakened to what was for him an ordinary day. Breakfast, lunch, and preperformance meals, the prospect of an enthusiastic audience, the beautiful music of Verdi, the satisfaction of another role sung to the hilt. His was a rich, rewarding life. And then it had ended on the sourest note of all—murder.

The rain had stopped, the clouds were drifting off to the west, and a sprinkling of stars dappled the night sky. The air smelled fresh and clean, with just a hint of autumn's decay. Judith waited for the police car to pull away. The neighborhood was quiet, the only sounds coming from traffic navigating the steep hill that made up the Counterbalance two blocks away. With unaccustomed reluctance, Judith went back inside, closed and latched the door, then wryly smiled to herself. What was the point of safeguards? Who was she trying to keep out? Judith was well aware that she could be locked inside her house with a killer.

# ELEVEN

"PHILISTINES," MUTTERED RENIE, whose only consolation for being up so early was the sight of a menu. Cheers To You was a no-nonsense eatery near the university campus with ample portions of hearty American food. The cousins had been fans of the cafe since their college days. "This is a conspiracy, just to ruin my day. Do you two twits know it was *still dark* when I got up this morning?"

Judith glanced at Melissa Bargroom. The music critic was fortyish, with a cascade of auburn hair and a lively expression. She was almost as tall as Judith, but the dancing eyes and the pretty face lent her a pixielike quality. Melissa tried to keep a straight face. "You know, Serena—yoo-hoo, Earth to Serena, Earth to Serena!" She pulled the menu away from Renie's eyes which had begun to glaze over. "Really, my dear, there are often literally hundreds, nay, *thousands* of people in this city fully conscious and at work by 9:00 A.M. Honest."

"They're certifiable, every one of them," asserted Renie, trying to refocus. *"What's the point?"*

Judith knew that arguing with Renie, especially before ten o'clock in the morning, was a lost cause. The three women gave their orders to the waitress, who had already brought them coffee. Renie dumped lots of sugar into her cup but both Judith and Melissa took theirs black.

"You go first," said Melissa to Judith.

As concisely as possible Judith gave a rundown of the previous evening for both Melissa and Renie. "There's nothing new so far this morning," Judith concluded. "Mrs. Pacetti was able to take tea and toast; Schutzendorf bitched all the time he was polishing off the bratwurst; and Plunkett acts like he lost his anchor. Which I suppose he has. Tippy was sleeping in. I figure she can fend for herself or ask my cleaning woman to fix her something."

Melissa switched off the tape recorder she had brought along. "According to my police beat comrade at the *Times*, we can't say for sure that Pacetti was poisoned with Strophanthin. We have to hedge and call it a 'digitalis-like poison.' But we *can* say that the empty vial was found on the buffet table. This is all new to me—I gather that homicide stories require a lot of dancing around, lest we impede the investigation, or worse yet, influence the jury if and when the case comes to trial."

"So dig us some dirt," urged Renie, who had come to life at the sight of a crab and cheddar omelette accompanied by toast and hash brown potatoes.

Melissa tilted her head to one side. "I feel like a fraud. I don't know much about this cast of characters, really. That is, not much of recent note. One thing, though—" she paused to lift her eyebrows in a significant manner—"Pacetti and Garcia-Green had a torrid affair that lasted at least a couple of years. It was going on the last time Pacetti sang here, which is how I know about it."

"Ah!" exclaimed Judith.

"Oho!" breathed Renie.

"Then they had a falling-out," Melissa went on, "at La Scala in Milan. Bear in mind that Pacetti wasn't the type to play around. Inez might have been the real thing for him. She's had a half dozen lovers since then, the most recent being—get this—an honest-to-God Swiss brain surgeon. I don't know what caused the breakup with Pacetti, but Inez is inclined to take lovers as the whim hits her. In any event, Mario was gone with the whim—so to speak." Melissa wiggled her eyebrows again.

"That explains the animosity with Mrs. Pacetti," said Judith, dipping toast into one of her two fried eggs. "It also explains why Pacetti asked Inez to sing with him when he came here for his return engagement. They were lovers when he was here the first time."

Melissa nodded over her Belgian waffle. "Once the contracts were signed five, six years ago, they were stuck with each other. In fact, they did some other performances together after the rift, mainly in Europe."

"That must have galled Amina," commented Renie. "I assume she knew if everybody else did."

"Oh, she knew—Inez makes no secret of her affairs," responded Melissa. "But Signora Pacetti has her own way of coping with infidelity."

"Not poison, I hope," said Judith.

"Probably not," replied Melissa as the waitress poured more coffee. "Tit, as they say, for tat." She gave the cousins a sagacious smile. "Let's say she enjoys a junket with Plunkett and let it go at that."

"Plunkett!" Judith was aghast.

"Plunkett?" Renie was incredulous.

"Plunkett," repeated Melissa. "Yes, yes, I know he has no blood in his veins and his flesh is made of *papier-mâché*, but he's *so* devoted. She made no bones about it in the slightly more broad-minded operatic circles of Europe. I would bet that Mrs. P. seduced him the minute she found out about Mario and Inez. Pacetti couldn't get along without Plunkett—or he thought he couldn't—and was in a bind. The truth of the matter is, he couldn't have got along without Amina. She was always the driving force behind his career."

"Hey, hey," said Renie, definitely on the alert now that the clock was edging toward ten. "How come Pacetti didn't insist that his wife and his business manager knock it off? He was a feisty guy, after all."

"Feisty, but neurotic," said Melissa, glancing at the clock. The small but crowded cafe still had patrons waiting in line at the door. "He probably couldn't bear to think what might happen to him if he lost either Amina or Plunkett. He was terribly superstitious. He was first a tenor, second, a husband. He must have preferred to put up with the *ménage à trois.*"

"Hmmmm." Judith finished her last rasher of bacon. "So it's been Amina and Winston all along. Does that mean Tippy de Caro isn't anybody's bimbo?"

Melissa had folded her napkin and set it next to her empty plate. "Not that I know of. She's just along for the ride. I've got to get back to the office if I want to have this story in by eleven." She began to rummage in her handbag for lipstick and compact.

Judith realized the meaning of Winston Plunkett's apparent indifference to Tippy. She was precisely what she was supposed to be—an assistant. Or was she? Judith still felt unsettled in her mind when it came to Ms. de Caro.

"Other than that old news, I don't have much," said Melissa, skillfully negotiating her wide mouth with bright crimson. "I feel like a real washout, but then we're pretty isolated out here when it comes to hot gossip from the opera world. The only recent tales I've been told are about Pacetti's backing out of two or three performances this past spring. That's not like him, but tenors are the most unpredictable species in the world. Otherwise, his career was going great guns, especially with that big new recording contract. This must be a terrible blow to old Schutzendorf. I had the dubious pleasure of sitting next to him at the opera house. They should have sold him two seats. I was pushed so far over that I was practically sitting in Mrs. Dunkowitz's lap."

Renie swallowed the last of her tomato juice. "Say— when did Bruno show up that night?"

Melissa shrugged. "I don't know. He was already there

when I arrived about five minutes before curtain time. He looked as if he was pretty well settled in, which, given his girth and garments, would take awhile."

Judith had a sudden inspiration. "What do you know about Justin Kerr?"

Melissa had picked up her bill and risen to her feet. "Justin Kerr?" She tapped her temple. "I heard him sing here last season. Very promising, good reviews out of San Francisco in the spring, raves from Salzburg last August. I should interview him in the next couple of days. We'll find out what he's made of tomorrow night when he takes over for Pacetti. He's on the spot."

The cousins agreed. After Melissa left, Judith and Renie had one last cup of coffee. "Extramarital affair or not," mused Judith, "I don't see Amina killing the goose that laid the golden egg for Plunkett's sake. Especially if Mario wouldn't stop them from carrying on."

"Or Plunkett doing ditto," agreed Renie, then gave a little shake of her head. "Wait—maybe that's more likely. Plunkett might be a dark horse, a snake in the grass, whatever. With Mario out of the way, he could have Amina all to himself—why, I couldn't say except that Melissa made it sound as if he were her sex slave or some damned thing—and collect the royalties and insurance and the rest of the Pacetti fortune."

Judith nodded. "That would make more sense. But I can't see Plunkett harming a fly, though he supposedly ties them. As for Inez, she wouldn't wait six years for revenge. Besides, Melissa made it sound as if Inez dumped Mario rather than the other way around. I wonder why, under the circumstances, Inez called on Amina?"

"To crow?" suggested Renie. "You know, to rub it in that Pacetti really loved her instead of Amina."

"Maybe." Judith couldn't discount the idea, but she wouldn't think much of Inez if that had been her intent. "Let's not leave Justin Kerr out of this. With Pacetti going sticks up, he gets his big chance."

Renie, however, scoffed. "If this were La Scala or the

Met, I'd say maybe. But international reputations aren't made in this town. Singers are strange, and tenors are the strangest of all, but the worst I'd expect from Justin Kerr is a bit of germ warfare. You know, to knock Pacetti out of a performance or two."

"That makes sense," Judith agreed, "unless the poison was meant merely to make Pacetti sick. If Kerr's involved, he might have misjudged the dosage. It seems to me that poisoners have to know something about the substances they use." Noting that the waiting line was finally gone, she guiltily got to her feet. "We've been hogging this table long enough. I better go check on the usual suspects back at the B&B, coz. What are you up to today?"

"Press check at the printer on the cancer research center brochure, 1:00 P.M." Renie grabbed her purse. "Visit our mothers. Do two loads of laundry. Fix dinner for Tony and Anne—Tom's working. Wait for Bill to call me tonight. I haven't talked to him since he and Joe left."

"I'm surprised Joe didn't phone last night," said Judith as they waited in line at the cash register behind two college students. "I thought he might be worried about me. You know, killer at large and all that."

Renie grinned at her cousin. "He figures you're used to it. Besides, he's got Woody playing guardian angel."

"True." The cousins went through the ritual of paying their bills and getting change. Outside, the sun was bright, the sky virtually cloudless. There was definitely a nip in the autumn air. Judith shielded her eyes as she sighted her blue Japanese compact parked on the far side of the lot. "We could get a frost before Halloween. I wonder if we'll have snow this winter."

"Remember six years ago when we had that blizzard on Armistice Day?" Renie hurried to catch up with her cousin's longer strides. "It was so hot right around Tom's birthday in October that I almost croaked, and then a month later we were up to our knees in snow. The schools were closed for a week. Bill and I *walked* to the opera. Hey," said Renie as they reached the car, "that was *Butterfly,* with Pacetti. We got a cab home, but the driver refused to come down our street and let us off up at the corner. I damned near slid on my butt all the way from . . ."

"Whoa!" Judith's head bobbed up. She stared at Renie across the roof of the car. "Snow? Armistice Day? *November?*"

"Right," replied Renie, wishing Judith would use the power locks to let her in the car. "You were still living with Dan out on Thurlow Street in that dump with the rats in the walls and the hookers using your front porch for a message drop."

"Are you *sure* Pacetti sang here in November?" Judith was leaning on the roof, her eyes narrowed at Renie.

"Yes! Hey, let me in, I can afford the fare! Next time I'll bring my own car!"

Judith finally complied. Once inside with their seat belts fastened, Judith turned to her cousin. "Then somebody's lying. Amina Pacetti has mentioned the beautiful flowers here. Not once, but twice. She specifically referred to the rhododendrons."

Renie's brown eyes grew round as understanding dawned. "Rhodies—April, May, even June. But never in November. What do you think?"

Judith started the engine. "I don't know. But the Pacettis made an unpublicized visit to our fair city somewhere along the line. I wonder when. And I wonder why."

With her nose in the air, Phyliss Rackley was sweeping off the back walk. "I won't talk to that awful man," she said haughtily, her eyes darting in Skjoval Tolvang's direction.

Judith looked over at the Swedish carpenter, who was ripping old boards out of the toolshed and hurling them onto the grass with the vigor of a man half his age. "What's wrong?" asked Judith, not really wanting to know.

Phyliss led the way back inside the house as Judith waved feebly at Tolvang. "He took the Lord's name in vain just because he hit his thumb with a hammer. Then he cursed again when he dropped some of those big boards on his foot. And after part of the old roof fell on his head, he cried out with the most blasphemous words I ever heard. I really think the man is possessed." Phyliss gave the broom a severe shake, as if she wished it were Tolvang's neck.

"He's a fine carpenter," said Judith lamely.

"The Lord was a fine carpenter," Phyliss asserted piously. "I'm sure He never used language like that."

Hanging her green jacket on a peg in the hallway between the kitchen and the pantry, Judith followed Phyliss into the kitchen. For all of the cleaning woman's complaints about Tolvang, she seemed to have the morning well in hand. Hoping to divert Phyliss from further attacks on Skjoval Tolvang, Judith praised her efforts.

"Well, thank you very much," said Phyliss, preening a bit. "I've just about got this floor done for the day. Not that it's easy for a woman of my age and poor constitution to keep up such a pace, but the Good Lord gives me extra strength to compensate for the crosses He's made me bear. Like bunions. You wouldn't believe how they ached when we had that rain. Praise the Lord for the sunshine. Even my lumbago is better. At least some," she added grudgingly.

"I'm glad," said Judith, starting to rewind her answering machine. As usual, there were calls for reservations, three from out of state, two from the other side of the mountains. Judith consulted her calendar. "I'll sure be happy when this bunch is gone," she said, more to herself than to Phyliss.

"Well, you got rid of one of 'em," the cleaning woman remarked, getting the hand vacuum out of the hall cupboard.

"I hardly intended to do it that way," Judith responded wryly. "Murder isn't my idea of canceling a guest stay."

"Oh, I don't mean that Eye-talian singer," said Phyliss,

checking to make sure the vacuum cleaner belt was in place. "I mean the slut."

"Slut?" Judith stared at Phyliss. "Who?"

Phyliss made an exasperated face at her employer. "The harlot. With her short skirts and tight clothes that would tempt a preacher. Skippy? Bippy? Trippy?"

Judith blocked Phyliss's exit to the back stairs. "Tippy? What do mean, Phyliss? Where did she go?"

Phyliss shrugged, sausage curls bouncing. "How do I know? I went up to tell her it was the last call for breakfast, waited half an hour, didn't see her come down, decided she'd gone out, went back to do up her room—and she was gone. Cleared out, luggage, everything. She must have left while I was in the basement doing the wash. Good riddance, I'd say." Phyliss barreled past Judith, using the vacuum as a wedge. "That lady was no lady, I tell you. She was a *tramp.*"

Even though Phyliss had disappeared up the stairs, Judith still stared.

Winston Plunkett was in the upstairs hallway, using the house phone. He had turned the wicker settee and matching end table into a makeshift office. Judith waited for him to finish his call, which he was conducting in what sounded like flawless French.

"Paris," he said five minutes later, when he had put down the phone. "It's evening over there, but I've had trouble reaching the director of the Paris Opera. Fortunately, I caught him just as he was leaving for dinner."

Judith sat down next to Plunkett, who seemed surprised at her apparent attempt at intimacy. Mrs. Pacetti's room, however, was a mere eight feet across the hall, and Judith didn't want to risk being overheard.

"Mr. Plunkett, do you know where Tippy is?"

Plunkett's face was blank. "No. I assumed she was overly tired and had slept in." He glanced at the door to Tippy's room which was at a right angle to Amina's. "She's not in there?"

Judith shook her head, then got up and went to open the door. Plunkett followed her. "See?" said Judith. "Everything seems to be gone, just as Mrs. Rackley told me."

To make sure, Judith checked the closet, the bureau, the dressing table, and under the bed. Phyliss hadn't yet finished doing up the room, but it was cleaned out as far as Tippy de Caro's possessions were concerned.

"Why . . . I'm flummoxed!" declared Plunkett. "She never said a word to me! I can't believe she left like this, without giving notice. Do you think she's been arrested?" Something akin to panic seemed to pass over Plunkett's long face.

Judith supposed that his reaction could be considered normal under the circumstances. But she thought he was wrong. If Tippy had been charged, or even taken downtown for questioning, Woody would have let Judith know.

"I think she left under her own power," said Judith. "Where's Schutzendorf?"

Plunkett looked uncomfortable. "Uh . . . we had a bit of a dustup. He insisted on using the phone, too, but I gather he hadn't asked your permission. *I* had," the business manager went on with the air of a schoolboy who has received a special favor from his teacher, "so I told him he'd better find another phone somewhere else. I suspect he went down to the bottom of the Hill to one of the business establishments that has a pay phone."

"I see." Judith nudged a bureau drawer that wasn't fully closed, then went back into the hall. She stopped to knock on Mrs. Pacetti's door. Edna Fiske appeared, holding a blood pressure kit. Beyond the nurse, Judith could see Amina, sitting up in bed with more magazines and yet another flowing peignoir. She did not seem to be overcome with grief.

"How's the patient?" Judith asked as Plunkett hovered behind her.

"Stable," replied Edna in hushed tones. "She was quite distressed last night. I had to give her a sedative. That was really dreadful news. In my opinion, poisoning people is unacceptable behavior." Her severe look indicated she blamed Judith for such social aberrations.

"It's pretty rotten," Judith agreed, not wanting to get sidetracked by Edna's moralizing. "Have you or Mrs. Pacetti seen Tippy de Caro this morning?"

Again, Edna looked disapproving. "I haven't." She turned to Mrs. Pacetti and repeated Judith's question. Amina glanced up from her magazine, gave a slight shake of her head, and again buried her nose in the pages of haute couture.

"Thanks," said Judith, starting to back away. But both Edna and Plunkett were on the move, almost colliding with each other as the nurse came through the door and the business manager tried to enter.

"Excuse me, so sorry," exclaimed Plunkett. "I just wanted a word with Mrs. Pacetti. If that's permissible, Nurse?"

It was. Plunkett continued on into the room, closing the door behind him. With a brief nod at Judith, Edna started for the stairs, still carrying the blood pressure kit.

"Where are you going?" Judith called after the nurse.

Edna looked up through the spindles of the bannister. "Mrs. Rackley feels an aneurism coming on. Or so she says. I'm going to check her out." Edna Fiske gave no hint of humor or irony as she headed off on another healing mission. Judith had the feeling that if asked, Edna would have taken the temperature of the maple tree in the front yard.

But Tippy de Caro was Judith's priority. She would have to tell Woody Price that the young woman had left Hillside Manor. Judith went up to the third floor to use her private line. To her surprise, the door to her bedroom stood open. Bruno Schutzendorf's voice rumbled out into the little foyer. Annoyed, Judith started into the room, then suddenly stopped. Schutzendorf was sitting on the bed, his bulk making the mattress sag, and his face turned away from the door. He was speaking in English; Judith retreated behind the potted weeping fig that stood between her room and Mike's.

"Clauses, clauses, clauses!" Schutzendorf was roaring into the phone. "I care not for your clauses! I know one thing, and one thing only—the man is dead! The police say murder, poison, deliberate! And that means you pay more, eh?"

Judith held her breath. Schutzendorf must be talking to an insurance company. Would Cherubim Records insure Pacetti's life? *Probably,* Judith reflected, thinking of various athletes and movie stars. At least there would be some compensation for Pacetti's loss.

"Vait? How long?" Schutzendorf had lowered his voice a notch, but Judith certainly didn't have to strain to hear him. "Six months! Ridiculous!" He paused, then continued on a more reasonable note. "Of course I understand your position. It is that I am upset beyond measure. Mario Pacetti is irreplaceable. Mere money is no consolation. And I do not like the red tape, the details, the *clauses.* I will be speaking with you again very soon. *Auf wieder-sehen.*"

Judith made a few quick steps around the potted fig, as if she were coming out of Mike's room. But Schutzendorf was making another call, asking for assistance from the international operator to connect him to a number in Hamburg. After a minute or more had passed, she heard him speaking in German. Judith decided to confront Schutzendorf.

"Ahem," she said from the doorway.

Schutzendorf barely looked in her direction. He held up a hand for silence. Judith leaned on the doorframe, tapping her foot. Schutzendorf continued speaking in rapid German. Judith emitted a series of impatient sighs. Schutzendorf took out a pen and started to write on Judith's flowered bedspread.

Judith resurrected two of the few German phrases she knew. *"Achtung! Halten sie!* Stop!" She flew into the room, barely able to refrain from pouncing on the German. "Don't you dare, that has to be dry-cleaned!"

"Vat?" Schutzendorf looked genuinely startled, even a trifle chagrined. "Oh, *ja, ja,* the counterpane. My apologies." He resumed his conversation, which fortuitously seemed to be at its conclusion. Judith strolled around the room, tidying up a bit.

*"Danke,"* said Schutzendorf, rising from the bed. The mattress remained in its sagging position. "Your housekeeper kindly permitted me to use this phone. I thank you many times."

Telling herself to give Phyliss a swift kick, Judith tried to keep her exasperation with Schutzendorf to a minimum. "Next time, ask me, not Mrs. Rackley," said Judith, making an attempt at a smile. "By the way, have you seen Ms. de Caro this morning?" Judith wasn't optimistic about the reply.

But Schutzendorf surprised her. "Yes, yes, so I did. I awakened early. Your bed is firm, it is comfortable—but small. I toss and turn in my sleep, like a ship on the ocean—roll, pitch, heave, twist." Judith was getting the picture; she marveled that Schutzendorf didn't just plain capsize. Dan had done that once, upending their mattress and sending Judith sliding feetfirst into a basket of dirty laundry at the foot of the bed. It had been a very strange way to wake up. "So," Schutzendorf continued, "I rose and went for a walk. The morning was fine, not like the rain of these past days. Upon my return, I saw Fräulein de Caro getting into a car and driving off."

"A car or a cab?" inquired Judith.

"A car," asserted Schutzendorf. "Not a German make, so I can't say what kind. But a man was driving, I believe."

Judith had a hand at her breast. "What color?"

"The man?"

"No, the car."

"Gray."

Judith was not surprised.

# TWELVE

WOODY WAS OUT to lunch when Judith called. Renie had already departed for her press check, but had left a message of her own on her cousin's machine. There would be at least two more press checks that afternoon, forcing Renie to stay at the printer's, or at least keep close to her phone. Could Judith do her a huge favor and run down to the box office at the bottom of the Hill to pick up the replacement tickets for Wednesday night? *Please?* Naturally, Judith would.

She took care of her business messages while waiting for a return call from Woody. Phyliss was upstairs doing the guest rooms. Her blood pressure had been normal. She refused to believe it.

"Not on a day like this," she had said, "getting off to such a bad start with that heathen in the backyard. I know I'm due for a spell."

Judith had made a sound of assent, then sat by the phone trying to guess Tippy's whereabouts. With typical German precision, Schutzendorf had pinpointed her departure at 6:26 A.M. Judith probably had been in the shower at the time. It was now after 1:00 P.M. In the ensuing six hours, Tippy could have gone just about anywhere, including out of the country.

Woody called back at ten minutes after one. Judith's news caused the usually stoic policeman to lose his composure.

"Darnit!" he exclaimed. "I told her not to go anywhere! Why didn't Schutzendorf tell somebody she'd left?"

"A fair question," said Judith. "I suppose he didn't realize she was going for good. That's assuming she has, but I would think that's the case as she took all her belongings with her."

Woody's sigh heaved over the line. "Okay, we'll do the routine check of the airport, the bus and train depots, the Canadian border. I take it Schutzendorf couldn't describe the car or the driver?"

"He was sure it was a man at the wheel, but he didn't get a good look at him. In fact, it was still dark and I guess the only glimpse he caught was when the light went on inside as Tippy got in. As for the car, all he knew was that it was gray but not a German make."

"Hmmm." Woody was back in control of his emotions. "No Volkswagen, Mercedes, BMW—what else? That still leaves a lot of automobile manufacturers."

Judith told Woody about the gray vehicle Arlene had seen the day the Pacettis arrived. She also mentioned that Inez Garcia-Green and Justin Kerr had arrived at Hillside Manor in a gray car.

"I think it was a smallish sedan," she said. "But it was dark and rainy. I couldn't see it very well."

"I don't suppose your neighbor noticed much about the car that was parked down the street," said Woody in a resigned voice.

"Arlene? She'd notice more than most people. I'd ask, if I were you. I didn't because it hadn't seemed important. Now, maybe it is."

Woody agreed, then rang off. He had a full plate, with no time for idle speculation. Judith wished Renie would get back from the printer's. She needed someone to help her toss around ideas.

Except, she realized as she went downstairs to forage in

the freezer, she didn't have any. There were no convincing
motives for Pacetti's murder. There was no one who ben-
efited more from his death than from his life. There was
no logic to the case, and the lack of orderly commonsense
hypotheses and conclusions cast Judith adrift. All she
could cling to were a batch of inconsistencies. The Pacettis
had made an unpublicized visit to the city; someone had
sent seemingly threatening missives to Hillside Manor; a
gray car was showing up on a fairly regular basis; Tippy
de Caro had defied police orders and fled; Inez Garcia-
Green had made not one but two visits to the B&B; Justin
Kerr had no knack for arranging flowers; Inez and Mario
were ex-lovers, while Amina and Plunkett were currently
engaged in an affair; Schutzendorf was merely . . .
Schutzendorf.

Judith gave herself a good shake, hauled a package of
pork chops out of the freezer, and trudged upstairs. It was
still sunny and clear outside, a perfect day for putting in
her spring bulbs. Judith grabbed the bags from the back
hallway, picked up a trowel from the porch, and headed
for the flower bed by the toolshed.

"No, you don't, Missus." Skjoval Tolvang waved a saw
at Judith. "Can't you see I'm vorking here?"

"Hey, come on, Mr. Tolvang," begged Judith. "It won't
take ten minutes. If I don't get these in now, we may have
a frost and then I won't be able to plant them at all. Have
you taken a lunch break?"

Tolvang looked at Judith as if she'd asked him if he'd
poured gasoline over himself and lighted a match. "Lunch
break? Vat kind of loafer no-good do you think I am? Coffee, that's all I need, strong and black, the kind that can
put holes in a two-by-four."

"But you're working inside now," Judith pointed out.
Indeed, the carpenter had already ripped out all of the old,
unusable parts of the toolshed and had begun to frame up
the new section. As always, Judith was impressed.

Tolvang squinted at Judith. "Ten minutes? Okay, do
your digging, goddamit. And a lot of good it vill do you,

ven those raccoons come and eat it all up. Vy don't you get that plug-ugly cat of yours to chase away these animals? At least he could tackle them pesky squirrels."

"I told you," Judith said staunchly, "Sweetums doesn't live here anymore. But he'll probably come back with Mother." She flinched at the thought.

"Then you got neighbor cats hanging around out here. Hunters, too. One of 'em got a bird." He handed Judith a big black feather. "Why can't they get together and scare off the other varmints?"

Judith glanced at the feather. "They aren't organized. You know how it is with cats; they're too independent."

"And so am I," Tolvang declared. "Are you going to dig or vat?"

Judith beamed at the carpenter. Down on her knees, she began to work the ground quickly and efficiently. She almost dropped the trowel when a voice sounded at her elbow.

"Gopher Purge," said Phyliss Rackley.

"Huh?" Judith swiveled. Phyliss had on her coat and was carrying her purse and a shopping bag. "You startled me, Phyliss. Are you leaving already?"

"That's right. I forgot to tell you I have an appointment with my dentist at three. My teeth have been acting up something cruel. It may be my gums, to tell the truth, or it could even be that neuralgia." She gazed through the open beams of the toolshed, where Skjoval Tolvang was hammering away like crazy. "The Devil's Workshop," she muttered. "I tell you, he's possessed."

"Mmm-mm." Judith started to put the bulbs into the holes she'd dug. "What did you say about gophers?"

"I said Gopher Purge. It works. And you've got 'em. Here," she went on, pointing to the strip where Judith was planting, "and over there by the bay window in the living room."

"Well . . ." Judith wasn't convinced. In her experience, gophers tended to dig all over the yard, not only in the flower beds, but under the lawn. Squirrels and raccoons went for the bulbs, none of which grew next to the house by the living room. That space was reserved for a half dozen rosebushes, several lupines, a couple of sweet lavender clumps, and her lilies of the valley. "I'll think about it," Judith said at last, not wanting to argue further with Phyliss.

"You do that." The cleaning woman plodded down the driveway, her purse in one hand, the shopping bag in the other.

"You talk too much," shouted Tolvang. "You got four minutes left."

Judith made a face. "Right, right," she grumbled. The last of the tulips went in; then two dozen daffodils. "Done," she called to Tolvang even as she started to crumple the paper bag that had contained the bulbs. "Wait—I forgot about the hyacinth bonus. I've got just three of them." Judith dug deeper.

Her trowel hit something hard. A rock, she thought, and swore under her breath. But the surface was smooth. Judith used the trowel to try to dislodge the object. It felt more like a piece of pipe. As the dirt fell away, she saw a shiny red surface. Putting the trowel aside, Judith started to remove the dirt with her bare hands. A moment later, she realized what she had uncovered. With a tug, she wrested the large thermos from the ground.

"Time's up!" shouted Tolvang. He hammered on a metal bucket for emphasis.

Hurriedly, Judith dumped all three hyacinth bulbs into the trough left by the thermos. She replaced the dirt in a haphazard manner and fled toward the house.

"You don't have to run, Missus!" Tolvang called after her. "I vouldn't chase you, py golly! You're no super-snooper city inspector! You're yust my customer!"

Over her shoulder, Judith tossed him a lopsided grin.

Judith's excitement was somewhat quelled when she still couldn't reach Woody. But she did manage to flag down the ubiquitous squad car. An impassive Nancy Prentice and a blank-faced Stanley Cernak put the thermos into an evidence bag and drove off to headquarters. Seeing them turn out of the cul-de-sac reminded her that she still had an errand of her own to run. Ten minutes later, she was at the box office window outside the opera house, waiting in a fairly sizable line for Renie's tickets.

She still had a dozen people in front of her when Inez Garcia-Green emerged from a beige limo right behind Judith's blue compact, which she had dared to park in the Passenger Load Only zone. Briefly, Judith struggled with herself. She was still wearing her gardening clothes, baggy green slacks and rumpled striped rugby shirt. But curiosity won out over vanity. She darted from the line and headed straight for the soprano. Inez was accompanied by two other people, a man and a woman, who wore the harried air of faithful retainers. Inez wore a black swing coat over an exotic black-and-ivory silk print concoction that was as casual as it was elegant. Circlets of seed pearls adorned her ears and another pearl, big enough to give an oyster a hernia, was set in a gold ring and surrounded with diamonds. In full regalia, Inez Garcia-Green was a handsome woman. Judith realized how Mario Pacetti could have lost his head.

"Señora Garcia-Green!" exclaimed Judith with enthusiasm. "What a surprise! I've got used to seeing you more often at my house instead of the opera house."

Inez's eyes narrowed at Judith as the retainers drew closer to their mistress, shielding her from the riffraff. *"Your* house?" The soprano looked as if she thought Judith lived in a septic tank. "Oh!" Apparently recognition dawned. "Yes, I know you. I return now to the world of music. The show goes on, as they say." She gave Judith a curt nod and started to walk off toward the opera house.

"Mrs. Pacetti has a question for you," Judith fibbed, trying not to be too obvious in blocking Inez's path. "She wanted to know where you got those marvelous flowers you brought her. She's got a funeral to plan, of course."

Inez scowled at Judith, then turned to her female retainer, a small gray-haired woman with a slit of a mouth and worried black eyes. Inez spoke in rapid Spanish; Judith couldn't catch more than a couple of words. The female retainer answered in an abrupt, yet deferential, murmur. Inez turned back to Judith. "Justin Kerr commandeered them from the opera house. They were used as the centerpiece in Act I. Naturally, they would not be fresh for the next performance. Justin managed to get them before they struck the set. He's a very considerate young man." Inez gave Judith an ingratiating smile that didn't match up with the chilly look in her eyes. "So you must tell Amina Pacetti that she should ask Mr. Layton of the opera company here. As for me, I know nothing about flowers. Absolutely nothing." The smile had fled. Inez Garcia-Green practically walked right over Judith as she continued her procession to the opera house.

With a frown, Judith got back in line. She was now number seventeen. And all she had got for her time and trouble was the fact that Justin Kerr had been hanging around the supper table where the vial of Strophanthin had been found. Had she missed something? Judith moved up to sixteenth place. As far as the investigation was concerned, she felt as if she were dead last.

"Woody said not to expect fingerprints," Judith told Renie as they indulged themselves in double mochas at Moonbeam's on top of Heraldsgate Hill. "But at least he can analyze the contents of the thermos."

"And were there contents?" asked Renie for the third time.

Judith nodded so vigorously that the people at the table next to her stared. "I shook it. I'd say an inch of liquid anyway. I was afraid to open the thing for fear of spilling it."

"Good work," said Renie, putting extra sugar into her cup, then sprinkling the whipped cream with nutmeg, cinnamon, and vanilla. "No word on Tippy, though?"

Judith shook her head. "No. But that's not all bad news.

Woody says, as far as they can tell, she didn't take a plane, bus, or train out of town. Of course she might have disguised herself. And Arlene gave a pretty good description of that gray car—assuming it's the same one. She thinks it was a fairly new, small Ford compact sedan. She recognized it because she says Jeanne Ericson's folks have one just like it, except in white."

"I guess that's progress," remarked Renie, oblivious to the whipped cream that sat on her upper lip. "I've been thinking—if Mario and Amina came to town somewhere along the line, where did they stay? Maestro Dunkowitz hosted them the first time; you got stuck with them on this visit. If Pacetti had such an aversion to hotels, where else would he hole up? Is there any way you can check through the state B&B association?"

Judith considered. "I suppose. There are close to forty B&Bs in the city, not counting the suburbs. Maybe I could get the central reservations agency to do some checking."

Renie took another swallow of her mocha, augmenting her mustache. "It's a real puzzler, isn't it?"

"It sure is. If I weren't afraid the murderer is—or was—under my roof, I'd run up the white flag and let Woody work his wonders."

"You consider Tippy a serious candidate?" Renie seemed dubious.

"I consider everybody seriously," replied Judith. "As I've often said, people are so unpredictable. And they certainly aren't always what they pretend to be. I already made one mistake about Tippy, figuring she was Plunkett's girlfriend. Now why would she do a bunk? Has she been embezzling? Is she a jewel thief? Did she use her job as a cover for dealing drugs? Or is she a killer? One thing I'm beginning to think is that she is not the ditz she seems. For all I know, she really did go to Harvard."

Renie finally noticed the whipped cream. "Yum," she said, lapping it up. "By the way, your mother wants you to bring her winter clothes over now that it's getting colder. I hemmed and hawed. When are you going to tell her about the toolshed?"

"I'm waiting to tell Joe first." Judith made a nervous little gesture with her hands. "Either that, or build a big fence between the back porch and the toolshed. Maybe he'd never notice Mother was living there."

Finishing their drinks, the cousins paid their bill and headed out into the pale golden sun of late afternoon. "How were the press checks?" inquired Judith as they walked across the street to their cars.

"Okay. Too much blue on the first one, too high on the red on the second, but they finally got it adjusted. So far, no major last-minute glitches," Renie noted, though she still had one more trip to go. "Thanks for picking up those tickets. I'm sorry you had to stand around for so long. Even if Inez turned out to be a zero, at least you didn't get ticketed for parking in the loading zone. But the brochure's going to look pretty sharp. A good thing, since this is a first-class operation all the way," said Renie. "After all, the Henderson Cancer Center is one of the best of its kind. Maybe *the* best. People come here from all over the world. The new complex will have an entire wing of apartments for patients and their families instead of the annex they use now. It'll be more like the set-up they have over at the Children's Medical Center." Renie had turned very serious, wearing her boardroom face. "You'd be surprised how many of the rich and famous arrive at the center incognito. It's all very discreet, with the utmost regard for the patient's privacy. If they're cured, the public never knows they were sick. If they're not—well, they usually go home to die, poor souls. But they know they've had the best treatment possible."

Judith, equally solemn, nodded. "I've heard the foundation has been very successful raising funds. It must take millions and millions." She stopped abruptly, almost colliding with a lamppost. "My eyes are deteriorating. I think it's this Pacetti bunch. Maybe I really am going 'round the bend."

"You're going 'round the lamppost, coz," said Renie. "Knock it off, or somebody who doesn't know you're Joe Flynn's wife will give you a DIP citation for too much vanilla in your mocha."

Judith laughed, albeit weakly. Renie might be right—the Pacetti case was getting to her. Meanwhile, as far as she could tell, the investigation was going nowhere. Judith got into her car and went home.

Judith was surprised to find Bruno Schutzendorf and Justin Kerr sitting in the living room, drinking her prize brandy.

"Join in," Schutzendorf urged, as if he were the host and Judith the guest. "We toast. The excellent Justin Kerr has agreed to sign a recording contract with Cherubim Records. Let me introduce you."

"Congratulations," said Judith, extending her hand. "Actually, Mr. Kerr and I . . ."

"I'm very pleased to meet you," Justin broke in, his smooth voice erasing Judith's words. "You have a lovely place here. But it *is* tucked away. I got a bit lost trying to find it." He gave Judith a quick wink.

"Oh—yes, well, it *is* a cul-de-sac. I mark it carefully on my advertising material." She hoped her face didn't look as puzzled as she felt. Why, Judith wondered, would Justin Kerr pretend he'd never been to Hillside Manor?

Schutzendorf was gesturing expansively. "This is Justin's first big contract. Before now, he got the chicken food. We are both well pleased." The German's teeth gleamed in his beard.

"I'm very happy," said Justin Kerr, who was looking at ease in a tweed sport coat, crewneck sweater, and casual slacks. "Mr. Schutzendorf is responsible for this breakthrough." He raised his brandy glass to the record magnate.

Judith made a few more complimentary remarks, then excused herself. In the kitchen, she quickly dialed the state

B&B association, hoping to catch somebody before the office closed at five.

Ingrid Heffleman answered. Judith knew her from the association meetings. For the past two years, Ingrid had been urging Judith to serve on the board. Judith had begged off, at first claiming that she was too inexperienced in the business, then using her newlywed status as an excuse. Now, Judith thought with a pang, she might have to trade her time for information. It would take a bit of trouble to contact all forty B&Bs in the city.

But Ingrid set Judith's mind at rest—at least as far as her request was concerned. "Heavens, Judith, if Mario Pacetti and his wife had stayed at any B&B in the county, we'd have heard about it. Everybody's been talking about your coup since the opera people made the reservation. Don't you remember, they had to go through us to do it."

They had, of course. "What about using assumed names?" Judith wasn't quite ready to give up on the idea that the Pacettis had somehow slipped into town and found haven in a discreet neighborhood hideaway.

Ingrid chuckled. "He could call himself Leonardo da Vinci and not fool anybody. Even people who aren't opera fans knew Mario Pacetti. I *am* sorry about the tragedy. You must be devastated. Again."

Judith thought she detected a hint of aversion in Ingrid's voice. The B&B association was like any other organization, with infighting, competition, and clashes of personality. Judith had to admit that in less than three years as a B&B owner, she had had more than her share of notoriety. Not everyone, especially within the hostelry business, would cite her as a shining example of innkeeping.

Hanging up the phone, Judith started in on the hors d'oeuvres. She was opening a can of Vienna sausages when Justin Kerr slipped into the kitchen.

"A glass of water," he said, a bit too loudly. "If I may?"

"Of course." Judith got out a glass. "Ice?"

"No, thank you." As the tap ran at full bore, Justin turned back to Judith and spoke in a whisper. "I didn't mean to interrupt, but I'd rather Mr. Schutzendorf didn't know I was here the other night. It's a long story, a typical, complicated, opera sort of thing I won't bother you with. I'm sure you understand." He gave an exaggerated shrug of his broad shoulders.

"Yes." Judith watched him fill the glass, turn off the tap, and take a swift swallow. The question she was about to pose was short on tact, but to the point. "Are you Pacetti's replacement?"

Caught in the act of putting the glass down, Justin spilled some of the water on the counter. "Replacement? Of course not. No one could replace Pacetti."

"But you could sing his roles," noted Judith, trying to keep her face innocent. "You're up-and-coming, I'm told, Inez Garcia-Green obviously likes you. She sings for Cherubim. Surely she'd be willing to make recordings with you."

Justin shifted about uncomfortably. "Inez has been very kind. It's possible that I could sing opposite her in the upcoming *Don Carlo*. But Schutzendorf has made no specific promises."

Judith nodded. "You have an agent? Or business manager?" To soften her prying, Judith offered Justin Kerr a Vienna sausage. He declined.

"Yes, a manager." The singer's gaze drifted away from Judith to the schoolhouse clock on the wall behind her. "An old friend of the family, in fact. Say, it's almost five-thirty. I'd better be going. We've got a performance scheduled for tomorrow night and I've planned an early dinner. We had to hold extra rehearsals today and yesterday to make sure I was set for tomorrow night. It's been pretty tiring. Many thanks." His handsome features grew more engaging as he smiled at Judith. "For everything."

Judith said it was nothing—but of course she knew Justin appreciated her discretion more than her hospitality. What she didn't know was why he should appear so concerned over Schutzendorf finding out about the previous visit to Hillside Manor. Noiselessly, she lingered in the

dining room while Justin bade the record magnate farewell. The parting took a while, with much effusiveness on
both sides. When the young tenor finally left, Judith went
to the front door and looked out. Her mouth twisted into
a wry expression as she noted that Justin Kerr drove off in
a gray Ford compact sedan.

The pork chops almost went to waste. Schutzendorf had
dinner out, Plunkett settled for a sandwich, Amina preferred pasta, and Edna Fiske ate her staple of green salad.
Judith put the pork chops, mushrooms, white and wild rice
into a container with the cauliflower and drove up the hill
to Aunt Deb's apartment.

"We already ate," announced Gertrude, leaning on her
walker and thrusting her chin at her daughter. "It's almost
six. We had milk toast. Do you think we sit around here
all night and starve ourselves?"

"Then warm it up for tomorrow," said Judith, struggling
to get past her mother, who seemed determined to bar the
way.

"We got mutton for tomorrow," growled Gertrude in her
raspy voice. "Thursday Deb's doing Shipwreck. You think
we're too old and daffy to figure out decent meals?"

"Then give it to the cat," said Judith between gritted
teeth. Even as she spoke, Sweetums sidled up to her,
brushing against her ankles. "Are you going to let me in
or not?"

In the small living room, Aunt Deb was maneuvering
her wheelchair from the hall. The apartment was crowded
with the furnishings of two lifetimes, a spectrum of seven
decades, from Edwardian antimacassars to a cordless
phone. "Judith, dear! How nice! Where have you been all
week?"

"It's only Tuesday," murmured Judith.

"Give me that," commanded Gertrude, holding out an
arm clad in a garish green and gold cardigan. "I'll put it
in the freezer."

"No, you won't," countered Judith, pulling the plastic

container out of reach. "You two will leave it there until it crystallizes. A trillion years from now, archaeologists will be trying to figure out what the hell you kept in your refrigerator. And you'll both be saying, 'We're saving it because we don't want to run out.' This isn't 1931, Mother. It's almost the twenty-first century."

"Bull," said Gertrude, deliberately lifting the walker and banging it back down within half an inch of Judith's foot.

"Now, dear," said Aunt Deb, pushing herself closer.

Judith held up the container, as if auctioning it off at a church fund-raiser. "Promise you'll eat this tomorrow or I'll give it to Mrs. Parker's poodle, Ignatz. Come on, you two, give in."

Gertrude eyes narrowed and her mouth worked from side to side. Aunt Deb leaned back in the wheelchair, her hands fretting the fabric of her blue and white housecoat. Sweetums snuggled against Judith in an uncharacteristic display of affection.

"What the hell," said Gertrude at last. "We can freeze the mutton."

"I'm very fond of pork chops," Deb admitted. "It's so sweet of you to think of us, Judith. You and Renie are such good girls. How can Gertrude and I be so lucky to have you?"

"Holy bat boils," exclaimed Gertrude, "you're enough to gag a goat, Deb. Why don't you put one of these pork chops in your kisser and choke yourself?"

Aunt Deb smiled sweetly, though there was just a touch of hostility in her brown eyes. "Isn't your mother a caution, Judith? Sometimes I almost think she means what she says. It's a good thing we know she's actually *senile.*" Deb kept right on smiling.

Furious, Gertrude made an awkward move with the walker, trying to turn around and go after her sister-in-law. Sensing blood, Sweetums crouched, growled and sprang—at Judith. Catching his claws in her black wool sweater, he squirmed and screeched, ears laid back and tail a-flying. Judith swore, trying to free the cat. Gertrude turned around again; Deb stopped smiling and stared. Finally, Judith pried Sweetums loose. It was hard to tell who was angrier. Judith scowled at the pulls in her sweater. Sweetums snarled at her feet.

"I hope it's not new," said Aunt Deb in a placating tone.

"I hope you brought my winter clothes," said Gertrude, apparently diverted from assaulting her sister-in-law. "It's supposed to get down to forty tonight. You want me to freeze my perkies off?"

"I haven't had time to get your things together," Judith lied. "I'll do it tomorrow." Another lie. She saw the genuine disappointment on her mother's face and suddenly felt guilty. "As a matter of fact, I've got a surprise for you. I know you're really going to like it."

Gertrude's eyes brightened. "You're getting a divorce?"

Judith sighed. "No, Mother. But I'm serious. I'll tell you in a few days; I promise."

Gertrude's forehead furrowed under the white curls of her latest permanent. "It better be good," she muttered.

"It is," said Judith, bending down to kiss her mother good-bye. "You'll both like it, I think." She moved past Gertrude to hug Aunt Deb.

"How nice," said Aunt Deb. "Does Renie know?"

"Yes." Judith started backing toward the door, one eye on Sweetums, who was arching his furry orange body and hissing like a small steam engine. With a deft movement, Judith made her escape. And wondered, all the way home, if she was making a mistake moving her mother back to Hillside Manor.

There was a call from Woody on the machine. He had left both his work and his home numbers. Judith tried police headquarters first and caught him just as he was leaving.

"We got the report back on the thermos contents," said Woody in his businesslike manner. "What was left of the tea had definite traces of Strophanthin."

"Ah!" Judith beamed into the receiver. "Now we're getting somewhere."

"Yes—and no," said Woody. "The pathologist told me something that doesn't mesh. Strophanthin is deadly, all right, but one of the antidotes is strong tea."

"Huh?" Judith screwed up her face.

"The pathologist doubts that there was a sufficient amount of Strophanthin in that vial to kill Pacetti if he was drinking a lot of tea. The residue in the thermos accounts for about a quarter of what was in the vial," Woody went on. "It just doesn't jibe."

Judith sat down on the kitchen stool, a hand to her temple. "I don't get it, Woody. The man died. Did he ingest the Strophanthin or didn't he? It *was* in the tea, after all."

"But when was it put there?" Woody's question was phrased so that it sounded as if he were asking himself as well as Judith. "Why was the thermos brought from the opera house and buried in your backyard? There are a ton of places to ditch something at the opera house, including several dumpsters outside. It doesn't make sense."

"I know." Judith stared at the calendar posted next to the telephone. The notes she had scrawled all over it were a blur. No wonder she had a headache. Scooting to the edge of the stool, she reached for the bottle of aspirin she kept on the windowsill above the sink. "If Pacetti had been poisoned with the tea, then Amina would be the prime suspect. But if he wasn't . . . or if someone else had access to that thermos, either here or at the opera house . . . Hell's bells, Woody, I feel like I'm on a merry-go-round." Judith popped two aspirin in her mouth and quickly poured herself a glass of water.

Woody gave a tight little laugh. "Tell me about it. I can't ask these so-called suspects to stick around much longer after tomorrow or the next day. They'll start to file complaints or threaten to sue or just plain get up and go. Like Ms. de Caro."

"No sign of her, I take it?"

"None. She's disappeared into thin air." A note of discouragement was creeping into Woody's voice.

Briefly, Judith mentioned Justin Kerr's meeting with Schutzendorf and the tenor's insistence upon secrecy about his earlier visit to Hillside Manor. She also told Woody that Justin had been driving a gray Ford.

"I think I'll do some homework on Mr. Kerr this evening," said Woody, his mood perking up. "Sondra's at a baby shower, so I might as well work late."

"Let me know if you find anything," said Judith. "Like Tippy."

An hour later, Amina Pacetti made her first foray into the living room since her husband's death. She wore a quilted robe of many colors, full makeup, and her hair was once again impeccably coiffed.

"I grow stiff," she announced, going to the piano and playing a few chords. "You need to have this tuned. It's rather flat."

Judith gave a nod of assent, but her mind was far from flats or sharps. Standing by the cushioned window seat a few yards from the piano, she racked her brain for an approach to the thermos question. At last, she picked up the evening paper, which was sitting on the coffee table.

"Have you seen the article in the *Times* tonight?"

Amina regarded the newspaper as if it were a plague warning. "No. Nurse Fiske asked if I wished to see it, but I declined. What should I need to learn? That my husband was most cruelly murdered? I know that." Her gaze fell back on the piano keys. This time she played a series of minor chords.

Indeed, Melissa Bargroom and her coworker's news story was pretty basic. The article had appeared at the bottom of page one, since the morning paper and the electronic media had beat the *Times* to the punch with the homicide angle. The duo had walked the fine line of journalism, presenting only the barest facts. Melissa, however, had dug a little deeper into her knowledge of Pacetti's career and written a second piece for the arts and entertainment section. As far as Judith could tell, the recap contained nothing pertinent to his murder.

The newspaper having flunked with Amina, Judith opted for shock tactics. "I found your thermos. It was buried in the backyard."

Amina slumped onto the piano bench. "What?"

Judith repeated her statement, noting that Amina's shock seemed genuine. "Where did you see it last?" asked Judith.

Amina brushed at her mouth, not noticing that she had smeared lipstick on her hand. "Oh . . . I'm not certain. I still had it with me when Mario went onstage. Then . . . I don't recall. I never thought about it again. How could I? My husband was dying!" She buried her face in her hands, but no sobs were forthcoming. Instead, she shook her head and swayed from side to side.

Judith held her own head, aware that the aspirin wasn't helping much. "I'm sorry, really I am. But it's so strange, finding the thermos in the garden. Someone must have taken it from the opera house. It was red, wasn't it?"

Amina nodded. "Madness!" she wailed through her fingers. "There is a madman loose! Am I next?"

Judith moved to Amina's side, but thought better of patting the other woman's shoulder. "The police are watching the house," she soothed. "I saw a patrol car go by just a few minutes ago. Mrs. Pacetti, do you have any idea who sent that rock?" Once again, Judith was careful not to mention the second missive.

Amina's head jerked up. Her face looked blotchy and her eyes snapped. "Of course I do! Who else but Inez Garcia-Green?"

Judith stared. "Inez? How can you be so sure?"

Amina gave a shake of her shoulders. "Because she told me, that's how. She tells everything to everybody. She thinks I would tell the police and she would be arrested. But the police know. So why do they not take her away to prison? The woman's mouth should be shut. Then she could not talk, or sing, and the world would be a better place. A curse on her! *Maledizione!*"

Edna Fiske stalked into the living room, her face set. "What's this? Too much excitement by far! Come, come, Mrs. Pacetti, it's back to bed for you. I warned you about eating that pasta."

To Judith's surprise, Amina allowed Edna Fiske to lead her away, looking not unlike a child under the thumb of a stern governess. They had just disappeared when the phone rang. Judith answered it in the kitchen and beamed as she heard Joe's voice at the other end of the line.

"I just ate twenty-four oysters," said Joe. "Will that make me sexy?"

"You *are* sexy, you nut," said Judith, draping herself over the kitchen stool. "Where are you?" She could hear quite a bit of noise in the background.

"Delmonico's," replied Joe. "Bill's at the next phone, listening to Renie crow about her hot new brochure. You caught any killers lately, or are you sitting back and letting Woody take the heat?"

"Woody's doing fine," said Judith, not wanting to spend time or money with mundane details such as murder when she could be listening to Joe tell her how sexy he was. Or better yet, how sexy *she* was. "Miss me?"

"Like crazy," said Joe. "I got so desperate last night, I tried to kiss Bill. He put me in therapy. Or was it in traction?"

The conversation moved on to the adventures of Lieutenant Flynn and Professor Jones in New Orleans. The weather was hot, humid, and occasionally rainy. The conference was informative, interesting, and enlightening. The food was terrific. They'd eaten French, Cajun, creole, even Chinese. They'd seen most of the sights, from Bourbon Street to Lake Pontchartrain. The hotel was great, right by the Superdome. Maybe they'd have time to get into the bayous. Or charter a fishing boat in the Gulf. Judith began to wonder when Joe had time to miss her. As she reluctantly hung up, she was well aware that he and Bill were having a heck of a lot more fun in New Orleans than she and Renie were having back home. Judith called Renie to say as much, but got her cousin's answering machine. That seemed odd, since Renie had just been talking to Bill. Judith was still frowning in puzzlement when the back door banged.

"Open up," shouted Renie. "I want to show you my brochure."

"How'd you get here so fast?" asked Judith, letting her cousin in.

"You know Bill," said Renie. "He hates talking on the phone almost as much as your mother does. As soon as he hung up, I raced over here to show you this little hummer. Ta-da!" Renie whipped the cancer center brochure out of her briefcase.

Judith admired it with appropriate awe. Indeed, it was a handsome piece, bearing the usual bold, yet tasteful, graphics of Serena Grover Jones. The cousins sat down at the kitchen table while Judith put on her glasses and flipped through the pages.

"I like the architecture," remarked Judith. "It's got a nice, solid look."

"Right," agreed Renie, going for the cookie jar. "I tried to carry that feeling throughout the brochure. Hey, you haven't baked!" Her voice had an echo as she spoke into the empty container.

"I haven't had time, you goof," said Judith. "Oh, here's the wing with the apartments. The rooms look pretty lavish. Did you do these sketches?"

"No, the architect did those." Renie replaced the sheep's head lid on the jar. "I toured the present facility last summer. Even in the old annex, they've got a couple of suites that are quite nice. One of them has two bedrooms, a living room, even a small study. It's usually reserved for visiting brass or celebrity patients who . . ."

Judith dropped the brochure. Renie grimaced. "I hope you or Phyliss mopped today. I only have a dozen file copies of that, you klutz," admonished Renie.

Reaching under her chair, Judith retrieved the brochure. "It's clean," she asserted, waving her free hand at her cousin and suddenly looking excited. "Call me crazy, but I just had the weirdest idea. What if Pacetti, a world-class worrywart, had checked himself into the Henderson Center this past spring? Melissa said he canceled performances about then. And it was springtime when the Pacettis were here on their unscheduled visit. Is there any way you could check?"

Renie was scowling. "Yes, you're crazy. I think. Well . . . I've got pretty tight with their P.R. person. I could give it a try, but you'd have better luck using Woody."

"Woody has a typical policeman's aversion to wild goose chases," said Judith, getting up to fetch a couple of cans of pop from the refrigerator. "I have to admit this idea falls into that category. But if you could do some probing, it might help."

"How?" Renie accepted a cold Pepsi. "Let's say you're right—heaven forbid—and Pacetti had cancer. Why kill him?"

"Lots of people survive cancer. Maybe he didn't have it but was afraid he did. Maybe it was Amina." The excitement was fading. "It's a long shot, but the Pacettis had to stay somewhere if they were here last spring. It wasn't in a B&B, they don't seem to know anybody besides Dunkowitz, who wouldn't invite them back, and we know they hate hotels. Do you really think they'd park one of those luxury RVs out on the edge of town and sleep with the tourists?"

"Probably not," admitted Renie. "But I think you're out on a limb on this one, coz."

"Maybe," said Judith, squinting at the list of donors on the last page. "Damn, I can't even read the boldface type. I think I'd better call Dr. Inouye tomorrow and make an appointment before I go blind. I haven't had my glasses changed since just before I opened the B&B."

"Inouye's moved," said Renie. "In fact, he's in the same

clinic as the Feldmans, next to the Children's Medical Center."

"Then I probably can't afford him any more," Judith lamented. "Speaking of my incipient poverty, was Tolvang still out there when you arrived?"

"No," Renie answered. "I passed him on my way in. He only dropped two buckets off his truck as he clunked away toward the Counterbalance. Fortunately, both missed me."

For the next half-hour, the cousins mulled over the latest developments in the murder case. Renie was troubled by the buried thermos, but not for the same reasons that had plagued Judith and Woody.

"I don't care whether the Strophanthin poisoned Pacetti or not," said Renie. "Who else but the murderer would bury that thermos? Coz, that really tightens the circle. It's got to be one of your guests."

Even though she'd had the same feeling all along, Judith blanched. Somehow, it was more terrifying to hear her worst fears voiced aloud, especially by someone else. Still, she had a quibble.

"Don't forget, Inez and Justin showed up after the murder. Either of them could have gone up to the second floor, used the back stairs, and slipped outside. They were here long enough to bury a dinosaur."

"They didn't know the layout of the house," Renie objected.

"They did if somebody told them. Look," said Judith, pulling her chair closer and sketching imaginary happenings on the table, "let's say there are two people involved. The gray car shows up when the Pacettis arrive, scouting things. Justin Kerr, just for a good guess. Somebody is inside—let's say Tippy, for another guess—and waves a nightie out the window—then drops it accidentally. It's a signal, okay?"

Renie looked unconvinced. "A signal for what? Can't these goofballs use a phone?"

"You know how my phones are set up—I've got the private line on the third floor, but the phones in the living room, the kitchen, and the upstairs hall are for business. Anybody could listen in on an extension."

Renie acknowledged that fact. "So you figure Tippy gave Justin some sort of high sign, then later told him—or Inez, or both—how the house is laid out. You're reaching, coz."

"Of course I am," Judith replied a bit testily. "All I'm trying to do is make sure we're not overlooking any of the suspects. Otherwise, we're down to the trio I have to sleep with. And Tippy, of course."

"Tippy," mused Renie. "It's too bad you never went through her luggage. You might have found another short negligee."

"I never thought of it," said Judith. "Anyway, it didn't seem important. More like a silly stunt." She stood up. "It's not too late."

"For what? Silly stunts?" Renie looked askance.

"Come on," said Judith, heading for the back stairs. "Let's go over Tippy's room with the proverbial fine-tooth comb. Phyliss was in a rush today because she had a dental appointment. Maybe she didn't do her usual bang-up job."

But rushed or not, it appeared that the cleaning woman had been thorough. Judith looked under the bed, the bureau, even the rug. Renie perused the closet and the drawers.

"Drat," said Judith, as the cousins craned their necks to see if there was any nook or cranny they'd overlooked.

"What about the bathroom?" asked Renie.

"Tippy shared it with Amina," said Judith. "I can't imagine she'd leave anything there."

Renie looked anyway, moving about quietly so as not to alarm Amina next door. Frustrated, Judith scanned the bedroom one last time. The bureau drawer she'd pushed in earlier still wasn't closed properly. Judith gave it another shove. Again, it didn't mesh. Annoyed, she tugged it all the way out. Wedged along the side was a credit card, apparently having fallen out of the drawer. Judith picked it up and examined the imprint.

Renie was closing the bathroom door. "Zip," she said, then stared at Judith. "What's that?"

Judith was wearing a strange little smile. "Bloomingdale's," she said, holding the plastic between her thumb and forefinger. "Made out to Victoria D. Kerr of Chestnut Street in Boston."

Renie's jaw dropped. "Huh?"

Judith's smile grew more cunning. "I think," she said as her black eyes danced, "we've found out who Tippy de Caro really is. Now, we need to find out where she's gone. Maybe it's not going to be as hard as we thought."

# THIRTEEN

RENIE SAT DOWN on the hundred-year-old wedding ring quilt that covered the four-poster bed. "Hold on," she said, giving Judith a dubious look. "You're jumping to conclusions. Victoria Kerr isn't necessarily Tippy de Caro. Nor, if I follow your line of logic, which I usually can, is Ms. Kerr somehow related to Justin the Tenor Kerr. Slow down. Think. Have you had any other Kerrs staying here?"

Judith, feeling only a mite deflated, joined Renie on the quilt that their maternal great-grandmother had laboriously pieced a century earlier. "I remember names, but I don't recall any Kerrs. Carr, yes—they were from Wisconsin, last spring. They stayed in the front bedroom. Besides, this credit card must have got stuck in the last day or so. I'd have noticed that drawer being out-of-kilter if it had happened earlier."

Renie gave a nod. "Okay. A point conceded. Two points, maybe. Now what?"

Judith got up. "We call Woody to see if he's talked to Justin Kerr yet. Then we check to find out where Justin is staying. He might be at the Cascadia. Inez is there, after all."

Woody wasn't in. A call to the Cascadia Hotel drew

a blank when Judith asked for Justin Kerr. Systematically, she worked her way through the city's other large hotels. After six tries, she was getting discouraged.

"That takes care of the top tier," Judith said, running her finger down the listings in the Yellow Pages. The cousins had retreated to Judith and Joe's room in the family quarters. "Justin isn't a big star, so I suppose it figures that he wouldn't be staying some place that costs two hundred dollars a night. But damn, there are at least a dozen smaller, but first-rate places in the downtown area. Here, coz, you give it a try. My ear's tired."

Renie, who was sitting in the dressing table chair, took both the directory and the telephone from Judith. On her fourth try she got a positive response from the Hotel Plymouth. Justin Kerr was indeed a registered guest.

"Now what?" she inquired, replacing the receiver.

Judith was on her feet, heading for the closet where she got out her good red winter coat. "We go browse. Come on, coz, let's hit it."

"Wait!" protested Renie. "It's after nine, I'm in my grubbies, they'll throw me out for vagrancy."

Renie was indeed wearing one of her more disreputable costumes, a faded Georgetown University sweatshirt over equally faded black sweatpants, which had a hole in one knee. Judith never understood her cousin's wardrobe, which seemed to consist of seven-hundred-dollar ensembles at one end of the spectrum and semirags at the other. There was absolutely no in-between.

"Here," said Judith, tossing her brown raincoat at Renie. "This'll be long enough on you to cover up everything but your ratty shoes."

Renie was still grumbling when they pulled into the Hotel Plymouth's parking garage. "Six bucks this will cost us, and I'll bet we can't find anything but compact parking spaces. That's the trouble in this town, the Japanese own everything these days and they don't allow room for real cars."

"It's your own fault you and Bill insist on driving an

American car only somewhat smaller than a superferry," chided Judith.

Eventually, Renie found a spot on the last level. After much fighting of the wheel and a great many swear words, she managed to get the car parked. In the lobby, the cousins gazed around somewhat furtively. The hotel seemed quiet, with only a handful of guests chatting among the tasteful old-world appointments.

Gathering her courage, Judith approached the desk and asked to see Justin Kerr. The clerk, a young black man who looked as if he were either working his way through college or on the first rung of a management trainee program, rang Justin Kerr's room. There was no answer.

Judith asked the clerk for an envelope. She slipped the credit card inside, sealed it, and wrote Justin Kerr's name on the exterior. Then she handed the envelope to the clerk. "You can put this in Mr. Kerr's box, but we'll wait a few minutes in case he shows up." As the young man turned away, Judith nudged Renie and nodded toward the row of message slots against the far wall. With a smile of thanks for the desk clerk, Judith led Renie over to a beige divan flanked with huge bouquets of fresh flowers.

"Boy, this is sure fun," muttered Renie, wrestling with the folds of Judith's too-large raincoat. "What do we get to do next, put alum on our tongues and pucker ourselves to death?"

"Justin won't be late," replied Judith in a complacent tone. "He has a performance tomorrow night, remember?"

The metal hands of the Roman numeral clock over the lobby archway inched toward ten. People drifted in and out of the lobby. The young desk clerk occasionally cast a surreptitious look in the cousins' direction. Renie squirmed inside the raincoat, bored and impatient. Judith watched the main entrance, but also glanced now and then at the door that led to the bar.

At two minutes after ten, Renie got to her feet. "Hey, let's forget it, coz. He may already be up there, not answering his phone. I got up at seven-fifteen this morning, in case you've forgotten."

Judith didn't spare her cousin any sympathy, but she did stand up. "Let's try a more devious approach," she said, heading for the elevators. "Did you notice the number of Justin's room?"

Renie sighed with resignation. "Yeah, 722. When are you getting your eyes checked?"

Inside the elevator, Judith punched the button for the seventh floor. "If we can't find a maid to bribe, we'll have to resort to my lockpicking skills."

Renie rolled her eyes, but offered no comment. It wouldn't be the first time that Judith had made an unlawful entry. The corridor on the seventh floor was empty. The only signs of life behind the rows of closed doors were an occasional tray of dirty dishes or a stack of clean towels. The cousins proceeded to Room 722, which was almost at the end of the hallway. Judith produced a crochet hook from her handbag.

"I came prepared," she said with an off-center grin.

Renie sighed again. "Great," she muttered. "Did you bring targets we could put on our backs so somebody can shoot us?"

With her ear to the lock, Judith didn't reply, but gave a sharp shake of her head to silence Renie. Although most of the hotel had been renovated in the last decade, the management had retained the original doors, and, surprisingly, the original, comparatively unsophisticated locks. In less than two minutes, Judith heard the satisfying click that signaled the inner mechanism's release.

The room appeared to be dark. Judith slipped inside, with Renie at her heels. On the right, Judith found the light switch.

"All right," she breathed, taking in her surroundings. It was a standard room, with a double bed, a desk, TV, two chairs, a small table, and three lamps. The only unusual feature was the woman who threw open the bathroom door. She was stark naked. She screamed—and so did the cousins.

Judith was the first to regain her composure. "Hi, Tippy," she said, feeling foolish. "I'm glad you're okay."

But Tippy had fled back into the bathroom. She emerged a moment later, wrapped in a big white towel. "What the hell is this?" she demanded, sounding not much like her usual bouncy self.

"We thought you'd been kidnapped," Judith said. It was not as big a fib as Judith had been known to tell in a good cause. If one of her guests had been murdered, it wasn't impossible that another could have been carried off by force. "In fact, I notified the police that you were gone."

"Great." Tippy glared at Judith, securing the towel around her bosom. "Well, I'm fine. I decided to get the hell out of your stupid B&B. It didn't strike me as a healthy place to stay."

"Mario Pacetti wasn't poisoned at Hillside Manor," Judith asserted, wishing she could feel free to sit down. "At least he didn't die there," she added, thinking about the thermos that had been buried in the backyard. "The problem with trying to find you was that we didn't know which name to look for—de Caro or Kerr."

Tippy's eyes widened. "What do you mean?" she gasped.

"Oh, I don't suppose you've done anything illegal," Judith responded breezily. "It's a stage name, right?"

Tippy had padded over to the bed where she perched on the edge. "You could say that." Her tone was dry, her voice much sharper than the cousins were accustomed to hearing from her previous persona. "All right, how did you figure it out?"

Judith risked sitting in an armchair; Renie followed suit, still struggling with the raincoat as she sat down on the other armchair. "You left a credit card in the bureau," said Judith. "It's in an envelope downstairs at the desk."

Tippy, her wet red hair hanging around her face, gave the cousins a look of chagrin. "Careless of me. But I was in a hurry. As you know, there's a killer on the loose. How the hell did you get in here?" The sudden alarm on her face indicated she hadn't excluded Judith and Renie from the list of possible suspects.

The cousins exchanged furtive looks. "It was sort of sneaky," Judith admitted, "but we were genuinely worried. Especially when the desk clerk couldn't get through to the room." Judith hoped her half-baked explanation would obscure the illegal method of entry.

"I was in the shower," said Tippy irritably. "I didn't hear the phone ring. Justin—my cousin—is out to dinner." She dropped her eyes, glanced at her wrist, realized she wasn't wearing a watch, and looked over at the TV where the digital clock showed that it was now ten-seventeen. Fine lines appeared on her forehead. "Justin ought to be back soon, though. It's getting late."

Noting that Tippy was swinging one foot in an impatient manner, Judith calculated that the other woman's mood was precarious. "If you're sure there's a killer at Hillside Manor, do you know who it is?"

Tippy clutched at the towel as if she were not only protecting her modesty, but her very life. "No! That is, I'm not even sure the killer is actually staying there. But I could make a pretty good guess, all things considered."

"So guess." It was Renie, speaking for the first time since the cousins had entered the hotel room.

But Tippy vehemently shook her head. "That would be slander, if I'm wrong. And worse, if I'm right. I told you, that's why I left the B&B." She was eyeing the phone, which stood on the desk near Judith's chair. "Look, I think you two had better go. If you don't, I'll call security and have them throw you out."

Judith gave a sad little shake of her head. "Sorry, Tippy. Then we'd have to call the police. They're looking for you. It's just a matter of time. Are you *on the run?*" Her face assumed a dire cast.

"Oh, for Christ's sake!" Tippy threw back her head, the damp hair flying. "Of course not! My name *is* Tippy. My nickname, I mean. When I was little, I couldn't say Victoria. I used de Caro because . . . well, because I didn't want Mr. Pacetti to think we were *obvious*. I suppose Plunkett's having a brain seizure about now. Is he the one who called the cops?"

Suddenly at sea, Judith gave an uncertain shake of her head. "No. He was concerned, of course. But let's face it, you're involved in a murder investigation. The police don't like losing track of suspects."

A light glimmered in Tippy's gray eyes. "Wait a minute—you mean Winnie hasn't figured out who I really am?" She saw the blank expression on Judith's face and laughed aloud. "Ha! That's rich! The poor twit!" Her merriment was interrupted by the arrival of Justin Kerr, who promptly froze upon seeing their visitors.

"Relax," said Tippy. "It's my landlady from the B&B and her cousin. They're cousins, too—like us." She gave Justin a meaningful look.

"We've met," said Judith, with a wry smile for Justin. "Twice."

Justin glanced at Tippy, who was suddenly looking uncomfortable. "My cousin forgot we'd been introduced. Our stay has been overly eventful. And tragic." He gave all three women a dismayed look, then zeroed in on Renie. "I'm sorry, I've forgotten your name . . ."

"Serena Jones," said Renie. "Hi, we were just grilling your cousin. What's up anyway? You two were conspiring to get into Pacetti's good graces? What were you after, a patron?"

Judith threw an admiring look at Renie. All along, she'd figured that her cousin was in a semimoribund state, merely trying to figure out how to beat a hasty retreat in the oversized raincoat. But Renie, with her superior knowledge of the opera world, had obviously been grappling with some conjectures. Judging from the Kerrs' resigned expressions, she was right.

"It's not a crime," asserted Justin Kerr, setting his

shoulders and jutting his chin. "Great singers often sponsor protégés. Who better than Pacetti?"

Enlightenment dawned on Judith. She turned to Tippy.
"So you wormed your way into Pacetti's entourage trying
to get him to help your cousin's career. Why not just come
right out and ask?"

Tippy laughed again, though on a different, more sar-
donic note. Justin's pleasant face twisted with irony. "You
didn't know Pacetti very well," he declared. "The direct
approach wouldn't do it. That's why Tippy used another
name. First, she had to convince Plunkett that Pacetti
should have a protégé, then she had to see that he got
through to Pacetti."

"And I damned near did," insisted Tippy. "Winnie heard
Justin sing in San Francisco. He was impressed. We figured that if he heard my cousin sing here, he'd be ready
to go after Pacetti's patronage. It should have all worked
out—if the little creep hadn't died. Justin's damned good."
She gave Justin a look that conveyed more than mere
pride.

Justin, however, appeared faintly embarrassed. "Tippy's
very loyal," he said. "She'd do anything for me. She put
up with the Pacettis for almost four months."

Judith wasn't completely satisfied. "What about Inez?
She must have a lot of clout."

Justin exchanged an uneasy glance with Tippy. "She
does," he replied, "but she's not a tenor."

Renie gave a halfhearted nod. "She records for Schutzendorf, though."

"Yes." Justin seemed unwilling to say more.

"So who were you signaling to?" The question spilled
from Judith's lips.

"Signaling?" Tippy frowned. "Oh! The nightie! It was
for Justin's benefit. He worries about me when we're off
on our own, so I always try to communicate with him
somehow to let him know I'm okay." To Judith's surprise,
Tippy actually blushed.

"I see." Judith spoke blandly as she got to her feet. "By

the way, Mr. Kerr, I don't suppose you noticed anything strange before the performance Saturday night?"

Justin gave a shake of his head. "I kept to my dressing room. Once Pacetti went on, there was no need for me to hang around in the wings. Being an understudy is tough. You half hope the singer you're backing up will break a leg, and then you hate yourself for being so opportunistic."

"But Pacetti did—in effect—break a leg," Judith pointed out. "Were you summoned at that point?"

"Oh, yes." Justin nodded vigorously. "I came out right away, but all hell had broken loose. The next thing I knew, an ambulance was on its way and Maestro Dunkowitz and Creighton Layton were arguing about whether or not to go on with the performance. Dunkowitz refused. He said he couldn't conduct if there was anything seriously wrong with Pacetti."

Renie seemed to have become completely swallowed up by the raincoat. Only her head showed, the curly chestnut hair making her look not unlike a small frazzled flower on a big brown stalk. "So what was going on at that point?" she inquired. "Did you notice anything out of the ordinary?"

Justin clapped a hand to his forehead. "It was all out of the ordinary! Everyone was going berserk. The chorus, the supers, the stagehands—I tried to find Tippy, but it took a while in all the confusion."

"Plunkett was giving me about a hundred orders at once," said Tippy, still gripping the towel as she got off the bed. "Most of them were contradictory. Finally, I had to join him and Schutzendorf in following the ambulance up to the hospital. Amina rode with Pacetti, of course."

Judith tried to piece the sequence of events together. "But you had time to rinse out Pacetti's champagne glass?"

"Yes, Winnie insisted I do that. Germs, you know—in case someone picked it up and drank from it by mistake." Tippy wrinkled her nose at such fastidiousness.

Judith did her best not to sound like an official interrogator. "Did you notice how much liquid was left in the glass?"

Tippy studied her bare feet. "Oh—I'm not sure. Half, maybe."

"Plunkett didn't tell you to retrieve the thermos?" Judith asked.

"I don't think he thought about it. Mrs. Pacetti always toted that around."

Judith nodded, then gave both Kerrs an ingratiating smile. "It's certainly wonderful for cousins to be so close. Renie and I have always been like sisters. We're both only children and we grew up within two blocks of each other. Our mothers were sisters. Were yours, too?"

Justin started to reply, but Tippy spoke for both of them. "Yes, they were very close. In age, as well as in feeling."

"That's endearing," Judith beamed. She extended her hand, first to Tippy, then to Justin. "Be careful. If you really think you know who the murderer is, don't broadcast it. You're not safe until you get out of town. Or until the killer does."

Victoria and Justin Kerr looked very solemn. In the elevator, Judith gave an annoyed shake of her head. "Damn! I'd like to believe that pair!"

"I don't believe *you*. What do you mean about our mothers being sisters? They're sisters-in-law, you idiot!" Renie slouched down in the raincoat, in apparent dismay at Judith's gaffe.

"Of course they are," Judith replied with an evil twinkle. "And their mothers aren't sisters, either."

"Huh?" Like a turtle, Renie's head shot up out of the raincoat. "What do you mean? Oh!"

"That's right. They both wouldn't be named Kerr. Either their fathers were brothers, which means they'd have the same last name, or else they're not cousins."

Renie gave a little shake of her head. "Then . . . what are they?"

"I don't know," Judith replied as the elevator glided to the lobby level. "We'll let Woody figure that one out. But

I do know this—Justin says Tippy would do anything for him. Pacetti dies, and Justin gets his big chance. Classic scenario, right? But with Pacetti gone, Justin loses a potential patron. So when is a motive not a motive?"

"When Pacetti has already refused to sponsor Justin?"

Judith raised her eyebrows. "I never thought of that. Oh, dear."

The cousins got out of the elevator. The raincoat flapped around Renie's ankles. They descended into the lower reaches of the parking garage.

"Inez may not be a tenor, but she's falling all over Justin and she's big news in the opera world. Why not let her be his patron?" Renie remarked as she got into the driver's side of the car. "Or is the price too high?"

Judith arched her eyebrows, then fastened her seat belt. "As in, His Body? It could figure, especially if Tippy is not Miss or Ms. but Mrs. Kerr."

"That makes sense," replied Renie, girding herself to back the big Chevrolet out of the narrow parking slot. "Maybe they're secretly married. And it's a secret because Justin doesn't want to antagonize Inez. Ooops!" Renie felt her bumper nudge the car parked on her left.

"It washes with me," mused Judith. "If they were brother and sister, the only person they'd want to keep that a secret from was Pacetti. And now that he's dead, what's the point? Unless it has to do with Inez. I guess I'm glad that Tippy's not as imbecilic as she pretended. But I sure don't like the idea of her being a serious suspect."

"She seemed really afraid when she talked about the murderer," Renie noted. "But we know she's a fairly good actress. Yikes!" The front of the car scraped the compact parked on their right.

"What bothers me is that if Tippy didn't kill Pacetti, why does she think she knows who did? I mean, she must know more about a motive than we do." Judith winced as Renie made another attempt at reversing.

"Dump all this on Woody," advised Renie. She struggled with the wheel, alternating between the gas and the brake. The car crept backward, narrowly missing everything except for the figure that had suddenly appeared right behind them.

"Help!" A man shouted in fear as he jumped out of the way.

"Whoa!" Renie tried to hit the brake, got her feet tangled in Judith's raincoat, stepped on the gas instead, and went whizzing out into the exit lane. She managed to stop the car just before it struck the far wall of solid cement. Rolling the window down, Judith leaned out and called to the would-be victim who was clinging to a concrete pillar. "Are you okay?" she shouted.

Renie took one hand off the steering wheel and gave Judith a whack on the arm. "Never ask that," she muttered. "You want to get me sued?"

The man stared at the Chevrolet, stiffened, and then turned to rush off toward the garage elevators. Judith blinked. Her eyes might not be in very good shape, but she didn't need twenty-twenty vision to recognize the gray eminence of Winston Plunkett.

# FOURTEEN

WOODY PRICE HAD some news of his own. Justin Kerr was from the Boston area, had studied at the New England Conservatory of Music and for two more years in Paris and Rome. He had made his debut in Philadelphia seven years earlier. The past year, he had sung at various European and American houses, drawing critical acclaim for his stint in Salzburg the previous August. He was obviously on the rise. And, Woody noted, he must have had money to back him. Study at the New England Conservatory and in Europe didn't come cheap.

Inez Garcia-Green was a tougher nut to crack. She had done nothing. She knew nothing. She said nothing. Woody thought otherwise. He had gathered samples of her handwriting and would match them against the warnings sent to the B&B.

"It sounds as if you did just as well, if not better, at the Plymouth with Justin than I did at the Cascadia with Inez," said Woody over the phone.

Judith, who was stretched out on her bed, responded in a dry voice. "Because we found Tippy? Now you'll have to find out if Justin and Tippy are married. I suppose Plunkett showed up to see Justin, though I'd like to know why. I wonder how he reacted to finding Tippy there, too. Unless she hid in the bathroom."

"We already checked marriage licenses, just in case. No Justin Kerr was married in Massachusetts during the last five years," said Woody. "We've covered the whole Atlantic seaboard, and now we're working our way west. Of course they might have got married abroad," he added on a dejected note.

"I doubt it. Tippy's only trip to Europe this year was to Salzburg in August. If they got married then, I doubt that she'd have credit cards issued in her new name so quickly." Judith yawned. It was midnight and she was bushed. There was no point in bringing up her theory about the Pacettis' earlier visit until she had some facts to back herself up. Like most policemen, Woody didn't get enthusiastic over ideas out of left field.

"You probably don't think we're making much progress," said Woody.

"Oh—early days, as they say," replied Judith, arranging the pillows under her head.

"We're trying to track down the source of the Strophanthin. We know the manufacturer because of the bottle. It's from Holland."

"A real Dutch treat." Judith felt her eyelids droop.

"We couldn't get any prints off that thermos. You probably guessed as much."

"Right." Judith switched off the lamp beside the bed.

"We've finished questioning all the witnesses at the opera house. There were literally hundreds. Well, two hundred or so. Lots of conflicting statements about who was where doing what. Nothing really solid, except confirmation of what we already knew. The mezzo-soprano who sang the role of Flora thought she saw the thermos sitting on a stool after Pacetti collapsed. Maestro Dunkowitz said he sat on the very same stool later after he came up out of the orchestra pit and got through arguing with Creighton Layton. No thermos in sight."

"Hmmmm. That's sort of interesting." Judith forced her

eyes to stay open. "In other words, somebody walked off with it during all the confusion over Pacetti. But how do you hide a thermos?"

"Do you need to? Who would question somebody running around carrying a thermos? Who would notice, with everybody concerned about Pacetti?" Woody's voice was beginning to fade.

"Where are you, Woody?" Judith heard noises somewhere in the house. Perhaps Plunkett or Schutzendorf had finally returned.

"I'm home. Sondra's in the bathroom. She got back from the baby shower just after I got in." It was his turn to yawn.

Judith's maternal instincts stirred. "Go to bed, Woody."

"What? Oh, yes, I will. Good night."

"Good night." Fumbling a bit, Judith replaced the phone. She went to sleep with her hand still on the receiver.

To Judith's astonishment, Dr. George Inouye had a cancellation for Thursday morning at ten-thirty. Judith jumped at the chance to see the eye doctor so soon. For the rest of Wednesday, she tried to pretend it was just routine at the B&B. Phyliss arrived at nine, complaining of excessive earwax, aching hip joints, and an unsatisfactory session with the dentist.

"Four shots of novocaine, and he drilled halfway to my hat," she groused, spraying polish on the breakfront in the dining room. "It's a crown, so I have to get along with a temporary for two weeks. It'll fall out, you can be sure of that."

Skjoval Tolvang had come to work even earlier, and his progress on the toolshed was remarkable. Judith knew she should have been pleased, but if he finished up by the weekend as promised, she would have to face Joe with a *fait accompli* as soon as he got off the plane. The prospect didn't cheer her. Would Joe blow? It was hard to tell.

As for her guests, all of them vacated the house for

most of the day. Bruno Schutzendorf was the first to leave, humming Franz Lehár and twirling his walking stick. Amina Pacetti announced that she must get outside and breathe real air or go quite mad. Winston Plunkett had hired a car and the two of them intended to drive off into the autumn sunshine. Before they could get away, Judith cornered Plunkett in the entry hall.

"You must be aware that Tippy has been found," she said, keeping her voice low in case Amina should appear from upstairs.

If Plunkett had recognized Judith in Renie's car the previous night, he gave no sign. "Really!" His manner proclaimed mild surprise, but Judith thought that a flicker of emotion sparked in his gray eyes. "We owe her money for her wages. I hope she contacts us."

Judith wanted to press Plunkett further, but Amina was descending into the entry hall. For the time being, Judith kept her own counsel.

Phyliss Rackley, however, did not. "This is the worst bunch of guests you've ever had," she announced, emerging from Amina's room carrying an overflowing wastebasket. "This one leaves cotton balls and tissues all over the place. Magazines, clothes, jewelry tossed this way and that. That bookkeeper fellow or whatever he is writes himself little notes and they fall on the floor, the bed, even the sink! What's he got, amnesia? And that German!" Phyliss sidled closer to Judith and lowered her voice. "Did you know he's drinking *wine* in his room? Three bottles I've thrown out! And dirty glasses all over the place. Drink is the Devil's own work. How do these people expect to get to heaven if they aren't sober and neat? Nurse Fiske is the only one who tidies up after herself. A fine woman, that." Phyliss huffed and puffed as she started toward the stairs. "Oh!" she added, turning to glance at Judith over her shoulder. "Some of the flowers have died. Shall I throw them out?"

"I'll do that," Judith replied. "Which ones?"

Phyliss started down the stairs. "That big ugly bouquet

in Mrs. P.'s room and the ones you put on the German's dresser. Waste of effort with him, if you ask me. He's probably too intoxicated to notice . . ." Her voice trailed off as she disappeared from view.

Judith went into Schutzendorf's room first. Sure enough, the dahlias and the asters were definitely drooping. She picked up the Wedgwood vase, then realized she could refill it with the flowers from Tippy's vacated room. First, however, she decided to take a quick look around Schutzendorf's quarters. Nothing struck her as particularly unusual. The small closet contained his evening clothes and top hat, a half dozen shirts, a plaid bathrobe, two vests, three jackets, four pairs of pants, dress shoes, sturdy boots, and walking shoes. Everything, it seemed, except the outfit he had been wearing, which consisted of his basic Tyrolean cape, pants, jacket, shirt, and snap-brimmed cap. His large suitcase was empty; the smaller one contained three bottles of Sekt. His briefcase was locked.

Judith decided to take a peek at Plunkett's room, too. His closet also revealed no surprises, though the uniformity of the business manager's wardrobe brought a faint smile to Judith's lips. So did the small, open wooden chest filled with fishing flies. Red, orange, black, and yellow lures reposed in separate compartments. Judith was reminded of Uncle Cliff, whose collection of fresh-and saltwater tackle had been formidable. The notes Phyliss had mentioned also intrigued her. Apparently the cleaning woman had picked them all up and tucked them inside the blotter on the dressing table. Leafing through them, Judith saw that they were mainly names, addresses, and phone numbers. Except for their universal scope, there was nothing of much interest. Even his random doodles were dull, a series of loops and an occasional rectangle. The one small slip of paper that made Judith pause showed a triangle. At each corner, Plunkett had written a name—Tippy, Inez, Justin. His own initials appeared in the middle. A love triangle? But where did Plunkett fit in with this trio? A conspiracy? To promote Justin Kerr's career? That seemed more likely. But there was always another, uglier possibility . . .

Judith fetched the flowers from Tippy's former room. They were on the wane, but would last another day or so. She threw out Schutzendorf's wilted bouquet, realized that there was no water in the Wedgwood vase, and went into the bathroom to fill it. She emptied what was left of the water from the Lalique vase that had been in Tippy's room, then quickly arranged the blooms for Schutzendorf. He'd probably never notice the change, but Judith hated wilted bouquets.

On a whim, she opened the medicine chest. The two men had divvied up the space. Plunkett apparently had taken the two bottom shelves, since they contained shaving equipment that the bearded Schutzendorf wouldn't need. There were also a toothbrush, toothpaste, mouthwash, aspirin, vitamins, dental floss, and an over-the-counter sleep aid. Schutzendorf duplicated several of the items, but had more medications: antacid, nasal spray, antihistamine, and a prescription for something called isosorbide dinitrate. Judith examined the last bottle closely. It had been prescribed for Bruno Schutzendorf Sunday and had come from Bayview Hospital Pharmacy. The directions were for "one tablet every three to five minutes at the onset of irregular heartbeat." The medication must have been prescribed for Schutzendorf after his overnight stay at the hospital.

Amina's bedroom was next, where Judith again made a quick perusal. Phyliss had done her usual crackerjack job of cleaning, and all seemed in order. The closet was crammed, the dresser was crowded, the bureau drawers were stuffed. A thorough search would take too long. Judith still had a heavy schedule of errands to run. She grabbed the crystal vase with the faded exotic flowers and took it down to the kitchen. The bouquet went into the garbage can under the sink; so did something else. Judith heard a soft thud. She extracted the plastic container in which Justin Kerr had brought the bouquet. She dug among the wilted ginger, heliconia, and bird of paradise. She felt a hard object, caught among the long stems. Judith clasped it in her fingers.

She had no idea what a vial of Strophanthin would look like, but somehow she had the feeling she was holding one in her hand. It was empty; it had no label. Judith went straight to the phone and called Woody. Predictably, he wasn't in. Judith sat on the kitchen stool for a long time, trying to figure out what the discovery meant. Something else was bothering her, too, something she had seen upstairs. Or not seen? She couldn't put her finger on whatever seemed to be wrong. Maybe she should have made a more thorough search of Amina's belongings. But she had no idea how long the bereaved widow and the business manager would be gone. Judith decided she'd better tend to business.

Putting the small bottle into a plastic bag, she zipped it into the inner pocket of her big handbag, then headed out on her errands. The list was long; time was short. Judith toured hardware and appliance stores, seeking fixtures for Gertrude's new lodgings. Despite her best bargain-hunting skills, she returned out of sorts and out of pocket. Another grand had gone down the drain, or at least into a new one, along with a toilet, sink, shower stall, small refrigerator, and toaster oven. The rest of the furnishings could come out of the house or the collection that Gertrude had moved into Aunt Deb's apartment.

Judith was holding her head in one hand and a stiff scotch in the other when Renie called around four. She had drawn a blank with the P.R. person at the Henderson Cancer Center.

"Ernestine wasn't being discreet," reported Renie. "She just flat out said that Pacetti had never been there. I've come to know her fairly well during the course of this project. If he had been treated and she didn't want to disclose the fact, then she'd have been coy."

"Another theory shot to hell," sighed Judith. "What's your reaction to the bottle in the bouquet?"

"*Two* Strophanthin bottles in the props?" Renie sounded a trifle incredulous. "On the other hand, why not? Why one in the first place? Why not forty-eight of the damned things? The question is, was it there when Inez and Justin brought the flowers to Amina? Did somebody else put in there after the arrangement arrived at the house? And, if tea is an antidote, and there wasn't enough Strophanthin missing from the original vial, would this second full shot have done the job? Now how's that for an answer to your question?"

"Whew," Judith replied, "I guess I won't ask you anything else. My brain feels like Mother's overcooked oatmeal mush. I'm about to give up on this one. I'd better go do something really fun, like clean out the fridge."

Some of the items her guests had purchased the previous week were going bad. Judith threw out romaine lettuce, radicchio, tomatoes, and half a cucumber. Renie's earlier remark about turning into their mothers had spurred her on. Judith was determined not to hoard items that might be mistaken for museum relics or laboratory specimens. On her way to the garbage can, she saw Corinne Dooley on the other side of the picket fence, raking leaves.

"Hey," shouted Judith, "you want your lily-of-the-valley pips?"

Corinne looked up, her wide, good-natured face flushed with exertion. "Sure. You know me, with this family, I've got a refrigerator that would hold a moose. I'll send Dooley over to get them after he finishes his paper route. I've got to start dinner."

Back inside, Judith searched for the plastic bag that contained Corinne's pips. Vaguely, she recalled that she hadn't seen them a few days earlier either, when she'd offered some to Renie. Surely they had got stuck behind the myriad jars and containers that filled the bottom shelf. Judith kept looking.

But after going over every inch of shelving, drawers and racks, she found no sign of the pips. It didn't seem likely that any of her guests would have thrown them out by ac-

cident. Indeed, they hadn't bothered to throw out their own
rotting produce. Judith was standing in front of the refrigerator, chewing on her lower lip, when Edna Fiske entered
the kitchen.

"I hope Mrs. Pacetti doesn't overexert herself," Edna remarked with a worried air. "She and Mr. Plunkett have
been gone for hours. Would you mind if I made a cup of
tea?"

"No, go ahead." Judith was still frowning at the refrigerator. "I don't suppose you noticed a bag of little
tuberlike things in here?"

"You mean shallots or something?" Edna was filling the
teakettle.

"Not exactly. They're thin, with a runner and roots.
Lily-of-the-valley pips, to be precise. I was saving them
for my neighbor."

Edna Fiske was shocked. "In the refrigerator? My, that's
risky! They're highly toxic, you know. A person can die
from merely drinking the water in which the flowers have
been placed. You should have kept them in a cool place,
like your basement."

Judith gave Edna a faintly remorseful look. "I had the
bag tied pretty tight. Anyway, I don't think anybody would
mistake them for . . ." Her jaw dropped and she gaped at
Edna. "My God! You say they're *poisonous?*"

"Oh, very," Edna replied, taking a tea bag out of the
cannister on the counter. "You'd be surprised how many
ordinary plants and shrubs and flowers are potentially dangerous. It's no wonder so many children get poisoned in
their own backyards. Or drinking the water that picked
flowers have been in. Why, when I was working the pedi-
atric wing at . . ." It was her turn to stop and stare in horror. "Mrs. McMonigle! Are you thinking that Mr. Pacetti
ate those pips?"

"I sure am," Judith said, running her hands through her
short silver-streaked hair. "There were at least two dozen
of them. Would that do it?" Judith knew she had turned
very pale; Edna also looked ashen.

"Oh, definitely." The teakettle boiled, making both women jump. With hands that were none too steady, Edna poured the hot water into a mug. "I'm not an expert in toxicology, but I know that lily-of-the-valley pips are often mistaken for wild garlic, and if used in quantity, can cause death."

Judith had already sat down at the kitchen table, drinking the dregs of her scotch. Edna joined her, dipping the tea bag in and out of the mug in a jerky motion.

"That's got to be it," breathed Judith, staring now at Edna's tea. "What do you know about Strophanthin?"

Edna wrinkled her long nose. "The heart medication? Not a great deal. It's uncommon in this country. I believe the antidote is ... strong tea." She gazed into her mug with a certain amount of revulsion.

"How much of it would it take to kill someone? Especially," Judith added with a lifted eyebrow, "if that person had drunk a lot of tea?"

"Oh, my." Edna's big teeth clamped onto her lower lip. "Quite a lot, I should think."

Judith got her purse form the counter and produced the empty bottle. "Does it come in something like this? Would a bottle this size be enough?"

The nurse examined the little vial through the plastic bag. "I couldn't say, really ... I don't know that I've ever seen it. Frankly, I'd be dubious. I presume you're talking about Mr. Pacetti? Besides taking the antidote, he was quite a big man. Around, I mean. I can only guess, but I would calculate that it would require three or four times that amount for a lethal dose. Under the circumstances."

"Ah." Judith leaned back in her chair. "That explains it. Or could. Except ..." She frowned again. The pieces were there, but they didn't yet fit together. "How would a person use those pips, I wonder?"

Edna Fiske considered carefully. "Any number of ways. Most likely, I should think, in food. A salad, a casserole, anything that had a lot of ingredients. I have no idea what they taste like." She shuddered. "Mr. Pacetti was the sort who bolted his food. Unhealthy, but typical."

"Very unhealthy," muttered Judith, wondering why Edna's statement should jar her any more than the nurse's usual pronouncements on health. Judith gazed at her refrigerator as if it had betrayed her.

"Strophanthin," mused Edna Fiske, apparently having composed herself. "It's a heart medication, a form of digitoxin. Which is interesting, given this particular situation." Having come to grips with the horror of it all, Edna Fiske's homely face brightened with professional zeal. She actually preened a little in her crisp white uniform. "Another thing I remember about lily of the valley is that it's often mistaken for digitalis. It wouldn't be unheard of for a medical examiner to come up with the incorrect poison."

In Judith's brain, the pieces shifted around, like peas in a shell game. "No kidding!" Suddenly, she was anxious for Edna to go away. Judith wanted to call Renie. And Woody, too.

But Edna Fiske was inclined to linger over her tea. "In nursing school, I was very intrigued by poisons," she said. "People don't realize that almost every ingestible item they have in their house or garden is potentially toxic. You realize, I assume, that Mr. Pacetti may have eaten those pips by accident."

Judith blinked. "I hadn't thought of that." It was, of course, possible. But somehow Judith didn't think it was likely. On the contrary, the accident theory sounded like a good cover-up for a murderer.

Dooley had arrived a few minutes later, his carrier's pouch still slung around his neck. The lanky blond teenager was a member of the Police Auxiliary, and as such, entitled to take on certain law enforcement duties. He had been an enthusiastic amateur sleuth during the fortune-teller investigation and had also joined in to help track down the killer of a fellow parishioner at Easter time. But over the summer, Dooley had found a new passion—

Brianna Stein, the fifteen-year-old daughter of Judith's neighbors at the end of the cul-de-sac. Dooley had thus far been indifferent to the poisoning of Mario Pacetti.

"Sorry, Dooley," said Judith, who had finally been left alone by Edna Fiske and was about to call Renie, "I'll have to dig up some more pips. The ones I was saving for your mother got . . . lost."

Dooley shrugged. He had, Judith decided, grown at least two inches since she'd seen him up close a few weeks earlier. At almost sixteen, he was well over six feet of arms, legs, and erratic blond hair. "That's okay," he said. "I don't even know what pips are."

"They're not the berry things you sometimes see on the plants. They're more like rootstock," Judith explained, surprised at Dooley's lack of botanical knowledge. Unlike the majority of his peers, Dooley was a voracious reader, with a retentive memory. Judith wondered if he'd given everything up in the name of puppy love. From the looks of his too-skinny frame, she decided that he'd definitely given up eating. "Have you quit Police Auxiliary work?" Judith asked as Dooley lounged in the doorway.

"Huh?" He shifted his gaze, which had drifted off toward the driveway which led to the cul-de-sac where the Steins lived at the corner. "Oh—yeah, sort of. That's kid stuff. They don't let you do much, except hang out at rock concerts and try to see who's sneaking in drugs and chains and booze and guns and stuff like that."

"That's pretty boring, all right," said Judith, trying not to look aghast. "I just thought that with Mr. Pacetti getting poisoned, you might have volunteered to help with the investigation. You know, being neighbors and all."

"Mr. Who?" Dooley blinked uncomprehendingly at Judith.

"Never mind." Judith started to explain that maybe over the weekend she'd be able to find some more pips in the garden, but Dooley was again staring at the partial view of the Steins' house. "According to Arlene Rankers, they're coming back Friday."

"I know." Dooley's beardless face somehow displayed both hope and desolation. "She's missed almost two weeks of school."

Judith wondered if *she,* who obviously must be Brianna, had also missed Dooley. As the veteran mother of a former teenage boy, Judith knew better than to ask. "It'll be hard to catch up," she said, seeking neutral ground.

"Not for Brianna," Dooley asserted. "She's a four-point student. We're going to build a Mayan ruin when she gets back. For our science project."

"Sounds great," Judith said with enthusiasm. At least it sounded as if Dooley hadn't given up entirely on the external world. With a bemused expression, she watched him lope off toward the picket fence, his gaze still lingering in the direction of the Stein residence. Judith went back inside and dialed Renie's number.

Renie wasn't home. Judith remembered that her cousin was meeting Madge Navarre for dinner before the opera performance. It was now after five-thirty. She called Woody Price, but he'd left work for the day. Debating whether or not to bother him at home, she jumped when the phone rang in her hand. It was Melissa Bargroom, sounding slightly breathless.

"Your adorable but ditzy cousin is out," said Melissa, "so I took the liberty of calling you. I'm on my way to a chamber music concert, but I heard something today that I thought you two would want to know, lest I get killed by a flying cello in the next few hours."

"I didn't know chamber groups were so violent," responded Judith, smiling into the receiver. She refrained from asking Melissa if ticket holders were patted down for weapons, booze, and drugs. "What's up?" Judith settled onto the kitchen stool, wondering if she dared fix herself a second scotch.

"I called a colleague of mine in New York this afternoon," said Melissa, speaking more rapidly than usual. "I felt like such a dunce not knowing more about the Pacetti lash-up. Well, I didn't glean anything more about Pacetti, but I certainly learned some interesting background on Inez and—" She took an audible breath and raised her voice. "—her stepson, Justin Green."

"Whoa!" Judith covetously eyed the liquor cabinet across the room. "Justin *Green?* To be or not to be confused with Justin *Kerr?*"

"To be the same." Melissa chuckled. "Justin Green changed his name when his parents split up about fifteen years ago. His father was dead set against his becoming a singer, but his mother thought it was a terrific idea. I suspect that's one of the battles that led to the war. In any event, Justin took his mother's maiden name, which was Kerr."

"So that's why the police can't find a marriage license under Justin Kerr," murmured Judith, hopping off the stool to stretch the phone cord so she could reach the liquor cabinet. "And it could explain how his mother could be Tippy's aunt and they'd still have the same name. I think," she added, muddled by the convolutions of her own brain.

"Marriage license?" Melissa's echo was breathless, but she didn't wait for a response. "I've got to speed this up, the concert's at seven-thirty. I'd rather be hearing Justin sing Alfredo, but the chamber group was prescheduled. Anyway, his father, Cornelius Green, married Inez Garcia after he and Justin's mother divorced. Ironic, what? They met at some big do at Faneuil Hall. The marriage lasted about seven years. I haven't had a chance to check dates. But the bottom line is that Inez is—or was—Justin's stepmother. *Voilà!*"

"Wow." Judith was all but chinning herself on the bottom cabinet below her liquor stash. The phone cord was stretched to its limits. So was Judith. "And where is Mr. Green? Cornelius, I mean. Corny Green? That's awful!" She struggled to reach the bottle of scotch.

"Right, but I don't suppose anybody except his old Ivy League cronies call him that. He's the CEO of a big insurance company in Connecticut. Halcyon Insurance of New Haven. He wanted Justin to follow in his footsteps as a peddler of policies, rather than a singer of songs. I've got to run, Judith. I can't imagine how this helps, but it *is* interesting."

Judith fumbled at the bottle, finally bringing it to rest against her bosom. "It sure is. Why didn't more people know there was a family connection between Inez and Justin?"

"They probably did, back East. But think about it— Justin hasn't yet made a name for himself. He was a musical nonentity while his father was married to Inez. And I can't imagine that she was much of a stepmother. She was too busy with her career—so was Corny, with his. That's why they split up, I'm told. They were hardly ever on the same continent, let alone in the same bed. Inez and Justin probably have seen more of each other on the opera stage than they ever did in the old family dining room."

"True." Judith bore down on the receiver, which was trapped between her ear and shoulder. The bottle of scotch slipped out of her hands, fell on the floor, but did not break. She grimaced, but tried to keep her voice carefree. "Thanks, Melissa. You've done good work."

"I owed you one," said Melissa. "As a source, I was a journalistic vacuum. Got to dash. 'Bye."

Judith, bemused by Melissa's news and grateful that the music critic hadn't pressed her for other developments, got down on her knees to pick up the liquor bottle. She jumped again when Edna Fiske's voice pealed in her ear.

"Really, Mrs. McMonigle, I had no idea you were so keen on spirits!"

Judith stared up at Edna. "When I break one of these, I just lap it up off the floor." She grabbed the bottle and got to her feet. "Actually, I was on the phone and I'd received some rather shocking news . . ."

"Yes, yes," Edna broke in. "I've heard all the excuses. I suppose you drink to settle your nerves." She gave Judith a sharp look of disapproval.

"Actually, I do. About twice a year." Judith's glance was equally sharp. "Murder affects me that way."

Edna pursed her lips, but her expression grew less severe. "It doesn't do to buffer shock or drown sorrow in alcohol. I've seen too many sad cases in emergency rooms and on the wards."

Standing up, Judith resolutely poured herself half a shot, added ice, and boldly drank. There was no point in defending herself. Like most people, Edna Fiske would believe what she wanted to believe. "You've had quite a varied career," Judith remarked conversationally.

"I have at that," Edna replied smugly. "Hospital work, private practice, public health—now private duty. It keeps me on my toes."

"For how long has Mrs. Pacetti engaged you?" It occurred to Judith that if Amina was well enough to go off gallivanting with Winston Plunkett, she didn't need a nurse.

Edna was quick to interpret Judith's question. "It's a twenty-four hour assignment. That is, it goes from day to day. I should think Mrs. Pacetti wouldn't need me after this evening."

"Maybe the police will let them all leave in a day or two," Judith mused, aware after the first sip of scotch that she needed food more than drink. It was past 6:00 P.M. She wondered if her guests were staying out for dinner. Perhaps they planned to hear Justin Kerr's local opera debut. Ordinarily, Judith's visitors weren't accountable to her, but this had not turned out to be an ordinary stay. Judith wished she had known their plans; she could have gone to the opera with Renie. On the other hand, she was anxious to relay Edna's information about the pips to Woody. Judith excused herself to go upstairs to use her private line.

No one answered at Woody's home. Maybe they'd gone out to dinner. Judith left a message, then went back downstairs to fix herself a halibut filet. Edna had made yet another salad, which she was taking up to her room. Judith considered inviting her to eat in the kitchen, but thought better of it. She preferred to be alone when Woody called back.

But he didn't. At eight-thirty, Amina Pacetti and Winston Plunkett returned. Obviously, they had not gone to the opera. Except for a trace of fatigue, Amina appeared to be in blooming health. Plunkett, as ever, looked gray.

"You certainly had a good outing," Judith said as Amina allowed Plunkett to help her with her coat.

"Yes, yes!" exclaimed Amina. "The art museum, the aquarium, a ferryboat ride with dinner at a picturesque restaurant across the bay. For those hours, my troubles melted away. But now," she went on, surveying the entry hall as if she'd entered a mausoleum, "they return. My grief descends like the storm clouds."

Winston Plunkett was gazing at Amina with sympathy. "This is such a difficult time. There can be no sense of closure until the funeral is held in Italy. Mrs. Pacetti feels suspended in time and place."

Judith agreed. For all of Amina's flaws, she was a new widow in a strange land. There were children, after all, who no doubt needed to be comforted and to give comfort. In fact, Amina had more in common with Judith than most widows. It appeared that she, like Judith, had not been madly in love with her husband. Judith felt as if she had given Amina short shrift. Unless, of course, the widow had poisoned her mate.

Plunkett and Mrs. Pacetti went upstairs. Judith tried to call Woody again, just in case his answering machine was broken. There was still no answer. Frustrated, Judith considered trying to reach Woody's subordinates, Corazon Perez and Ted Doyle. But Woody should be the first to hear her news. She started up to the family quarters again, but at the door to the third floor staircase, she met Plunkett, coming out of his room.

"The police have released Mr. Pacetti's body," he said in a low, mournful voice. "If we can get permission, we'd like to leave for Rome on Friday."

Judith's reaction was mixed. She'd be elated to have her guests depart before Joe got back. But she was disturbed by the decision at headquarters. If the medical examiner had made a mistake about the kind of poison that had killed Pacetti, the murderer might never be apprehended.

"Is Mrs. Pacetti still up?" Judith asked.

"Nurse Fiske is with her," Plunkett replied. "By the way, is there any word from Ms. de Caro?"

Judith hesitated. "She's still in town." Plunkett's face was impassive. "She got scared, I gather," Judith added. Plunkett gave a little shrug that might also have been a shudder. "Did you mean to get in touch with her?" asked Judith.

The question stirred some speck of interest in Plunkett's gray eyes. "I should. Do you know where she can be reached?"

"The police know," Judith hedged. "You assume she's actually quit her post?"

"Wouldn't you?" Plunkett's thin eyebrows lifted. "With Mario Pacetti gone, the ship has sunk, Mrs. McMonigle. Anyone abandoning it shouldn't be considered a rat, but merely prudent." His thin face showed genuine emotion. And, Judith noted, a certain shrewdness that bordered on the ruthless.

The door to Amina's room opened, revealing Edna Fiske, medical kit in hand. "The patient seems none the worse for her strenuous day. I'll be staying on through tomorrow, however."

Judith put one hand on Plunkett and the other on Edna. "I'm sure you two will want to confer about that. Excuse me, I must speak with Mrs. Pacetti." She slipped between the pair and went into Amina's room, closing the door behind her. Attired in the peach peignoir with its feather trim, Mrs. Pacetti was seated at the dressing table, brushing her hair. She looked at her visitor with mild curiosity.

Judith was aware that if her lily-of-the-valley pips had caused Mario Pacetti's death, there might be some legal liability involved. Amina Pacetti struck Judith as the type who wouldn't hesitate to call in her lawyers. Judith had to be circumspect in phrasing her questions.

"Mrs. Pacetti," she began, pulling Edna's bedside chair

closer to Amina, "do you recall seeing some ... uh ... flower tubers in the refrigerator last Saturday? They were in a plastic bag."

"Tchaah! Tumors?" Amina's eyes grew round. "What is this of which you speak? Diseased plants?"

Judith winced, thinking Amina wasn't all that far off the mark. "No, no. They're like small roots. There were two dozen of them, tied up inside a baggie."

Amina looked again into the mirror and plied the hairbrush anew. "You have many things in your refrigerator. I know about cutting, I know about arranging, but of growing, I do not know. These plants I do not recall."

"They weren't precisely plants ..." Judith stopped herself. Either Amina had seen them or she hadn't. Or, possibly, she had pounced upon them as a method of dispatching her husband to the next world. Judith tried a different tack. "I removed the flowers from Madame Garcia-Green. They were certainly an unusual arrangement, didn't you think?"

Amina twirled the brush through her thick hair. "Oh—not so much. Mario and I are—were—accustomed to exquisite flowers. These were not well arranged. I asked Nurse Fiske to redo them, but she said it wasn't part of her professional training. Lax, is that not?" She put the brush down and stared at her reflection as if coaxing her image to agree with her.

Judith gave up on following the flower lead. Amina didn't seem the least bit perturbed by questions about the bouquet. Again, Judith struck a different note. "I understand your husband had a fascinating series of rituals before a performance. Did he ever eat anything after he arrived at the opera house?" she inquired, trying to sound casual.

Amina frowned at Judith. "Why do you ask? Because you are a policeman's wife? These questions have already been put to me by the black man, the brown woman, and the white man. Every race and creed has interrogated me, except for the Orientals and your Native Americans. They will come next, no doubt, from your FBI. I am sick of questions!"

Judith ignored the diatribe. "Don't you want the answers?" she asked innocently. "Would you rather your husband's murder went unavenged?"

Amina's face stiffened. "Of course not. But I have no answers. I am not a policeman!"

"What happened to your thermos?" Judith maintained her guileless expression.

"I don't know," Amina responded on a cross note. "I left it at the opera house. It was of little concern to me at the time. What's a thermos when you've lost your beloved husband?"

*About twenty bucks,* came the answer into Judith's head. She was ashamed of herself, but the reaction was entirely natural. She still remembered when the undertakers had come to carry Dan out of their squalid Thurlow Street rental and had gone right through the rotting kitchen floor while transporting his body to the hearse. *Not another makeshift patch-up job I can't afford—why do these things always happen to me?* she'd thought—and immediately been overcome with remorse. It appeared that Amina Pacetti operated on a loftier plane.

"That's okay," said Judith mildly. "I'd just like to know why it ended up buried in my backyard. With poison in it." She gave Amina a flinty smile.

"I do not know. Mr. Plunkett has told the police I do not know. We stopped at headquarters this morning on our way to the museum. Someone—the killer, I must presume—put poison in the thermos when I wasn't looking." She spoke coldly, almost detached from the heinous crime she was describing.

"I thought you never let that thing out of your sight," Judith remarked.

Amina lifted her chin. "I don't. I didn't. If I set it down, it must have been after Mario collapsed. And no, he did not eat anything at the opera house. He never does—never *did."* The small word seemed to cause Amina genuine pain. Her face crumpled and she turned away.

Judith felt a pang of sympathy. She wondered if she should tell Amina that it was possible her thermos had not contained the poison that had killed Mario. But Judith didn't know for sure. She kept her mouth shut, stood up, and moved to stand next to Amina.

"I'm so sorry I upset you. I feel responsible—in a way," Judith added quickly, envisioning a horde of lawyers from both sides of the Atlantic descending on Hillside Manor. "That is, you and your husband came here to find safety, under my roof. And it didn't turn out that way."

Amina raised her head. She saw the havoc wreaked by her emotions in the mirror and passed a hand across her forehead. "You ask questions of the wrong person," she said in a weary voice.

"Oh?" Judith frowned. "What do you mean?"

Amina gazed up at Judith with a dark expression. "Ask me no more. Ask," she said in a brittle tone, "Inez."

# FIFTEEN

"HE'S GREAT," RENIE declared over the phone through a mouthful of popcorn. "Not in Pacetti's class yet, of course. But Justin Kerr has a beautiful voice. Melissa should have been there to give him a rave review."

"I'm sorry I missed it," Judith said, standing at the sink to rinse out the kettle in which she'd just made herself some hot cocoa. "Nobody died, right?"

"Nope," replied Renie. It was after 11:00 P.M., and she had just returned from dropping Madge Navarre off at her condo on the other side of town. "Inez was in fine form, Sydney Haines sounded terrific and Maestro Dunkowitz made sure the orchestra played the same notes at the same time. However," she added, suddenly sounding mysterious instead of merely muffled, "Madge had an interesting note of her own to add."

"Madge? Such as what?" Judith blew on the mug of cocoa to cool if off.

"I should have remembered, but all these years I think of Madge's employer as the Weisenheim Agency," explained Renie. "Which it is, but it's affiliated with Halycon Insurance of New Haven. Is your picture coming into focus, coz?"

It was. "Interesting. So Madge really works for Justin Kerr's father, Corny Green. Next I ask, so what?"

"So . . ." Renie paused, munching on more popcorn. "Damned if I know. I said it was interesting, not informative."

"Did Madge know anything about the Justin-Corny-Inez connection?"

"Heck no, I can barely get her to divulge any local gossip, let alone the home office rumor mill," said Renie. "But to be fair, she was genuinely surprised that there was a connection. Cornelius Green is not unknown to her, but he seems to be some sort of mythical, Zeus-like figure sitting on top of a Revolutionary War monument in New Haven. Unlike most insurance company CEOs, he owns a big chunk of stock in the firm. In fact, his grandfather founded it back in the early part of the century. I suppose that's why Corny wanted Justin to go into the business."

Judith gave a murmur of acknowledgment. Justin was well-heeled, which explained his expensive musical studies. Justin was probably married to Tippy, the license having been taken out under his real name. Maybe, just maybe, Justin and Tippy were keeping their status a secret not because of the late Pacetti, but for fear of alienating the enamored Inez. As an ally, a live singer would be a lot more help than a dead one. Maybe that help had already arrived, in the form of a recording contract from Bruno Schutzendorf. Judith and Renie tossed these ideas back and forth for several minutes. Then Judith updated her cousin about what had been happening at the B&B. Edna Fiske's revelation about the lily-of-the-valley pips elicited a squeak of surprise.

"Let's back up," said Renie. "You're saying that somebody pinched the pips and fed them to Pacetti for lunch?"

"Could be. I couldn't find them when you were here Saturday night, remember?"

"Hmmmm. So what's with the Strophanthin? A backup, just in case?"

"Maybe," said Judith. "Or a blind. Whatever it was, we're

dealing with somebody who knows a lot about poisons. Of all kinds. Damn, I wish Woody would call. I wonder if he's been sent out on a more urgent case."

"What could be more urgent than a world-famous tenor?" Renie pointed out.

"In this town?" Judith uttered a wry chuckle. "How about somebody throwing garbage in the fish ladders over at the ship canal locks? Or small children feeding stale bread to the ducks down at the lake. You know what we're like around here—serial killers may come and go, but don't muck with the wildlife."

Renie conceded that their hometown did indeed have a reputation for getting riled up over some pretty odd doings. "Bill says it's our inability to deal with the darker side of human nature. This part of the world is so blessed by natural beauty that we can't face the fact that people can be ugly. So we avoid real evil and concentrate on comparatively petty misdeeds which . . ."

"Hold it, coz," interrupted Judith, who often found Renie's secondhand lectures from Bill a bit tedious. "There's somebody at my door."

"At eleven-thirty at night?" Renie sounded incredulous.

But to Judith's own amazement, her fiction turned to fact. The front door opened and the unmistakable tread of Bruno Schutzendorf was heard in the entry hall.

"That's right," said Renie, somewhat abashed. "I forgot—he was at the performance, fourth row center."

Judith hung up and went out to greet her guest. Schutzendorf was unburdening himself of his Tyrolean cape, tweed jacket, and snap-brimmed cap.

"A splendid evening," he declared, his booming voice heedless of whoever might be asleep upstairs. "Inez was magnificent. Sydney Haines is superb. And this young Kerr—he is a pleasure! I am shaking my own hand for signing him to a contract."

"I feel left out," Judith lamented. "How was the acting?"

Schutzendorf, now mired under his pile of outerwear,

gave Judith a bleak look. "Passable. Especially the two Americans. But you cannot see the acting on a recording. The interpretation, yes. The gestures, no."

"I was merely curious," Judith said in a self-deprecating manner. "I mean, it must be amusing for Justin to play the lover of his former stepmother."

The bristling eyebrows knit together. "Ah! You know about that, eh? It is no secret. Inez, naturally, is somewhat sensitive. She is too young to be Justin's natural mother, but the association might lead the uninformed to think otherwise. Still, there is an affection between them. Yet it is not just to do her the favor that I sign up her former stepson. He is a fine tenor in his own right. Had I needed Inez's advice earlier, I would have made a better bargain. But after Salzburg . . ." He gave a vigorous shake of his head. "Hindsight, that. And there was no choice." His rumbling voice had dropped to a mere mutter.

"No choice?" Judith evinced surprise. "Don't you run Cherubim Records?"

Schutzendorf would have thrown up his arms if they hadn't been full of clothes. *"Ja, ja,* but these singers! The temperament, the jealousies, the suspicion! But times change, people pass . . . into history. We have certainly lost a great tenor this week, have we not?"

"We have indeed," Judith replied. "Pacetti's death must cause you a lot of problems. I mean, you must have had recording sessions scheduled."

"We did." Schutzendorf nodded gravely. "Three in the next few months. They will have to be postponed unless we can find someone of equal stature. Not that there is anyone quite like Pacetti. Young Justin is a possibility for the less taxing roles, but not Calaf in *Turandot,* not even Don Alvaro in *Forza del Destino!* If we do not get appropriate replacements, we are lost. The other singers cannot be expected to rearrange their commitments." He hugged his stack of clothing and sighed deeply. "This has been a terrible blow to Cherubim Recordings. I am desolated."

Judith could see why. She allowed Schutzendorf to

mourn his loss for a few more moments, then waved him good night. With a heavy step, he ascended the stairs. She wondered if, police permitting, he, too, would leave Friday.

Giving up on hearing from Woody, Judith went to bed. The sky was clear except for a few wispy clouds off to the north. A half-moon hung over the Rankers's house. There was little wind, and the night air was mild. Any threat of frost seemed remote. Judith made a mental note to buy bags of candy for the trick or treaters. Halloween was only a week away.

It was no wonder that when she slept she dreamed not of Italian widows or German impresarios or Spanish divas, but of a witch riding on a broom above the toolshed. "Mine, all mine!" the creature cackled.

It wasn't exactly the Voice of Doom, but it was definitely the cry of Gertrude.

Dr. George Inouye's offices were so new that he wasn't yet listed on the building registry. The sleek structure that housed at least a dozen medical and dental specialists was situated across the street from the Children's Medical Center and had its own underground parking garage. Judith inquired at the bank located in the building's lobby, but the sloe-eyed teller had never heard of the eye specialist. Judith got into the elevator and rode up to the third floor, where Dr. Feldman held sway. But Mike's orthodontist was no longer in the same place. A smiling blond receptionist whose name tag read "Carol Carsten" made apologetic noises to Judith.

"This is the other Dr. Feldman's office now," Carol explained, as if she and Judith were on the most intimate terms. "You know, his wife, Sheila. Her practice has grown so that she's taken over the entire floor. Dr. Harold Feldman is on Four."

"It's Dr. Inouye I'm trying to find," Judith said. "He just moved in here. Eye guy?"

The receptionist kept smiling. "Dr. Inouye is on Five.

We've added two floors and just about everybody has moved. It's been a regular merry-go-round!" She uttered an exuberant laugh, as if to indicate that this was about as much fun as you could have in the medical profession.

"Thanks, I'll go up . . ." Judith was interrupted by the receptionist who had, in turn, been interrupted by a young nurse carrying a chart. The two consulted, with the receptionist dispensing more smiles and an overdose of information.

"Darilyn is new," Carol explained. "Everybody is new, it seems; we're all in new places. Really, it's one thing after another! But she's wonderfully eager and takes advice so well." The receptionist suddenly snapped her fingers and stood up. "Darilyn! Don't even try to decipher Edna's handwriting. Just let me see any of the charts she did and I'll translate. I got used to Finicky Fiske and all her strange ways."

Darilyn nodded and headed back into the examining room area. Carol sat down again and looked up at Judith. The young woman was clearly surprised to see the startled expression on her visitor's face.

"Are you all right?" she inquired, turning serious.

"Hold it," said Judith, leaning on the counter. "Did you say—I mean—could you be referring to Edna Fiske, R.N.?"

Carol's blue eyes widened. "Why, yes! Do you know her? Oh, my, I hope she's not your best friend or something! It's just that Edna was such a stickler about everything! The old school and all that. And her handwriting was so tiny and cramped." She gave Judith an appealing look.

"Edna's working as a private duty nurse to someone I know," Judith said, wondering how much she should reveal. "When did she quit her job here?"

"At the end of September," Carol replied promptly. "Don't get me wrong, she's a wonderful nurse. In fact," she went on, lowering her voice, "she got an excellent recommendation from Dr. Feldman. Dr. *Sheila* Feldman, I mean."

Wheels were spinning in Judith's head. Unfortunately, she wasn't sure in which direction they were going. "How does that work?" she asked. "Do patients request certain nurses or do the names just come up on a bureau list?"

"It depends," Carol said, her earlier giddiness now flown. "Edna free-lances. She's had quite a broad background in nursing and has built up a certain reputation. We refer her, as do a number of other doctors she's worked for."

Judith asked her next question boldly. "Did you refer her to Mrs. Amina Pacetti?"

"Let me look." Carol got up and walked over to a bank of file cabinets at the rear of the reception area. A moment later she returned with a beige file folder. "Here it is," she said, running her finger down a sheet of paper. "The request came in last Sunday. Dr. Feldman must have been called at home. She made the referral herself."

Judith became aware of the direction in which the wheels were spinning. She also understood why Edna's comments on certain occasions should have indicated that the nurse not only already knew her patient, but her patient's husband as well. "Why was Dr. Feldman called? Had one of the Pacettis been treated by her?"

Carol not only closed the file folder abruptly, but her expression shut down, too. "I can't violate doctor-patient confidentiality," she declared in a prim voice. "I've already said too much." Judging from the aggrieved look in her blue eyes, she felt that Judith had violated her.

"No problem," Judith said lightly. "Mrs. Pacetti is staying with me. So is Edna. Thanks for the help. I'm off to Inouye." She gave Carol a friendly wave. The receptionist gaped at Judith's departing figure. Judith figured her visit would probably provide Carol Carsten with entertainment fodder for at least a week.

* * *

Two hours later, Judith was armed with a new prescription for glasses and a bill from the optometrist for $127.56. She was also armed with some new theories about Mario Pacetti's murder. Her call from the pay phone in the lobby had gone for naught where Woody was concerned. He still wasn't in the office. Judith's status as Joe Flynn's wife had got her nowhere in terms of trying to find out where her husband's erstwhile partner might be. The woman on the other end of the line at headquarters insisted she didn't know.

Renie, however, had been at home. The lure of lunch and new developments brought her out of her lair. The cousins would meet at the Cascadia Hotel, call on Inez Garcia-Green, and eat in the Terrace Room. Renie wanted to reverse the order, but Judith insisted on seeing Inez first.

"What's our gig this time?" asked Renie as the cousins approached the hotel desk.

"Amina sent us. Which she did. Sort of."

Surrounded by marble pillars and Flemish tapestries, the cousins waited for the Brooks Brothers–suited clerk to tend to their needs. A phone call to Inez's suite elicited an ambiguous response.

"Madame Garcia will be down in a short while," said the clerk, with a professionally impassive expression. He turned his attention to a Japanese couple at the checkout section.

"We'll be in the Terrace Room," said Judith, before Renie could beat her to it. "We'll get a table for three."

"Good work," murmured Renie as they climbed the wide marble stairs that led into the restaurant. "It's almost one o'clock and I could eat a mule."

"Right," replied Judith somewhat vaguely. "At least I'll have time to fill you in."

"And I'll have time to fill me up," Renie noted, all but smacking her lips.

As it turned out, the cousins had a great deal of time to devour their crab cakes and spinach salads. Indeed, they were at the coffee and we-really-shouldn't-have-dessert stage when Inez Garcia-Green glided into the Terrace Room. She wore midnight blue, a tunic over slacks, and a matching turban. The handful of patrons who were still lingering in the Terrace Room watched her progress behind the maître d'.

"Mrs. Flynn?" Inez gazed past the cousins, surveying the rest of the room as if to make sure there was no one of importance that she might have missed. With a regal smile for the maître d', she allowed him to pull out a chair. "I have lunched. Cognac, please. Warmed."

Sapphire earrings sparkled on her perfect lobes. Gold and platinum rings set with diamonds, rubies, and more sapphires gleamed on her long, strong fingers. She wore her black hair neatly coiled at the base of the turban.

"You requested a meeting, no?" She surveyed the cousins as if they were unworthy of her presence.

Judith cleared her throat. "Mrs. Pacetti felt you knew something about her husband's death. She suggested we talk to you."

"Talk to you? Why?" Inez's piercing look changed to a smile for the waiter who had hurried over with her cognac.

"My husband is a homicide detective. I sometimes assist him in his inquiries," Judith explained, stretching the truth. "The woman's touch, you see."

"And this one?" Inez gazed at Renie. "She was also at your establishment the other night. Your maid?"

Renie's brown eyes snapped, but she held her temper. "Companion. You know, like a duenna. I carry her fan and dispense largesse."

Inez did not appear to have a sense of humor. Nor did she understand when she was being teased. "I see no fan. To whom do you dispense this largesse?"

Aware that Renie could string Inez along for hours, Judith broke in. "Why should Mrs. Pacetti feel you have information about her husband's murder?"

Inez waved a hand. "Oh! That Amina! She talks without knowing what she says! I sing with Pacetti; I see him two or three times a season. We are colleagues, no more. What would I know about why the poor man was murdered?"

Renie wasn't about to let Judith hog all the questions. "But you were lovers at one time," she said, wearing her middle-aged ingenue's expression. Seeing Inez's hostile reaction, she continued. "Everybody knows that. It follows then that you would know more about him than your average soprano."

"I am never average!" declared Inez. "I am a *prima donna assoluta!*" Obviously, she was more annoyed at being termed run-of-the-mill than by the accusation of an illicit love affair. "And who is Amina Pacetti to cast stones? Has she not also taken a lover?"

"Well—maybe," Judith murmured, feeling very unworldly. "But I heard she took up with Plunkett as an act of revenge." Watching carefully for Inez's reaction, Judith was startled when the soprano threw back her head and laughed aloud.

"Plunkett! That miserable creature of repressed passion! You jest, of course." Inez shot Judith a contemptuous look.

Judith uttered a disconsolate sigh. "Oh, well, I guess I was mistaken. And Amina must have overrated your powers of perception. What a shame."

Picking up her snifter of cognac, Inez's dark eyes flashed. "I have excellent powers, of perception and otherwise. I know this much—Mario Pacetti was called a fighting cock, but he was all cock-a-doodle-doo. And often, it didn't do. Much." Inez's face set in hard, sharp lines.

Judith, somewhat mystified, stared at Inez. "Didn't do . . . Never mind. Or," she hurried on, seizing the opportunity, "do you mean he wasn't a well man?"

"He was well when we were lovers." Having had the subject broached, Inez now seemed quite comfortable with it. "You have a phrase in your language—'able-bodied.' It was that he was not always able, if you take my meaning. But his health was excellent otherwise at that time."

Fascinating as Mario Pacetti's sex life might have been as a topic of general gossip, Judith pressed on. "You seem to be qualifying the status of Pacetti's health. Do you mean that he later became ill?"

Inez was sipping her cognac and visibly relaxing. She struck Judith as the type who put up barriers to protect her private self from her public image. Having determined that the cousins were less interested in Inez Garcia-Green's personal life than in Mario Pacetti's, she was beginning to unbend.

"Ill, no, not that I know of. But we singers are always worrying about our voices. Mario worried even more than most. A mere cold to us is a tragedy. A sore throat is near death. Despite his reputation for accidents, Mario enjoyed superb health. Until these past few months, that is. Then there were cancellations. Not many, but starting in the spring, at Teatro Fenice in Venice. Rome, too. A severe cold, I heard." Inez shrugged, the midnight blue tunic rippling over her impressive figure. "There were rumors, too, that he was postponing *Otello* next season at La Scala, and that he had backed out of doing Radames in *Aïda* this winter at the Met. Instead, he requested Rodolfo in *Bohème*." She gave the cousins a meaningful look.

It was lost on Judith, but Renie, with her deeper knowledge of opera, leaped into the void. "In other words, he was avoiding the demanding parts. Rudolfo is comparatively easy, as opposed to Radames or Otello."

Inez nodded gravely. "So it seems. For those of us who knew of his enormous self-confidence—despite his neurotic behavior—there was a feeling of concern. Why was Mario pampering himself? Was he fearful about his voice? He was too young to worry yet about his talent diminishing. Yes, he has been very cautious, avoiding difficult schedules. If anything, he should have gone on for another ten years at least, perhaps not truly peaking until he reached fifty. That's why he'd put off singing Otello this long. He was waiting until his voice had achieved the proper maturity."

Judith nodded. Her idea was taking shape. "Do you know if he remained in Italy after those cancellations?"

Inez looked puzzled by the question. "I was in Venice to sing Minnie in *Fanciulla del West*. We were not at the same hotel, of course. Mario and Amina had taken a villa near Arsolo, outside of the city." Her high forehead furrowed in an attempt at recollection. "Now that you mention the fact, I don't recall hearing of his presence in Italy until after the Rome cancellation. That would have been a month, perhaps six weeks, later."

"Would he have gone home to . . . Bari, is it?" asked Judith.

Again Inez shrugged. "It is possible."

Judith couldn't think of anything more to ask Inez. But Renie had another question.

"In all honesty, have you noticed any deterioration in Mario's voice this past six months?"

The soprano considered the inquiry with great care. It was, after all, tantamount to passing judgment on a Raphael Madonna or a Michelangelo sculpture. "No," she said at last. "No deterioration. But more exertion. That is, he seemed to work harder at producing the notes. Before, it was all effortless, as natural as water from a mountain spring."

"Ah." Judith uttered the exclamation softly. "What does that mean to you? As a singer."

"It could mean many things." Inez turned the snifter in her long fingers. "It could mean a vocal problem, an incapacity of the lungs, a gain or loss of weight, even a mental condition. What do you call it? A block?"

"Right." Judith fervently wished she could get in touch with Woody. There was so much she had to tell him, so many things she wanted to ask him to do . . . She gave Inez Garcia-Green her most gracious smile. "You've been a lot of help. The police will be very grateful."

It didn't seem to occur to Inez why her musings on Pacetti's vocal status should have anything to do with his murder. It was enough that she had been consulted and appreciated. Renie added to the diva's sense of well-being by complimenting her on her performance of the previous evening. They left Inez in the lobby, where a trio of opera buffs jumped for joy at the sight of her and humbly requested autographs.

"You didn't mention the vial or the rock," said Renie as they headed for the parking garage elevators.

"I'm waiting for the handwriting expert to figure out the rock," Judith replied, stopping abruptly at a row of pay phones. "Those two separate but seemingly equal Strophanthin bottles stump me. I don't even know what to ask anybody. And I didn't want to jar Inez out of her garrulous mood."

"Who are you calling?" Renie asked as Judith deposited a quarter in the nearest pay phone slot.

"Woody. If he's in, we're going to swing by headquarters. It's only three blocks from here." She heard another unfamiliar voice answer. Judith's request to speak to Woody was again turned down, but this time an excited explanation was given. Judith hung up the phone and turned to Renie with a wry expression. "It's a boy. Woody won't be in until tomorrow."

"What!" Renie gaped at Judith. "The baby came early? Oh, rats! What do we do now?"

Judith started for the elevators. "What do you think? Go buy a baby gift. We're headed for the hospital."


Sondra Price was delighted with the blue-and-white checked romper suit from Judith and the green-and-yellow striped coverall from Renie. The cousins had purchased both garments in six-month sizes, causing Sondra and Woody to laugh at the idea that their tiny son would ever fit into such enormous outfits.

"Three months, and he'll be wearing them," Judith declared. "After all, he weighs over eight pounds now. You'll be surprised at how fast they grow."

Sondra, a pretty woman just past thirty, with a master's degree in speech therapy, beamed up at her husband. "He's going to be a pilot. I can tell by the way he squints, like he's looking into the sun through the windshield of a 747.

He's wrinkled, too, as if he's been out in the sun too long. Have you seen him yet?" she asked the cousins.

They had. Renie assured the new parents that the wrinkles would go away. Judith said he'd stop squinting soon and start seeing. Woody insisted their baby already did. At the age of eleven hours and fourteen minutes, Woodrow Wilson Price III was obviously a precocious child.

Half an hour later in the hospital cafeteria, the cousins did their best to bring the new father down to earth. As professional as Woody usually was, it took a few minutes to get him off pablum and onto poison. Even then, he was somewhat skeptical about Judith's pip theory.

"You aren't one-hundred-percent positive those pips weren't in the refrigerator Saturday night, right? Isn't it possible that your cleaning lady threw them out? Would she remember doing it? Did you check your garbage?"

Judith couldn't categorically refute the points Woody raised. As for the garbage, it had been collected Monday as usual.

"It's possible," Woody allowed after Judith had made another pass at convincing him she might be right. "Anything's possible. But somebody had Strophanthin in their possession. Why not use it instead of a bunch of flower roots?"

Briefly, Judith was stumped. Then the answer dawned on her. "Because of the tea. Our killer is careful. He or she probably read up on poisons. If the murderer got hold of the Strophantin to use it on Mario and then discovered he always drank what was in effect an antidote, there had to be a shifting of gears. And of poisons."

"So why leave the empty vials on stage?" asked Woody. "Why one bottle on the table and the other in the flower arrangement? Why put some of the stuff in the thermos and bury it in your backyard?"

"To confuse the issue," Judith answered promptly. "Those pips are often mistaken for a form of digitoxin. If you're off looking for someone who was running around backstage before the performance leaving vials among the champagne glasses and the exotic blooms while also dumping toxic substances in thermos bottles, then you're never going to zero in on the killer. It's a smoke screen. The big obstacle is that nobody saw anything suspicious going on before . . . Oh!" Judith jumped, almost knocking over her Styrofoam coffee cup.

"What?" Woody turned curious brown eyes on Judith.

But Judith shook her head. "Never mind. I'm probably having a minor brain seizure. Let me think this through. What about your handwriting expert?"

Momentarily, Woody looked blank. "Oh—the rock and the sheet of paper. Corazon's tracking that for me. Give her a call."

"Okay. Can I ask her to check with Customs and Immigration to see if Mario and Amina entered this country in April or May?"

Woody raised his eyebrows. "I suppose. Why?"

Judith settled back in the orange modular plastic chair. "I think Mario came over here to consult with Dr. Sheila Feldman, world-renowned throat specialist. He was having vocal problems, it seems. Now I don't know what that has to do with his murder, but it suggests several possibilities to me. Can you get a warrant to go through Dr. Feldman's records?"

Woody's face broke into a big grin. He shook his head slowly. "Mrs. Flynn—Judith—you come up with the craziest ideas! A singer like Pacetti probably consults a throat specialist at least four times a year. I'll go along with the Customs and Immigration notion, but I'm not getting mixed up with doctors. They always stonewall, if only because they think we're fronting for the IRS."

Somewhat deflated, Judith shot a quick look at Renie. "Okay, Woody," Judith said, "just don't blame me when Joe gets back from New Orleans and finds out this case is looser than a galloping goose."

A brief expression of alarm crossed Woody's face. "Mrs. Flynn . . . *Judith* . . . I'm not trying to be a pain; I'm just following police procedure. And," he added on a wounded note, "having a baby."

Stung, Judith grew remorseful. "I know. I'm sorry. I just want to get this thing solved. Not only have I lost a guest, but the contents of my refrigerator may be responsible."

"She's right," chimed in Renie. "What's really surprising is that it hasn't happened before. With her mother's leftovers, that is."

Judith gave Renie the evil eye. *"Et tu, Brute,"* she muttered.

"Et pips," Renie replied, turning to Woody. "Wait and see, Dad. I'm with Judith. I think Mario et them and if I've got my cousin figured, I also think she may know who dished them up. Right?" Her gaze returned to Judith.

Judith didn't respond.

# SIXTEEN

CORAZON PEREZ HAD left a message, so Judith called her back. The policewoman answered on the first ring. The handwriting expert had had some problems with the analysis.

"The surface of the rock gave him fits," Corazon reported. "He had better luck with the paper. But bear in mind that the drawings were impossible to work with. He had no basis for comparison. At least the musical score gave him a couple of letters."

"And?" Judith leaned away from Renie, who was practically on her neck trying to hear the conversation.

"He couldn't come to a conclusion." Corazon sounded apologetic. "He won't discount Inez Double G—as they call her in the homicide division—but he really can't be sure. I'm sorry."

Sensing that Corazon was eager to move on, Judith quickly asked her to describe the original bottle of Strophanthin. Sounding puzzled, Corazon sketched a brief word picture.

"That's it," said Judith, more for Renie's benefit than for Corazon's. "When you see Woody Price," she said into the receiver, "remind him I've got its mate. Empty. It may not be as cute as a baby bottle, but it could turn out to be evidence." Judith put down the phone. "Let's see if that doesn't get Woody back in the groove."

"What about the rock?" Renie asked.

Judith grimaced at her cousin. *"Nada,* as Inez would say in her native Spain. Now I wish I'd asked her about that rock when I had the chance at the Cascadia this afternoon."

Renie strolled to the refrigerator. "It's almost six. Aren't you doing hors d'oeuvres?"

"My guests are out," Judith replied, fingering a note that had been left on the bulletin board. "They're all being hosted by Maestro Dunkowitz this evening. I suspect they're under the impression they may get to leave tomorrow. Woody didn't say so, though."

"Woody's in Babyland," Renie replied, scrutinizing a jar of extra small oysters. "What do you say we fry these up for dinner? I don't have anybody hanging around my house tonight either."

"Fine," Judith agreed, heading for the back stairs. "But first we grill Edna Fiske. After Corazon Perez, Edna's my next priority."

But upstairs, there was no sign of Edna. The front bedroom she had taken over from Mario Pacetti was empty of personal belongings. Judith swore under her breath and hurried back down to the kitchen.

"She's flown the coop." Flipping through the phone book, she found a listing for E. D. Fiske at an address only three blocks from Madge Navarre's condo. To Judith's relief, Edna answered on the third ring.

"I just got homc," said the nurse. "Mrs. Pacetti was somewhat ambivalent about my leave-taking, but patients shouldn't be babied. She clearly no longer requires professional nursing care. I prefer to offer my services to those who genuinely need me. Thank you, by the way, for your hospitality."

"It was a relief for me to have you here," Judith responded. "Medical assistance isn't a standard option at a

B&B. It must have been a great comfort for Mrs. Pacetti to have a nurse who had also treated her husband."

There was a slight pause at the other end. "I can't say I *treated* him. Not in that sense. I merely assisted Dr. Feldman. Not that she could do anything, under the circumstances."

Judith eyed Renie who was wearing an anxious expression. "I suppose not. Surgery was ... uh ... out of the question?"

"Definitely," Edna asserted. "It leaves such scar tissue. Of course that was Mr. Pacetti's decision and he was free to change his mind."

Judith rubbed at her forehead, trying to figure out in which direction she could go without sinking into the quicksand of ignorance. "Is it certain the scar tissue would have affected his voice adversely?"

"Almost always. For an ordinary person, it doesn't matter that much. But for a singer—well, you can imagine. Benign polyps wouldn't frighten most of us in the least. We could get along quite nicely with a bit of a rasp in the voice. But not someone who sings professionally. The condition was quite recent. In fact, I understand he'd had an insurance physical last December and they hadn't shown up then. He might have continued his career for a year or two. If he'd lived." Edna's own voice struck a professionally bleak note.

Judith stifled a sigh of relief. It had been a guess, but a good one, considering Sheila Feldman's specialty and her referral of Edna Fiske to Mrs. Pacetti. After exchanging a few pleasantries, Judith hung up.

"Eureka!" she cried. "Now we're getting somewhere!"

"Are we on the same wavelength?" Renie inquired. "Pacetti with vocal cord trouble, right? Voice going before its time?"

"You got it." Free from Edna Fiske's scrutiny, Judith made for the liquor cabinet. "Customs and Immigration will show that the Pacettis entered this country in April, probably, with the rhododendrons in bud. I don't know where they stayed, but my guess is that somehow they got into the family housing at the Children's Medical Center across the street from Dr. Feldman's offices. Rules can be bent for somebody of Pacetti's stature."

Renie had got out a pair of glasses and was putting ice into them. "So you're figuring that Pacetti's vocal problems may have something to do with his murder?"

Pouring bourbon for Renie and scotch for herself, Judith nodded. "It's possible. The trouble is, I can't figure out *what*. If money is a motive, which it often is, who benefits from his early demise? Amina, for one."

"Schutzendorf, maybe," suggested Renie. "Madge told me last night that his recording company would carry insurance on him. You know, like sports teams carry for their players."

The cousins had gone into the living room where they sat on the matching sofas. Judith considered building a fire, but decided it was too warm. "Edna mentioned an insurance physical, last December. But the polyps didn't show up."

"Let's check out motives," Renie said. "Amina— unfaithful wife who collects insurance, estate, freedom. Not bad, huh?"

"Somehow I don't see Amina as seriously unfaithful. I mean, it sounds to me as if she took up with Plunkett just to get back at Mario for having the affair with Inez. Then he became a habit, like wearing mismatched socks. Unless . . ." Judith's forehead furrowed as she recalled Inez's reaction to the suggestion that Winston Plunkett was Amina's lover. "What if Melissa was wrong?"

"Melissa?" Renie looked askance. "Her reliability percentage is almost as high as Madge Navarre's."

"But Melissa is working with gossip, not hard facts, like Madge." Judith frowned at the bright little pumpkin lights that adorned the mantel. "What if Amina was having an affair—but not with Plunkett? Faithful old Winnie might make a good cover for something more serious. Let's face it, we've always had trouble swallowing the Passionate

Plunkett story. I can't help but figure that the only thing he does with his fly is tie one for fishing."

Renie made a strange, bewildered face. "So Amina might have somebody else waiting in the wings. Hmmmm."

"Could be. But then we need another motive for Plunkett," Judith reminded her cousin.

"Did he know Mario was losing his voice?" Renie mused.

Judith inclined her head. "Possibly. Plunkett may have accompanied them in the spring to see Dr. Feldman. And now that I think about it, he didn't criticize Tippy for taking off after Pacetti got killed. In fact, he acted as if she'd made the right choice. I wonder . . ."

Renie sipped at her drink. "But why would Plunkett kill him? He could always quit—like Tippy did—and get another job."

The jumbled blur of the past few days swirled around in Judith's brain. Words, so many words, in accents foreign and domestic . . . She couldn't remember all of them . . . And yet, there were snatches that came to mind.

"The night Pacetti died, Plunkett said something out in the kitchen . . . It was about his life's work, and then he . . ." With a sharp shake of her head, Judith gave the coffee table a kick. "Damn, I've lost it! Why do I keep feeling that if only I'd paid closer attention, I could put this thing together in logical order and figure it all out?"

Renie gave Judith a sympathetic look. "We know who was in the kitchen last Saturday—everybody. Among the guests, that is. The Pacettis, Plunkett, Tippy, and Schutzendorf. But Schutzendorf was also the only one of this crew who wasn't backstage before the performance Saturday night. Still, if he knew that Pacetti's career was going down the drain, he might have done him in out of sheer pique."

"Not pique," Judith countered. "He'd have done it for gain. I keep getting hung up on Justin Kerr and Inez Garcia-Green. Why did they show up here with a stolen stage prop and an empty Strophanthin vial after Mario was murdered?"

Renie's short chin dipped toward her chest. "They grabbed the bouquet as an excuse. Did they know the bottle was in the plastic liner? If they—or one of them, either Justin or Inez—put it there, was the intention to get rid of evidence? Were there always two bottles, and whoever put the one into the bouquet dropped the other one by mistake? And if so, why was one empty and the other half-full? Then we get back to the big question—did the Strophanthin kill Pacetti, or was it the pips?"

"The medical examiner—and Edna Fiske, for that matter—aren't keen on the Strophanthin theory," Judith noted. "So why in the world are these bottles floating around? I opt for them as a red herring. Then who does the Strophanthin point to?" When Renie didn't reply at once, Judith continued, her dark eyes suddenly glimmering with the kernel of an idea. "Schutzendorf has a prescription—don't ask me to pronounce it, it's probably got an ordinary name like 'Blood Pump'—for heart problems. He got it at the hospital after he stayed there the other night. What if he needed it because somebody had swiped his Strophanthin?"

Renie's mouth twisted as she thought this latest theory through. "He shares a bathroom with Plunkett, but Amina and Tippy could have gone in there. Or ..." Her face lighted up as she pummeled the arm of the sofa. "Inez and Justin could have done it while they were upstairs."

Judith inclined her head. "*After* Pacetti was killed? Come on, coz, your brain is compost."

Renie's eager expression changed to one of chagrin. "Well, if it were a red herring ..."

Judith gave Renie a curious little glance, then sank farther into the sofa cushions. "I'm guessing, but I think Inez and Justin were looking for something. I still think Inez sent those so-called threats, just to be annoying. The woman has no sense of humor, and whatever amusement she gets out of life—other than performing, that is—has to be some weird kind of thing, like getting people riled or scared or just plain put out. For all of her seeming indifference to the breakup with Mario, she may have been hurt. Or at least her vanity was wounded."

Renie raised her eyebrows. "So she sends threats? I don't get it."

"You're being dense, coz. Remember crank-calling boys in our youth?"

Renie made a wry face. "I don't remember our youth."

"Emotionally, some women never get beyond that stage. If they feel wronged or rejected, they do strange things. Cousin Marty's ex-girlfriend sent him a pair of ostriches via UPS."

"Marty is such a dope she should have sent a pair of brain surgeons to operate and find out if he had one. Yeah, I remember that now. Okay, okay, I'll buy petty harassment as a form of revenge. Rejected males beat the crap out of people—but females deliver. Or something."

"So I think that after Mario was killed, Inez got scared. That's assuming she didn't do it, of course," Judith said by way of clarification. "She came here to see if she could find the rock and the sheet of paper and make off with the evidence. Think how silly that would have looked in the press. If there's one thing Inez Garcia-Green doesn't want to be, it's belittled."

"And after six or seven years, the Spurned Woman Theory doesn't wash, I suppose. But," Renie went on, "what if she acted on behalf of her former stepson? Doesn't it strike you as odd that the minute Pacetti keels over, Schutzendorf signs up Justin?"

Judith regarded Renie with a quizzical expression. "It *is* odd. I wonder if Pacetti blackballed Justin with Cherubim Records? To spite Inez, maybe. Or at Amina's behest, to do ditto."

Renie spread her hands. "Pacetti buys the farm, Schutzendorf has to buy himself a new tenor. And Justin trots along at Inez's side because he doesn't have that contract inked yet. Ambition can be a terrible thing."

"True." Judith had leaned forward, fingering her chin. On the coffee table, the jack-o'-lantern leered at her. "Maybe that's why Inez came the second time, to tell Amina that with Mario gone, Justin was going to get his big chance." She stopped abruptly as a loud banging sounded at the back door. Both cousins hurried to the rear entrance.

Skjoval Tolvang, who had not been in evidence upon their return to the house, was standing on the porch, lighting his pipe. Out in the yard stood several large cartons. The carpenter sucked at his pipe, then gestured at the boxes.

"I collected your sink and shower and the rest," he announced. "Tomorrow, they go in. Then I paint on Saturday and finish up the rest. I vork Sunday, if needs be. You vant a look-see?"

Judith—and Renie—did. The bed-sitting room was finished off, the small bathroom awaited its conveniences, the closet boasted shelving. New glass had been installed in the original casements that faced the garden. The cousins admired Tolvang's meticulous old-world craftsmanship.

"This is really wonderful," breathed Judith. "Mother will be thrilled."

" 'Thrilled?' " Renie snickered. "Come on, coz, she'll say it's about time and why didn't you add on a sauna?"

Judith acknowledged the bald truth of Renie's observation. "Well, *I'm* thrilled," she said, turning to Skjoval Tolvang. "If you're done by the weekend, we can start moving the furniture in Monday."

"You vant me to help Sunday night?" asked Tolvang, making another stab at starting his pipe.

"Oh—my husband can do it when . . ." Judith paused and swallowed. ". . . When he gets back from his trip." She still hadn't come to grips with confronting Joe. "But it might be a good idea if you give me the bill before he gets home." Judith gave Tolvang a sickly smile.

"Okay, vill do," the carpenter agreed. "I stick to my price. Except for them pesky bedpost beetles."

Judith gaped at Tolvang. "Bedpost beetles? What on earth are they?"

Tolvang had finally got his pipe to draw. In the dusk, a haze of gray smoke encircled his white head. "Like termites, only vorse. They vere chewing avay at vat vas left of your foundation."

"Oh." Judith had a vision of their relatives marching across the lawn to make a meal of Hillside Manor. She could see the entire house crumbling around her ears. "Okay, that's extra, right?"

"Only two hundred bucks. And then the viring. It vas all shot."

"The wiring? How much?"

Tolvang shrugged. "It's not done yet, but I'm figuring maybe another five hundred. Not bad, all things considered. Like the plumbing."

Judith was beginning to feel numb. "That was included," she said a bit testily.

"Ya, sure, youbetcha. But ve veren't figuring on the roots." He pointed not to Judith's fruit trees, but to the weeping willow in the Dooleys' back yard. "Those veeping villows, they are the nuts. The roots go all over the place. I had to dig and dig. Four places, then I finally got a free spot to run the pipe to the sewer line." He shook his head at the memory of his perseverance. "Four hundred."

Judith's shoulders slumped. As near as she could calculate in her head, the bill was going to come to another twelve hundred dollars above the carpenter's original estimate. That was beyond the grand she had put out for the appliances and other appointments. And wasn't even counting what she would have to add—again—to her insurance. Gertrude was turning out to be a luxury that Judith wasn't sure she could afford.

"Uh . . ." Judith shifted awkwardly, glancing at Renie, as if in appeal. "Mr. Tolvang, would you mind terribly if I waited a couple of weeks to pay the extra thousand or

so? It may be out of pocket because of this murder situation."

Murder and millwork, poverty and plumbing—they
were all the same to Skjoval Tolvang. He shrugged again.
"Vy not? I trust you. You know vere to find me; I know
vere to find you." He pulled on his pipe and dug around
in his overalls. "Reminds me, here's some change I found
vile I vas digging. Maybe it'll help you out, py golly."

With a feeble smile, Judith accepted the handful of
coins and put them in the pocket of her slacks. It was
mainly pennies, a dime or two, and one quarter. No doubt
Dooley and his friends had dropped the money on one of
their forays over the picket fence. It seemed to Judith that
these days, kids didn't bother to retrieve small change.
Even Mike wouldn't bother picking money off his bedroom floor unless it was paper. Sometimes Judith de-
spaired of the younger generation's attitude toward their
finances. But right now she was despairing over her own.

"Maybe you can write all this off, when income tax
time rolls around," Renie said when they were back in the
kitchen, starting dinner.

"Oh, Lord, everything's such a mess!" Judith exclaimed,
wielding a frying pan for the oysters. "I'm in debt up to
my ears, Joe doesn't know Mother is moving back, *Mother*
doesn't even know it, and I may or may not have guests
staying through the week! I could lose almost two grand
on this Pacetti deal if they pull out tomorrow. I've already
lost money on Mario and Tippy."

"Yeah, dying is sure a hell of an excuse to get out of
paying your bill," Renie remarked dryly. "I thought you
wanted this bunch to hit the road."

"I do," Judith answered doggedly. "If I knew they were
going for sure, I could hustle up some fill-in business.
Maybe. But it's all up in the air. Just like this damned
murder investigation. Wouldn't you know Woody's wife
would have that kid early and screw up his schedule?
Drat! Everything's a wreck, especially me!"

"Stop beating yourself up," urged Renie, who was slicing potatoes to make homemade french fries. "When we were talking to Woody this afternoon, I got the impression you had an inkling whodunit." She gazed at Judith, who was dipping raw oysters into milk, egg, and bread crumbs. "Do you?"

"No," Judith answered promptly, "but I have this ridiculous feeling that I *should* know. Then I think that if all these people go away, maybe nobody will ever know. And so what? Whether the killer is caught or not, I'm going to end up on a street corner with a tin cup selling pencils out of a shoe box. Oh!"

"Oh what?" inquired Renie. She started dumping pieces of potato into a small deep-fat fryer.

Judith's black eyes were wide as she stood in front of the refrigerator with a cucumber in one hand and a beefsteak tomato in the other. "Shoe box. Boot box. *Dan.* I put him in the basement when Tolvang began the remodeling. When are we going to take him to the cabin and . . . uh . . . lay him to rest?"

Renie was unperturbed. "Next weekend? The weather will hold. We shouldn't get frost until November."

"Next weekend it will *be* November," Judith reminded her cousin. "It could snow up on the river by then. Heck, it's over sixty miles away."

"It won't snow," Renie replied, draining the french fries. "Here, ready for your vat o' fat?"

Judith allowed that she was, at least as ready as she was for anything about now. The cousins sat down to eat, discussing not the murder, but the family cabin, where Dan McMonigle had, in one of his maudlin moods, asked to have his ashes spread. Although the family vacation home was ideally set on a riverbank with Mt. Woodchuck towering over the surrounding forest, the present generation had not made much use of it. Joe Flynn wasn't a nature lover; Bill Jones wasn't keen on outdoor plumbing; the rest of the cousins had other interests. Judith often wondered if it wouldn't be smart to sell the property.

"You'd never get everybody to agree on that," said

Renie. "And even if they did, then there'd be a hell of a
row over who got how much. Leave it be. As you already
pointed out, you've got plenty of other problems just
now."

Renie was right. After she went home around ten, Judith
trudged up to the family quarters. Her guests still had not
returned from Maestro Dunkowitz's dinner party. Just as
she was getting undressed shortly before eleven, Judith
heard them come in. Maybe, she thought with mixed emotions, for the last time. Perhaps by tomorrow night, the
Pacetti party would be gone from Hillside Manor.

Judith tossed her sweater on the back of a chair, but
draped her slacks over a hanger. Something fell out of her
pocket. Puzzled, she bent down to see what it was. The
change that Skjoval Tolvang had found in the garden lay
on the braided rug. Judith scooped up the coins and laid
them on the dressing table. One of them caught her eye. A
closer look revealed it was not a Lincoln penny as she had
thought, but a foreign piece. She picked it up again, wishing she had her new glasses. But by holding it under the
lamp on the dressing table, she saw the word *"Groschen."*
All the pennies were foreign, Judith realized, and the quarter was actually a clip of some kind, perhaps a family
crest. Judith closed her hand over the little item and leaned
against the dressing table. Fragments of knowledge danced
in her brain. *When* had she heard *this? Where* had she seen
*that? Who* had said *what? Before* or *after . . .?*

With a sigh of frustration, she paced the bedroom. On
the dressing table, she noticed that her yellow rose had
bit the dust. Had she forgotten to put fresh water in the
little bud vase? But of course it had been almost a week
since she'd picked it. It was due to die. Unlike other
flowers, roses never seemed to last too long inside the
house.

Judith stopped pacing and stared at the drooping petals.
Some of them had fallen onto the dresser scarf. She stared;
she blinked; she took a deep, ragged breath.

Moving quickly, Judith went over to the small bookcase

that stood in the corner. She took down her much-used copy of Webster's *Biographical Dictionary* and flipped to the headings under *F*. As a librarian, she had been asked many, many questions over the years. Students, especially, had required her knowledge and requested her help. Weights and measures, Colonial Africa, Babylonian religion, Paul Revere's ride, Best Supporting Actor for 1956, the final score of the first Super Bowl—there was hardly a subject that Judith had not touched on during her twenty-year career in the public libraries.

Judith squinted at the small print. Unlike siblings, she and Renie weren't competitive. But like their mothers, they, too, could enjoy a good argument. Judith was convinced that Renie was wrong about Schutzendorf's uncle, Emil Fischer. Or that *something* was wrong. Judith was determined to prove her point. Her eye strayed to the listings under Fiske: John, originally Edmund Fisk Green, 1842-1901. American philosopher and historian, b. Hartford Conn. . . . Fiske, Minnie Maddern, 1865-1932. American actress, b. New Orleans . . . Fiske, Haley, 1852-1929, President, Metropolitan Life Insurance Co., New York . . .

Judith curbed her natural curiosity and moved up to Fischer. Sure enough, there were two Emils, one an operatic basso, 1838-1914, and the other, a German chemist who had won the Nobel Prize in 1902. The cousins were both right—Renie had remembered the voice of Wagner; Judith, the savant of science.

In the silence of her room, with the autumn air fresh and crisp outside her dormer window, Judith stared at the silver moon. The wind was picking up again, blowing clouds in from the west. A crow called from the maple tree, then flew off into the night. Leaves fluttered in the brisk breeze, like feathers drifting to earth. Judith bit her lip, leaned against the casement, and closed her eyes tight.

Fiske. Fischer. Fish . . . Something was fishy, all right. All along, Judith knew the killer had to have a sophisticated knowledge of poisons. And access to them. Judith felt as if she had been blind. Reaching for the phone, she started to dial Edna Fiske's number, then thought better of it. Judith would bide her time, though it was swiftly running out. It wouldn't be wise to alert Edna too soon.

Or was it foolish to wait?

# SEVENTEEN

Judith didn't expect to reach Woody Price, but she definitely wanted to get hold of Corazon Perez and Ted Doyle. They were off duty, Judith was informed, but would be paged.

After putting her clothes back on, she sat on the bed for a few moments, but was too nervous to stay still. Renie might be up—she was a Night Person, after all. She tended to work late, insisting that she got her best creative ideas after dark. Consequently, she often turned the phone off after ten o'clock. It was now almost eleven-thirty. Renie might be in bed; she could be in the bathtub. Judith didn't want to take the chance of making the call. She was, after all, already taking more of a chance than most ordinary mortals would. Her almost certain knowledge of the murderer's identity made her feel like a live target. Except, she tried to console herself, the killer didn't know that she had figured it all out . . .

Perhaps she'd feel safer downstairs. Eventually, she'd have to let the police officers in. But first, they'd telephone. Dare she risk being overheard on the kitchen phone? Judith decided she did. Being cornered in her own bedroom didn't appeal to her. The tension in the old house seemed to seep from the very walls.

But the familiar kitchen cheered her somewhat. She could hear the wind in the trees and the Rankers's hedge rustling between the houses. Judith poured a small glass of tomato juice and wished, not for the first time, that she hadn't quit smoking. She was about to change her mind about calling Renie when the phone rang. She snatched it up and answered in an uncharacteristically breathless voice.

"Hello, Mrs. Flynn," said the sleepy voice of Corazon Perez. "What can I do for you?"

Judith hesitated. Obviously, Perez had been in bed. "Well—I had some information I should relay to you and Ted. I didn't want to disturb Woody after he stayed up last night with Sondra. I'm afraid I woke you up, though."

"That's okay, it's part of the job." Perez's tone was philosophical. "Can you give me the data over the phone?"

Again, Judith paused. Overhead, she heard footsteps. Not all of her guests had settled in for the night. "I'd rather do it in person. Is Ted Doyle off duty, too?"

"That's right. In fact, he was coming down with a terrible cold this afternoon." The policewoman's voice had become more alert. "Look, why don't I get dressed and drive over to your house? It won't take half an hour."

The footsteps were coming down the back stairs. Judith tried to assume a casual, cheerful air. "That sounds great. It'll be terrific to see you again. 'Bye."

Winston Plunkett wandered into the kitchen, looking vague. His hostess's presence didn't seem to surprise him, not even at such a late hour.

"I can't sleep," he announced. "Actually, I'd just drifted off when something woke me. I thought I might get a glass of mineral water."

"Sure," said Judith, going to the refrigerator and trying to conceal her nervousness. "Maybe the noise you heard was the wind. Or me, coming back downstairs."

But Plunkett shook his head. "No, it was much closer. Doors opening and closing. I'm a very light sleeper."

Judith's hands shook as she opened the bottle of mineral water. She kept her back to Plunkett as she poured the liquid into a glass. "Are you leaving tomorrow for sure?"

"I hope so," said Plunkett, with more feeling than usual. "I'd like to be done with all of this, once and for all."

Judith finally turned and handed the glass to Plunkett. "Oh? Have you resigned?"

Plunkett thanked Judith, then sipped slowly. "It's not a question of resigning. I signed a lifetime contract with Mario Pacetti. It expired when he did." The faintest hint of a smile played around Plunkett's thin mouth.

"Really. What will you do now?" Judith kept her shaking hands behind her back.

Plunkett didn't meet her gaze. "I'm considering a new post."

"With Justin Kerr?" Judith phrased the question innocently.

Now, Plunkett stared at Judith. "Why—yes. How did you know?" Before she could reply, he actually smiled, giving his normally lackluster features a certain gray wolfish charm.

"It would be an obvious choice, since Justin has just signed a recording contract and appears to be on his way up. He can't let Tippy manage him forever. It must have been tough on her these past few months doing two jobs. And they'll probably want to start a family one of these days."

Plunkett took a big swallow of mineral water. "My, you seem to know a great deal about this whole situation. How did you get the Kerrs to confide in you? I didn't realize that Tippy and Justin were married until I went to see him at the Hotel Plymouth the other night."

"Oh," Judith replied on a forced note of calm, "people tend to talk to me. I guess I invite confidences."

"Yes," Plunkett agreed, studying Judith more closely. "You have a very open face. I suppose that's why your business is so successful. People feel welcome here." He set the glass down, then reached out to touch Judith's arm. Involuntarily, she winced. "Excuse me," he apologized, "I wanted to extend my thanks. You've been very gracious, considering you've had to put up with a terrible situation."

Judith removed her hands from behind her back, but leaned against the sink counter for support. "It's been terrible for everyone," she said, shaking hands with Plunkett. "Especially Mrs. Pacetti."

Plunkett sighed, then released Judith's hand. "Yes," he said in a dolorous voice. "Especially Mrs. Pacetti. But I'm not sorry I won't be working with her anymore. She's extremely spoiled." Again, he gave Judith that incongruous smile.

Judith girded herself for what was to come. "Tell me, Mr. Plunkett, was it you or Tippy who put the Strophanthin bottle on the prop table after Mr. Pacetti died?"

If there had ever been any color in Winston Plunkett's face, it now drained away. "I don't know what you're talking about," he mumbled. "What's this Stro . . ." He made an effort to sound bewildered and look amused.

"Both of you admitted going back to the opera house Saturday night," Judith said in a calm voice. "I'm just curious about which of you dropped the bottle on the table."

Winston Plunkett started backpedaling for the stairs. "Really, I'm quite flummoxed. Perhaps you should talk to Tippy. Good night, Mrs. Flynn."

"Good night," Judith responded, watching him head for the back stairs in a state of near-panic. "But," she added under her breath, *"you'll* be the one to talk to Tippy . . ."

As soon as his frantic tread faded, she went to the back door and stepped out on the porch, taking in deep gulps of fresh air. Quietly closing the door behind her, she made sure that it wasn't locked. Clouds now rolled across the moon; the old orchard trees cast eerie shadows. The wind had grown sharper, colder. A few doors away, a garbage can blew over; nearby, shutters banged; the old house seemed to groan.

From her vantage point on the porch, the toolshed looked all but finished. Skjoval Tolvang would complete the interior work the following day. According to his last report, he needed to install the sink and shower, then put on the finishing touches. Judith walked down the steps to gaze more closely at Tolvang's handiwork. She had to stop calling it *the toolshed*. It was now what? The word "folly" came to mind, and Judith shook her head. This was no time to deal with what she and Skjoval Tolvang had wrought. Corazon Perez would arrive at any moment and Judith would deliver a murderer's destiny into the police-woman's hands. Judith wandered over to the birdbath and watched for headlights in the driveway.

Instead, a car pulled slowly up to the curb in front of the house. A furtive figure hurried down the walk and got in. Judith frowned. Should she let them go? They wouldn't get far, though. She nodded in satisfaction as the gray Ford sedan drove out of the cul-de-sac.

Judith was sure it was Tippy who was driving. She was sure, too, that Tippy had put the half-empty bottle of Stro-phanthin on the stage table. It had been risky, not because of being seen—the vial was too small to catch anyone's attention—but because by the time Tippy returned from the hospital and got the bottle from Justin, there was al-ways the chance that the police would have finished their search. It had been a clever plan. Unfortunately, it hadn't worked out the way they had hoped.

The back door opened slowly. A figure moved onto the porch, darted a look in the direction of the garage, then marched down the steps. Judith held her breath and didn't dare budge. The other person also appeared to be waiting, large suitcase in hand. *Waiting for what?* thought Judith frantically. A cab? A hired car? Corazon Perez would pull up at any moment; almost thirty minutes had passed since the two women had spoken on the phone. Judith decided to act.

"Hello there," she called, brazenly stepping out from the

shadow of the old apple tree. "Are you a late-night stroller?"

A hearty chuckle grated on Judith's ear. "No, no, I am merely . . . *leaving,*" replied Bruno Schutzendorf, his cape caught by the wind. "I catch what you call the red-eye to your East Coast."

"I see." Judith took in the flapping cape, the snap-brimmed cap, the walking stick with its handle carved into a boar's head. "I didn't realize you were free to go. That is, Mr. Plunkett indicated you would all hear from the police in the morning."

Schutzendorf gave a scornful shrug. "*He* has already gone. Why should I not go, too? I await my cab."

"Oh." A sudden inspiration struck Judith. "Which company did you call?"

Schutzendorf frowned at Judith. "Which? The Checkered one, who else?"

Judith waved a hand in a disparaging gesture. "Oh, no, Mr. Schutzendorf. Not Checkered Cabs. They can't go to the airport. You see, we have taxi zones in this town. It's been done to eliminate fighting over fares at the terminal," Judith explained, fibbing only a little. "You have to call a different company. Here, I'll do it for you." She brushed past Schutzendorf and hurried into the house.

It seemed to take forever for the Checkered Cab dispatcher to answer. When he finally did, Judith canceled Schutzendorf's request. Then she dialed Perez's number to make sure the policewoman was on her way to Hillside Manor. To her dismay, Judith got not Corazon's answering machine, but Perez herself.

"I'm just leaving," said the policewoman, now fully awake and sounding perky. "I checked in with Ted and he thought I should have him as backup. I'm on my way to collect him, then we'll be right over."

"Listen, Corazon," Judith said in desperation, "our suspects are leaving in droves. You folks had better get over here before it's too late. In fact, maybe it already is."

"Oh." Perez paused, then spoke rapidly into the receiver. "I'll have a squad car there right away. Unless they're still sorting things out at the Heraldsgate Tavern. They had quite a ruckus up there a few minutes ago. That's why they haven't been cruising around your place in the last hour or so. Hang tight until they get there."

"Hurry!" urged Judith. But Perez had already hung up.

Starting back outside, Judith wondered if she should rouse Amina Pacetti. But would Amina help or hinder? Judith couldn't take that chance. As casually as possible, she sauntered through the door. Schutzendorf startled her. He was standing on the back porch. His briefcase and luggage rested on the walkway.

"You have sent for the proper cab?" he asked.

Judith could have sworn that there was suspicion in his eyes. "Right. It'll take a few minutes. I had to give directions. Sometimes the cabdrivers get confused. Because of the cul-de-sac, you see. Heraldsgate Hill is a bit of a maze, once you get off the beaten track." She realized she was speaking much too fast. Her eyes darted to the driveway; her ears pricked for the sound of sirens.

"Which cab did you summon?" Schutzendorf's voice was remarkably soft.

Judith jumped. "Yellow? Green? One of them, they both go to the airport. It took a while for them to answer." Frantically, Judith wondered how much Schutzendorf had heard from the back porch. What had she actually said to Corazon? "I told them to hurry. And that it was getting late . . ." She gave Schutzendorf a ghostly smile.

He inclined his head. Despite the wind, the houndstooth cap remained in place. "Yes, you said all those things." In the bushy beard, his teeth looked almost like fangs. "But not to the taxi man, eh?"

Judith gulped. "The dispatcher."

"No. *Nein,*" Schutzendorf added on a more emphatic, but still soft note. "You dispatch the police!"

"The police?" Judith tried to laugh, at the same time darting glances around the backyard. Rankers's house was dark; so were Dooleys' and Ericsons'. Had Amina Pacetti been awakened by the wind? Judith opened her mouth to scream, but Schutzendorf deftly tucked his walking stick under his left arm, and grabbed her with his right.

"March!" he growled, all but pushing Judith down the porch steps.

Schutzendorf's grasp was like steel. She wanted to scream, but no sound came out of her mouth. Feeling numb, Judith willed her legs to propel her from the porch. She kept moving, straight into the howling wind, aware that her captor was shoving her in the direction of the toolshed.

"Open," he commanded, releasing her just enough so that she could reach the door.

Judith could scarcely breathe. Fumbling at the brand-new brass doorknob, she finally got it to turn. Schutzendorf pushed her inside, still holding her tight. The wind blew the door shut behind them.

"You pry," he muttered. "You ask too many questions. So you know the truth. You spoil everything, all the precise plans. For your interference, you must die." His tone was more vexed than furious. Judith would have preferred outrage to calm. But of course he was a most calculating man.

The wind groaned and moaned over the new roof of the toolshed. More banging and bumping could be heard outside. It was turning into a typically stormy October night. *Almost Halloween,* Judith thought dazedly. Her head grew light; her knees went weak. She almost fell when Schutzendorf abruptly released her.

In her terrified state, Judith couldn't remember if Skjoval Tolvang had turned on the electricity in the toolshed yet. But her eyes were growing accustomed to the darkness. So, apparently, were Schutzendorf's. He unscrewed the boar's head from his walking stick. A lethal six-inch blade shot out, the steel catching the sudden glimmer of moonlight through the window.

"So you scream," Schutzendorf said complacently. "Who will hear you with this clamor of wind and flying objects?" As if to prove his point, the door blew open, then slammed shut again. "Tell me this, what mistake did I make? I hate mistakes!"

Judith felt as if she were exploring her throat to see if she still had a voice. She knew her reply would doom her, but she had to say it. Schutzendorf knew she had learned the truth. "Your only mistake was poisoning Mario Pacetti in the first place." She could hardly believe the words had actually come out. They felt dry and thin on her tongue. "And, of course, your hat."

The walking stick weapon never wavered in Schutzendorf's right fist, but he clapped his left hand to the snap-brimmed cap. "My hat? What do you mean?"

Judith cleared her throat as the wind slammed some objects together outside. "You wore a Tyrolean hat when you arrived at Hillside manor. It was perfect with the cape and walking stick." Her eyes darted to the dangerous blade and she swallowed hard before she could go on. "Then, a couple of days later, you started wearing that cap. It didn't look right, it didn't fit your jolly German image. My carpenter found a black feather in the garden. He thought my cat had killed a bird. But my cat's been gone since the end of June. And the feather was too fancy—it looked like an osprey or something. Oh, there were other people here with feathers—Amina and Tippy—even Plunkett, with his fishing flies and Inez with Violetta's fan. You lost that feather when you were digging up more pips. Maybe the medallion, too. Then Mr. Tolvang handed me a bunch of coins. They turned out to be Austrian *Groschen*. All of you probably had been in Salzburg, so that didn't mean anything. I suppose the coins came out of your pocket when you were burying the thermos. You probably didn't notice until later. You'd already ditched the hat because it wouldn't look right without its feather and medallion. It wasn't in your closet. Maybe you put it inside that locked briefcase." Judith was leaning against the small partition that walled off Gertrude's would-be bath and changing room. She shut her eyes briefly, trying to figure out how to keep stalling Schutzendorf. If the on-duty police car could get away from the melee at the Heraldsgate Tavern, they might arrive at any moment. And Corazon Perez and Ted Doyle should be along soon. But of course they would never think to look in the toolshed.

Schutzendorf was nodding. "Clever. *Ja, ja,* you are no *Dummkopf.*" He took a step forward, raising the walking stick. "But now you vill be merely . . . *dead!*"

Judith ducked as Schutzendorf raised the weapon. She only glimpsed the door swinging open again. She had slipped to her knees at the moment her attacker was struck from behind. She was cringing on the floor when she heard the voice from above.

"No sneaky-pete city inspector comes after dark to check up on Skjoval Tolvang's vork! That's trespassing! I don't need no permit, py golly! This is an inside yob!"

Stunned, Judith dared to gaze up at her savior. "It sure was," she croaked. "In more ways than one. *Py golly!*"

# EIGHTEEN

JUDITH'S FEELING OF triumph wasn't diminished one whit by the arrival of Patrolpersons Nancy Prentice and Stanley Cernak. The petite policewoman and her gangling sidekick performed their duties swiftly and efficiently. Indeed, Bruno Schutzendorf was still lying on the toolshed floor when the squad car rolled into the driveway. And Judith was still trying to convince Skjoval Tolvang that Schutzendorf wasn't a snoopy city inspector, but a cold-blooded killer.

"Vich is vorse?" sniffed Tolvang, returning his hammer to the tool belt he wore around his grimy coverall.

By the time Schutzendorf had come 'round, Prentice and Cernak had been reenforced by Corazon Perez and Ted Doyle. Arlene Rankers showed up in her bathrobe, rousted not by the police cars or Tolvang's rattletrap of a truck, but the arrival of the Checkered Cab, which had never received word of the cancellation and was sitting out in the cul-de-sac, horn blaring for its would-be passenger. At that point, Amina Pacetti had also appeared on the scene, cursing Schutzendorf in Italian, German, and French. Judith's backyard looked like an all-night circus.

After Schutzendorf had been handcuffed, read his rights, and hauled off in the Prentice-Cernak vehicle, Judith had time to thank Skjoval Tolvang properly. The carpenter, however, dismissed her gratitude with a wave of his metal tape measure.

"T'ink nothing of it," he said. "I came to check out the shingles in this vind. And vile I vas about it, I'd a mind to make sure the electricity vorked. That vay, the rest of the yob can be done tomorrow. Donahues vant me to start early. But I see that briefcase outside," Tolvang went on, "and I t'ink, *Vell, vell, it's The City, goddamit.* This is a free country and they von't get avay with that!"

"And they didn't," Judith said less than forty-eight hours later as she and Renie joined their husbands for a postflight dinner in the high-rise dining room of a posh hotel near the airport. "At least Schutzendorf didn't. But of course he also planned on getting away with Amina. Instead, she rolled off yesterday in the mauve RV, with Edna Fiske holding her hand. I had a feeling Amina would need a nurse to help her recover from Bruno's treachery. Edna will probably enjoy the trip to Italy—and the funeral. Plunkett met them at the airport. After the services in Bari and winding up Pacetti's affairs, Winnie will come back to work for Justin Kerr."

Joe signaled for the waiter to bring a second order of drinks. His round face was bemused as Judith summed up the events that had led to her unmasking of Mario Pacetti's killer. "You deduced all of this from a *Tyrolean hat?* Come on, Jude-girl, give me a break! Everybody at headquarters is going to point and laugh when I walk in the door Monday morning."

Judith shot Joe an indignant look. "The hat was the clincher. Only two people had serious motives—Amina and Bruno, both for big bucks. Justin Kerr was ambitious, and Tippy shared his goals, but even for the world of opera, murder is a bit extreme. Inez wasn't exactly broken up over her affair with Mario, though she, too, was pushing Justin, not only because he was her former stepson, but because she had the hots for him. That's why Tippy and Justin had to keep their marriage quiet. If Pacetti wouldn't help Justin, there was always Inez to fall back on, though I'm sure Tippy wouldn't have liked the price her husband would have had to pay to show his gratitude. As for Plunkett, I considered him more seriously—if he was stuck with Pacetti in a lifetime contract and Pacetti was losing his voice—well, figure it out. The future looked a bit bleak. These seemingly bloodless creatures often have a darker side. But Winston Plunkett had an emotional side—and he wasn't a killer."

"Money, money, money," chirped Renie, who had chosen this night of reunion and celebration to switch to Harvey Wallbangers. "Amina got piles of it, but so did Schutzendorf—from the insurance policy he'd taken out on Pacetti. I finally tortured Madge Navarre into telling me the amount. It was ten million dollars, with half again as much more because death was externally caused. There was a rider or some such clause." Her voice faded as she got off into technical jargon beyond her understanding.

Bill Jones frowned over his old-fashioned. "I suppose that would have saved Cherubim Records from financial disaster. If Pacetti had lived, and yet had not been able to fulfill his contract, would Schutzendorf and his company have had to bite the bullet?"

Judith nodded. "That's right. Pacetti had had an insurance physical back in December. The throat condition didn't show up. Schutzendorf very likely wouldn't have got any more recording sessions out of Pacetti. It was a ten-year contract. Cherubim would never have made up the millions they'd paid to sign him. That," said Judith, sipping at her scotch, "would have been pretty hard for Bruno Schutzendorf to—excuse the expression—swallow. But with Pacetti's death, he got more than his money back. And he planned on getting Amina, too."

The waiter arrived with another tray of drinks. Joe promised they'd consider perusing the menu very soon.

Their table overlooked the airport. A 747 soared off into the clouds. A DC-10 taxied along the runway, coming to rest at the south terminal. The sun, which had appeared after almost two full days of rain, was going down behind the mountains to the west. It was a perfect autumn evening, typical for the Pacific Northwest. More rain was in the forecast for Sunday.

"So," said Joe, hoisting his second martini, "Amina was using Plunkett to cover up her affair with Schutzendorf. Why bother?"

Judith gave her husband a little smile, not so much for his question, but for the sheer pleasure of having him back at her side. "Who could take an affair with Plunkett seriously? Besides, Mario depended on Plunkett as much as he did on Amina. But Schutzendorf was another matter. Pacetti could have signed with any major recording company in the world. Schutzendorf wanted him badly. I suspect he begged Amina to keep their relationship quiet."

"Now just a minute," said Bill, who liked his information free of clutter and without obvious holes. Bill Jones tended to think not only clinically, but analytically. "Explain the part about the Strophanthin. And the thermos."

Judith took a deep breath. "Schutzendorf did in fact have a mild heart condition. He alluded to it once or twice. I suspect he kept the stuff with him. Maybe he originally intended to use it, but he saw those lily-of-the-valley pips in the refrigerator, and it gave him a better idea."

"Whoa," interrupted Joe. "Why *two* bottles? One was enough to throw everybody off the track."

Judith nodded, and brushed lint off Joe's navy blazer. "That was really puzzling. Schutzendorf put the vial in the floral arrangement. He didn't want to make it too obvious, just in case the medical people really believed Pacetti died of a heart attack. Why draw attention to the possibility of unnatural death? And the flowers might have been thrown out, plastic liner and all. If the medicine was traced back to him, he could say it was stolen. Which, as it turned out, was true."

Renie gave a little snort. "Talk about cross-purposes! Plunkett, Tippy, Justin, and Inez all thought they were doing the right thing when in fact they were only confusing the issue."

Bill Jones gave his wife a skeptical look. "Are you two saying they knew it was Schutzendorf who killed Pacetti?"

Again, Judith nodded. "They were pretty sure. Plunkett and Tippy were aware of Pacetti's vocal condition. They also knew about the huge amount of insurance. And both had dealt with Schutzendorf before—Plunkett via Pacetti, and Tippy when she was with the Boston Pops. In fact, the Pops refused a big Cherubim recording contract because Tippy recommended against it. She knew that under that jolly German exterior he was a very ruthless man. But they didn't dare go to the police. First of all, Justin might not get his own contract if Schutzendorf was out of the picture. Cherubim will survive without Schutzendorf. Secondly, they *might* have been wrong about him. If they made an unfounded accusation, think how Schutzendorf would have reacted! All of them—Justin, Tippy, Plunkett, Inez—had plenty to lose by riling Bruno Schutzendorf. So instead, they made their desperate attempt to point the police in the right direction by swiping his Strophanthin *after* the murder and having Tippy leave it on the prop table. Then the other bottle turned up, and chaos reigned. Not to mention the quantity of Strophanthin in the thermos."

"But originally it was the pips that were in the tea?" Joe was looking uncharacteristically puzzled.

"Not exactly." Judith smiled at her husband. "That's where the wilted flowers came in." She paused just long enough to let Joe hold his head. "Mario would have noticed the pips. Schutzendorf took them out of the fridge and trotted them upstairs to soak in the bouquet I'd placed in his room. In a few hours, the water would turn toxic. Then he probably poured the lethal liquid into one of those big tumblers he was using to guzzle his Sekt out of, and brought it back to the kitchen and poured it into the teakettle. I saw him fiddling with the teakettle and trying to get

Amina out of the way, but of course I just thought he was being his usual bumptious self. Pacetti bolted his food and gulped his beverages. If he noticed an odd taste to his tea, it would be too late. But of course Schutzendorf had to get the thermos back, rinse it out, put the Strophanthin in— and ditch it in a place where it just might be found to further throw everybody for a loop. The giveaway—which didn't hit me until I noticed the wilted rose in our bedroom—was that his dahlias and asters had died. Nobody else's had. It meant that Schutzendorf had emptied the vase and not bothered to refill it. Why? The answer was very simple."

"Sheesz!" Joe rubbed vigorously at his high forehead. "What are you trying to do, Jude-girl? Make the rest of us look simple?"

"Gosh, Joe," Judith said innocently, "how can you say that? You and Woody are the ones who solved the fortune-teller murder, remember?"

"What?" Joe's green eyes hardened slightly.

Judith bit her lip. "Never mind."

Bill was looking askance. "Don't tell me Schutzendorf was some sort of plant expert! The man ran a recording company." If Judith relied on logic, Bill's byword was reason.

"He was, as a matter of fact." Judith darted an amused look at Renie, who was squirming a bit. "Schutzendorf told me early on that his great-uncle was the famous Emil Fischer. We'd been talking about music—at least I had— and when Renie told me Emil Fischer was a well-known German opera singer, I assumed that's who Schutzendorf meant. But something bothered me—somewhere along the line, I'd heard that name, but it had nothing to do with opera. Finally, I looked it up the other night and discovered there were *two* Emil Fischers who lived at the same time. One was a singer specializing in Wagnerian roles— the other won the Nobel Prize for chemistry by synthesizing simple sugars. That's the august relative in whose footsteps Bruno's papa wanted him to follow.

Schutzendorf admitted to studying his great-uncle's work but said he had no aptitude for it. I thought he was talking about singing, but he was referring to chemistry. He did, however, learn enough from Uncle Emil's plant research to know that flower pips can be deadly."

Bill Jones adjusted his steel-rimmed glasses; Joe Flynn entwined his fingers over his budding paunch; Renie gazed up at the ceiling with its tiny lights made to look like twinkling stars; Judith burst out laughing.

"An honest mistake, coz. The point is, Bruno took the pips—and maybe some more from the yard, where Phyliss Rackley noticed that somebody had been digging by the living room window. The stuff can take a bit of time to work. Then he took the Strophanthin to the opera house and *after* Pacetti collapsed, he put the vial on the table."

Joe was making a face. "And nobody saw him running around on stage?"

"Oh, yes," Judith replied. "Everybody probably did. But he was helping Inez. She was in a minor state of shock. All eyes would be on her, the great soprano. Who would pay any attention to some minor gesture on Schutzendorf's part? The important thing was that Inez shouldn't pass out, too. After all, at this point, nobody knew what was going on with Pacetti."

Joe gave a little shake of his head. "It was after that when he swiped the thermos?"

"He put it under that big cape. It was easy to do, I imagine, in all the confusion," Judith said, noticing that the waiter was attempting to hover. "He buried it outside, just to create confusion and spread suspicion around. He was the only one who had *not* been backstage before the opera, remember? Everyone would assume that the vial of Strophanthin had been put there before the performance. Meanwhile, Schutzendorf discovers that his backup bottle of medication has disappeared. I don't know what he made of that, but I presume he had to scoot back to Bayview Hospital and get them to write him a prescription for something similar."

"Proof," said Joe, suddenly looking very official. "I don't see anything solid. It's all circumstantial."

Judith gave her husband a jab in the arm. "Hey, he tried to kill me! What more proof do you need?"

But Joe didn't relent. "Big deal. Attempted assault with a walking stick. *Schutzendorf* could walk. What I really don't get is why he panicked and tried to kill you in the first place. He could have taken that plane and got away with everything."

Judith nodded. "In retrospect, maybe. What are the keys to finding a killer? Motive, opportunity, means." Judith ticked the trio off on her fingers. "Schutzendorf bailing out his company, Schutzendorf in the kitchen when Amina Pacetti prepared Mario's lunch, Schutzendorf knowing about poisons, discovering the pips, taking Strophanthin under doctor's orders. Tippy seeing him in the garden. And the decorations from that damned hat. Woody found it mashed down inside the briefcase. The feather and the medallion can be traced back to Bruno Schutzendorf. Tyrolean hats are often custom-made. The feathers are chosen individually, the medallions are sometimes engraved with a family crest. Check it out, Lieutenant Flynn, even if you have to call Salzburg or Innsbruck. Now what else do you need? Polaroids of Bruno Schutzendorf rearranging my dahlias?"

"That would help," Joe agreed. But his expression conveyed grudging acceptance. And not-so-reluctant admiration. "I still find it strange that Schutzendorf didn't take a chance and just get the hell away from Heraldsgate Hill."

But Judith gave a firm shake of her head. "He didn't dare. Not after he overheard my phone conversation with Corazon. He figured the police must be after him. Amina probably told him the thermos had been found. Schutzendorf couldn't bury the thing the night of the murder because he was still at the hospital. Then it was raining—he was afraid of leaving footprints. Woody and his crew showed up Monday night, the squad car kept going by, and Schutzendorf had to plan his move very carefully. He didn't count on Tippy's taking off, especially so early Tuesday morning. It had stopped raining, but it was still dark. She saw him digging around while she was waiting for Justin, but she couldn't be sure of what he was doing. Naturally, it confirmed her suspicions, which she had already shared with the others. That's what that triangle doodle of Plunkett's meant—Inez and Tippy and Justin were in fact a triangle, but Plunkett put his own initials in the middle because they were all part of the group that suspected Schutzendorf. Tippy is very sharp, not the least like the goofball she pretended to be. She seems to think that some of those recent 'accidents' might have been staged."

Joe remained intransigent. "Tippy isn't one-hundred-percent sure of what she saw. Schutzendorf could have been digging for gold or chasing gophers. None of this will stand up in court. And Schutzendorf knew it. His reaction doesn't make sense."

Judith fanned herself with her linen table napkin. "Now, now—it does if you're more afraid of an insurance company than you are of the local police." She threw her husband an arch little glance.

"Wait a minute . . ." Joe began, but Judith shushed him with a wave of the napkin.

"I overheard Schutzendorf talking to the insurance people in New Haven. He had to wait six months to get his money.

"That's right," Renie chimed in, fully recovered from her embarrassment and trying to get the waiter's attention. "Madge Navarre says that with a big payoff like this— especially since it was a fairly new policy with not that many premiums paid in—the insurance investigators would make you guys down at headquarters look like amateurs. No offense, Joe. But when was Madge ever wrong?"

Madge Navarre's reputation for being both astute and accurate bordered on the legendary. "She should have been a cop," muttered Joe, finally allowing the waiter to present himself.

Renie ordered six hors d'oeuvres, presumably to share. Judith wasn't quite sure what her hungry cousin's intentions really were, but Bill Jones was checking his watch. It was perilously close to six o'clock. His recurrent ulcer had to be fed on time. Renie passed him the bread basket; she'd only eaten half of its contents so far.

"What you're saying then," Bill said, buttering a crust of sourdough bread, "is that Schutzendorf didn't dare take any chances. If he'd actually"—Bill had the grace to grimace at Judith—"managed to kill you, would Tippy have been next?"

Judith shook her head. "I don't think so. He'd have figured that her testimony didn't have any weight without mine. About the hat, I mean. And Skjoval Tolvang had no idea that the leavings he picked up in the yard could nail a murderer." Judith paused, sighing a little. "If it hadn't been for that tea being an antidote . . . or for Edna Fiske realizing that the pips could be lethal . . . or Tolvang digging up the backyard for the toolshed renovation . . ."

"The what?" Joe had set his martini glass down very carefully.

It was Judith's turn to look up at the star-studded ceiling. "Uhhh . . . Ummm . . . Gee, didn't I mention that part?" She turned to Renie in an apparent appeal for help.

"Crime prevention," said Renie firmly. "You do believe in stopping homicide before it happens, don't you, Joe?" She beamed at the waiter, who was placing several dishes of hors d'oeuvres, both hot and cold, before her.

Joe was looking puzzled. "It depends," he replied, snatching a Teriyaki chicken wing away from Renie.

"It's like this," Renie explained through a mouthful of mushroom stuffed with crab. "Our mothers are about to kill each other. We could put them into a Home. But that costs too much and then we'd all have to visit twice a week. Or we could let one of them do the other in. Then you'd have to arrest one and bury the other. Very embarrassing. And also costly. Of course we could keep Aunt Gertrude in the apartment and move my mother in with us." She paused just long enough to see Bill Jones start to turn purple. "Here, have a prawn." She shoved the nearest appetizer plate at her husband. "But we don't want to see Bill have apoplexy before our very eyes, do we?"

"What about *me?*" demanded Joe, whose color almost matched Bill's.

"*Joe . . .*" Judith's voice held a pleading note. "Mother is *old*. She's crippled. She wants to hang on to her independence. She'll be completely separated from the main house. But at least she'll be on her own . . . ah, turf. Don't be so selfish."

Joe sipped at his martini, his green-eyed gaze drifting off across the crowded dining room. "First Herself, now Itself. What will become of poor Joe?"

Judith gave his arm a little shake. "You've got me. *Myself*. Isn't that what you swore you always wanted?"

Slowly, Joe turned to look at his wife of four months. His color had returned to normal; the gold flecks sparkled in his magic eyes. "Did I say that? Hmmmm." He leaned over and kissed Judith lightly on the lips. She kissed him back, harder.

Renie turned to Bill. "Did you eat *all* those prawns?"

"Why not? It's past my dinner hour."

Renie gave an exasperated toss of her head. Bill stole her last stuffed mushroom. Judith and Joe stopped kissing. The waiter went into reverse and a moment later, showed up with champagne.

"Who ordered this?" asked Bill.

"Not me," Joe replied.

From across the room, someone waved a hand. All four heads turned. Two people sat at a corner table. They lifted their glasses in a toast.

It was Tippy and Justin Kerr.

Judith grinned; Renie clapped.

Joe nodded approval at the label. The waiter uncorked

the bottle. Glasses were produced, Joe took a sample sip, and nodded again.

*"Libiamo!"* cried Renie. They all drank, and Verdi refrains danced through their heads.

Four days later, Gertrude returned to Hillside Manor with Sweetums growling at the foot of her walker. Gertrude didn't quite allow her daughter to see how pleased she was, but Judith knew from the sparkle in her mother's eyes that this was a happy day. Joe was still not reconciled to the idea of installing his mother-in-law in the remodeled toolshed, but at least he felt the timing of her return was appropriate.

It was Halloween.